THE FRIENDS OF EDDY RELISH

PAUL DALZELL; GERARD RADLEY

authorHOUSE®

AuthorHouse™
1663 Liberty Drive
Bloomington, IN 47403
www.authorhouse.com
Phone: 1 (800) 839-8640

Published by AuthorHouse 04/15/2019

ISBN: 978-1-7283-0793-0 (sc)
ISBN: 978-1-7283-0792-3 (e)

Library of Congress Control Number: 2019904283

CONTENTS

1. Pit 1
2. Sabbatical 6
3. Pickle...12
4. Scrap 20
5. Fish..22
6. Deal 27
7. Rock 33
8. Weed 39
9. Aloha..46
10. Gnome...50
11. Sandman..53
12. Passport 56
13. Folksong...62
14. Mistakes 67
15. Breakfast 70
16. Meditation 73
17. Fruit..77
18. Reunion 80
19. Proposition 86
20. Plot 89
21. Barbecue 93
22. Porn..95
23. Samovar 104
24. Clubbing..110
25. Faith..117

26. Script 120
27. Reception 125
28. Debate 128
29. Screenplay 142
30. Comprehension 144
31. Steppe...147
32. Metal 150
33. Anxiety 155
34. News...158
35. Sorrow 162
36. Karma 165
37. Excrement 170
38. Remembrance 174
39. Education 176
40. Trip...182
41. Vegas..185
42. Ache 188
43. Website 193
44. Hamper..199
45. Rendezvous 206
46. Scars...208
47. Meat 212
48. Kit 218
49. Deal 221
50. Email 229
51. Plush 231
52. Party 234
53. Terrain 236
54. Debate 240
55. Payback 242
56. Gatecrasher 244
57. Feds 248
58. Film 249
59. Syndrome 251
60. Surprise...254

61. Producer 256
62. Language 259
63. Nerve 261
64. Chalk 266
65. Family 268
66. Threads 271
67. Fin 273

CHAPTER 1

PIT

"**A**nother drink?"

"No, thanks," said Eddy Relish.

"Are you waiting for someone? Only you don't look well," said the barmaid.

The pub door opened. Eddy gave the door a glance and tried to smile. "I'm okay, but thanks for asking."

The pub's front door swung open again. Eddy's eyes scanned the newcomers.

"You should go home. I swear your skin is green," said the barmaid.

A large man emerged from a corridor and settled into a chair at Eddy's table. He dropped a bag that clunked heavily on the floor. "Hello, Eddy," he said. "Came in the back door. Thought you might do a runner if I came in the front."

"Oh, fuck," said the barmaid. She scurried back to the bar.

"Hello, Bill. It's good to see you. How've you been keeping?" said Eddy. There was a tremor in Eddy's voice, and his gut was heaving.

Bill had a purple swelling around the right side of his lower lip. "I know what you're thinking. *Who'd smack Bill?* Well, you should see the other bloke."

"What happened? I mean, who—" said Eddy.

"Bloody dentist. I go in for a checkup and come out looking like this. I gave the dentist a choice: malpractice suit or nail gun earrings.

1

To be honest, there was no choice. Anyway, what's this I've been hearing about your good fortune?"

"What good fortune, Bill?"

"Your new motor. I was down the allotments this morning and bumped into Doug Down. He said you'd got a new motor. He'd seen you on Slag Lane yesterday."

"I … I don't know what he's talking about."

Doug Down was a homeless autistic man who haunted the Knockney Municipal Allotments, which had been renamed the Muammar Gaddafi Agricultural Collective. Doug stood at the entrance to the gardens. If asked, he would report everything he saw that day.

Bill shifted in his seat. "Come on, Eddy. No secrets from the reverend? 'We have renounced secret and shameful ways; we do not use deception.'[1] I should take you down to the allotments some time. Maybe you could help fertilize my vegetable patch."

Eddy winced at the threat. "It must be a case of mistaken identity. I do not own a car; I have not driven anything in weeks."

Bill leaned his large frame back into the chair and stared at Eddy with a half-smile on his scarred face.

"Eddy, Doug was not the only one who saw this mysterious double of yours. Some of my associates also saw you driving your new motor. Speaking of doubles, get yourself a scotch—a large one. I think you'll need it."

Eddy slunk off to the bar to order a double scotch. While waiting, he racked his brain. Why was Bill toying with him? The only car he had driven recently belonged to the mother of his girlfriend, Sharon Constable.

He caught sight of Bill's reflection in the mirrored wall behind the bar. Eddy noticed something deforming the side of Bill's leather grip. Eddy tried to ignore the contents of the bag. He heard the barmaids talking about Bill Blake as he ordered the drink.

"Yeah, they call him 'Reverend' Bill Blake," one said. "He's a

---

[1] Corinthians 4:2.

loan shark, among other things. My boyfriend says he was raised in a church orphanage, right? Bill knows the Bible back to front. My boyfriend says if you default on a loan, he nails you to a wooden board. Yeah! For real! Bill calls it crucifixion. He says it's not punishment but time for reflection."

The barmaids stared at Eddy, their eyes wide with fear and pity.

Eddy returned to his table, placing the whiskey on the table before sitting back down.

Bill shifted his bulk, leaned forward, and noticed the newspaper on the pub table. "What was this you were reading when I came in?" he asked.

Bill had no interest in the paper; he was drawing out the moment, a cat toying with a wounded bird.

"It's about the latest political infighting. Always makes a good read. Might make a good play."

He nodded to the front page of the paper on the table. His mouth was arid, and it hurt to talk.

Bill kept staring at Eddy.

Jesus Christ, thought Eddy, *I should never have borrowed money from Bill.*

Both Sharon and her mother had pleaded with him. He thought he had a firm offer of work from a local theater group that had just received an Arts Council grant.

Bill leaned back in his chair and closed his eyes for a few seconds. Then he fixed Eddy with his malevolent stare.

"Drink up," said Bill.

Eddy's stomach rebelled at the thought, but he drank down the scotch, which set his stomach alight.

Bill said, "Be a good lad. Tell me why you were driving a new motor through Knockney. Tell me why you could not steer that motor around to pay me back five hundred pounds *plus interest.* Before you answer, remember: 'Thou shalt not raise a false report.'[2]"

Eddy said, "Oh, last Tuesday. Sorry. Getting my days mixed up."

---

[2] Exodus 23:1.

Bill heaved the cast iron table aside with his right arm. It flew in an arc and smashed down on the floor. The whiskey glass shattered next to the bar. Bill reached into his leather grip. He pulled out an industrial nail gun loaded with six-inch nails. Eddy was pressing himself against the wall. Bill's left arm lashed out like a cobra, grasping Eddy around the throat.

The whole pub was silent. Eddy's eyes flickered back and forth among the pub's clientele. He could see their concern, but he knew no one would help him or risk calling the police.

Bill jabbed the nail gun muzzle down hard between Eddy's legs.

Eddy let out a yelp.

"Where's my fucking money, you little slag?"

Bang!

Bill drove a six-inch nail into the pub bench.

Eddy spread his legs wide apart to get them away from the nail gun.

"Where's my fucking money, you worm?"

Bill kept the nail gun stationary and fired again.

Bang!

Bill moved the nail gun toward Eddy's crotch, midway between his inner thighs.

Eddy let out a long scream.

Bill cut this off.

"Where's my fucking money, you useless turd?"

Bang!

Bill rammed the nail gun hard into Eddy's groin, with the barrel still pointed at the seat.

Eddy convulsed with pain, writhing and flailing his hands. His eyes were full of tears. He took sharp gasps of breath as the pain spread from his groin into his abdomen. He threw up on his jeans and shoes.

"Where's my fucking cash, you miserable Hollywood ponce?"

Bang!

Eddy had felt the gun's recoil and the punch of the nail.

Bill hefted the nail gun and jabbed it down onto the front of

Eddy's jeans, midway up the zipper. Eddy could feel the heat from the gun barrel diffuse through his jeans. A nail would pierce the bladder, rectum, and lower spine. He was beyond terror, writhing in Bill's grip. A dark stain spread across his crotch and down his inner thighs.

Bill stared at him, watching the spreading urine and sniffing at the smell of vomit and whiskey. He released Eddy and stood up. "I think you and me had better go for a little walk, my son. 'Beloved, I wish above all things that thou mayest prosper.'[3]"

Eddy doubled up to relieve the pain in his groin and massaged his throat.

Bill gazed around the pub at the clientele and staff. "What are you looking at?"

No one answered him.

Bill raised his voice. "I said, 'What are you looking at?'"

There was another breathless quiet as Bill surveyed the room, his left hand now resting firmly on the back of Eddy's neck.

Bill roared, "I said, 'What the fuck are you looking at?'"

He raised the nail gun and fired along the length of the pub. The nails bounced off the dartboard and shattered a drink on a nearby table. A woman squeaked with fear.

The pub landlord raised his hands in surrender. "Bill, Bill, we're not looking at anything."

"Right answer. You saw nothing. If I hear a peep about this little bit of fun, I will come back with this. I have plenty of nails and plenty of time. I know who you all are, and I know where you all live."

As the two men left the pub, Bill supported Eddy, who walked in a crouch from the pain and from the shame of wetting himself.

---

[3] John 1:1.

CHAPTER 2
SABBATICAL

Three days later, Eddy's long-suffering girlfriend was wondering where he was. Eddy's little disappearances were not unusual, one or two days at most, especially if he was trying to evade the law. But this was three—getting on for four days—forcing Sharon to check with the police. Sharon Constable picked up the phone and dialed the Knockney police station. She asked to speak to Chief Inspector Charlie Clore.

"Clore," said a gravelly voice.

"Inspector Clore, it's Sharon Constable. I need your help. It's about Eddy. I think something might have happened to him."

"I was wondering when I might get a call from you," said Clore.

"I haven't seen Eddy for nearly four days. He's vanished."

"Seems to me your Eddy's done a runner. If I were you, Sharon, I'd forget about him. Find yourself a nice new bloke and settle down. This is no way to live your life, lurching from one crisis to the next."

This advice was not new to Sharon.

"You don't know him like I do, Inspector. Eddy's better than you think. If he's in trouble, I want to know about it."

"Listen, love, you can bet your life he's in trouble. *He is trouble.* Just forget about him. I don't want to see you dragged down because of Eddy Relish. Do you want to be another wife or girlfriend queuing at the prison gates on visiting day, with a nipper in tow?"

There was a pause.

"No," replied Sharon in a small voice, "but he needs me."

Clore said, "Okay, if it was anybody else, I'd tell them to talk to Missing Persons." He sighed and said, "I wouldn't do this, but I've known your mum and Aunty Jan a long time. Do you know the Plume? Can you meet me there in thirty minutes?"

"Yes. Thanks, Inspector," said Sharon. "I'll be there."

Sharon fetched her coat and handbag and checked her appearance in the mirror. She went out of her apartment onto the balcony. Two of her Rastafarian neighbors were smoking large spliffs and listening to throbbing dub reggae.

"Sharon, love, how you doing?" said one of the Rastas in a Jamaican burr. "Where's that man of yours, him that was in all the films like, not seen him for a long time you know?"

"That's what I'm going to find out," said Sharon.

She left the Robert Mugabe Heights apartment complex, crossed the street, and descended into the tube station. Sharon wondered what shit Eddy had stirred up this time.

Clore was almost a family friend due to a former romance with Sharon's mother. This had not prevented Clore from an unhealthy preoccupation with Eddy Relish. He always made an appearance when Eddy was engaged in some shady activity.

Arriving at the Plume, Sharon noted that the bar traffic was light for a midweek evening. The presence of Clore was making the usual clientele nervous. Clore was sitting alone at the back of the pub, with empty tables either side of him. He was attracting dark glances from the Plume's landlord.

"Evening, Inspector, I see you're making the local wildlife nervous," said Sharon.

She smiled at the landlord, but this was not returned when he saw her sitting with Clore.

The inspector had a permanently furrowed brow, a receding chin, and a ginger-tinged comb-over. Sharon knew that Clore based his dress sense on fictional British TV detectives. He wore a blue blazer, cavalry twill pants, and a silk tie. A Burberry raincoat lay beside him on the seat. Clore was trying to be more interesting than what he was: an aging police detective stuck in a nondescript, decaying London borough.

"What're you having to drink?" said Clore.

"Gin and tonic, thanks."

Clore got the drinks and sat studying Sharon, as she pecked at hers.

"Okay, Mr Clore, when you finished checking me out maybe you'll let me know about Eddy," said Sharon.

"You know how the stupid bastard got himself into debt to Bill Blake?"

"Of course; I was trying to find Bill and pay back the money, but he's disappeared as well. Please don't tell me Bill's done something horrible to him."

"Yes and no. Reverend Bill Blake decided to collect on his debt about two weeks ago. When Eddy couldn't pay back the money, he put the frighteners on him and put him on a plane to Hong Kong."

"Hong Kong?"

"Yes, Bill's linked up with some of the local villains out there. Eddy was supposed to swallow a number of heroin-filled condoms and bring them back to Britain. We found this out by leaning on a few local snitches when Eddy disappeared from view."

Sharon said, "Go on."

"We talked with our Chinese police counterparts and the Chinese Embassy. They found out which Hong Kong villains were likely to be doing business with Bill. According to the Chinese Embassy liaison, Nancy Liu, Bill was linked up with the Three Fingers Triad. They are one of the more ambitious criminal gangs. They were hoping to get a new heroin outlet in the UK, through Bill, using a chain of Chinese takeaways as distribution points.

"Bill bastard Blake, he's got his fingers in so many pies. I didn't think heroin was in his line of business. Still, I shouldn't be surprised," said Sharon.

Clore said, "I know what you mean, but apparently the Triad wanted a reliable 'round-eye' contact in the UK."

He paused for a moment.

"Anyway, the local Hong Kong police watched the Three Fingers, and, sure enough, they led us to Eddy, who was holed up in a flea pit hotel, some place called Chunking Mansions."

"Is he safe now?" asked Sharon.

"For the time being," replied Clore.

Sharon visibly breathed a sigh of relief, and then a thought occurred to her.

"Were you keeping Eddy under surveillance? I know you have a passion for nicking him, but he's not some master criminal, just an unlucky one."

"First things first," said Clore. "What do you know about an Albanian refugee called Stefan Globtic?

"Only that Eddy told me he met him in Paris when were there on a weekend break, three or four months ago. Eddy had made a bit of money at the dog track, so we went on a short holiday. I think it was to make up for him fooling around with a barmaid in the Blind Beggar.

"I had a headache from the sun, so I had a lie down. Eddy went out for a walk by the River Seine. He met Globtic, who was drawing portraits, so Eddy gets his done. Its framed and hanging over my mantelpiece. You know how Eddy is; he gets talking to this Globtic, who speaks good English, and who tells him he wants to get into England. Eddy told me he wished him luck; I think he knew the guy was an illegal and was going to slip into England in a container truck."

Sharon took a sip of her drink.

"About six weeks later Eddy was walking down Knockney high street, and Stefan Globtic pops up. He'd just arrived in England. Globtic remembered that Eddy lived in Knockney, so was wandering around the area hoping to bump into him. He told Eddy that he wanted to claim refugee status. Then he would be housed courtesy of Her Majesty's government; and given forty quid a week to spend on cigarettes and booze."

Clore laughed and said, "Did Eddy help out Globtic?"

Sharon said, "Yes, but not all that much. Eddy helped to find his way to the mosque in Chumleigh. He thought that some of his countrymen might be worshiping there. So he borrowed my mum's car and took him over to Chumleigh."

"And that was it?" asked Clore

"Yeah, so what's this all about?"

Clore said. "The French police fished a body out of the River Seine not too long after you and Eddy were in Paris. They determined that this was the real Stefan Globtic. However, a man using a French passport in the name of Stefan Globtic had legally entered the UK. So we know he's a villain.

"So who was the man that Eddy met in Paris and here in London?"

"I'm getting to that," said Clore. "The French security service began questioning Albanians and narrowed down the search to a cell of Islamist terrorists. They found out his real name is Abdul Madbul. He was working as a portrait artist along the banks of the River Seine to earn money to get to the UK."

"And Madbul was the man that Eddy met and who drew his portrait?"

Clore nodded "The French searched through their close circuit camera images of every artist working the tourist beat. They narrowed it down to one bloke who they cannot identify. He keeps his back to the camera and wears sunglasses when not working. This Madbul is not stupid. He was a crack Albanian secret agent. Now he has gone rogue and fallen in with an Islamist terror group. Madbul is in Britain to create mayhem."

Sharon was puzzled, "Okay, but why is Eddy so important in all this?"

Clore said, "No one knows what this fellow Madbul looks like. The French recognized Eddy Relish as one of Madbul's customers. An undercover operative at Chumleigh mosque recognized Eddy driving out from the car park. He recalls the Madbul-Relish connection, and Special Branch put Eddy under surveillance.

"Bloody hell, you don't think Eddy is involved with Islamist terrorists do you?"

"Course not, but he was the bait we had hoped to use to smoke the bastard out. We began putting the rumour about at Chumleigh mosque that Eddy had cottoned on to him being a terrorist."

Clore continued looking amused.

"Do you know we even had a look-alike driving around Knockney to increase the possibility of Madbul making a move? Just in case, we were keeping tabs on both you and your boyfriend."

"I'm not sure if I should say thank you or be angry," said Sharon. "When do I get to see Eddy again? When is he coming back to England?"

Clore looked uncomfortable. "I've already told you more than I should."

"Come on, Inspector, you can't just leave me hanging like this," said Sharon.

Clore looked more uncomfortable but continued. "Okay, but I trust you'll keep all this to yourself; don't tell your mum or Auntie Jan."

Sharon nodded.

"It was decided that Eddy should disappear for the time being, while our double continues to try and lure Madbul out of hiding. The Chinese leaned on the Triad to keep their mouths shut, and let us set up Bill Blake. Eddy is in a secure compound somewhere in South China. He will load up with refined heroin in condoms but won't actually swallow them. Eddy will fly into London, along with his special packets of Trojans. We will apprehend him when he shows up at Bill's place with the heroin.

"You're going to arrest him?"

"Well he is a heroin smuggler; okay, relax, bad joke. What do you think Bill is going to do if we do not go through the motions of arresting Eddy? We'll take them both in, but let Eddy out quietly when Bill goes to prison, and Knockney can breathe easily again. Eddy will have to spend a few weeks as a guest in a safe house."

"Yeah, but what about the bloody Albanian?" asked Sharon.

"Another reason for keeping Eddy in a safe house," said Clore.

Sharon sighed. "How does he do it? Only Eddy Relish could get himself into such a pickle."

CHAPTER 3
PICKLE

How do I do it? thought Eddy Relish. He sat on the edge of a narrow wooden bed in South China. He was still woozy with jet lag and not used to the humid tropical heat.

I can see the headlines, "Relish in a Pickle," except that nobody gives a toss about me, he thought glumly.

Eddy lay down on the bed but was tired beyond sleep. He got up and opened the bedroom door.

"Turn that bloody noise down!" he yelled at his minders in the next room.

Four Chinese men in singlets and shorts were playing mah-jong on a table in the center of the room, while listening to *Teresa Teng's Greatest Hits*.

"I'd get more peace if I was in a biscuit tin with a troupe of dancing skeletons. Put a sock in it, will you? I'm trying to get some sleep," he shouted.

Fat Pong pulled a toothpick from his mouth, pointed at Eddy, and belched. The others started laughing. One of them revealed a mouthful of broken teeth. In frustration, Eddy walked over to the fridge in the corner, grabbed one of the bottles of Singha beer, opened it, and took it outside.

Eddy knew there was no point trying to deal with the minders; they spoke little to no English. They had no reason to pay any attention to him. Fat Pong was supposed to be the point man—the one who would take care of him and get him out of there. All Fat Pong had done since they had arrived this morning was hang out with his three annoying friends.

Eddy went outside the sparsely furnished house and sat on a stool. The house was one of many buildings in a compound bordered by a tropical forest. Eddy could still hear the music, but this was now competing with the thrum of crickets and cicadas at dusk. The forest stretched in all directions over hilly terrain beyond the compound. The peaks were shrouded by a leaden sky. The overcast sky matched Eddy's glum mood.

Eddy tried to recall all the events that had happened to him since he arrived in China. Everything had passed in a blur. One minute he was in the company of silk-suited Chinese gangsters. The next, he had been seized by green-uniformed policemen and bundled into a military aircraft. The only explanation he had received was from a flint-faced Chinese police officer.

"No more Triads, Mr. Relish; you go home with heroin, but first you go to Hainan."

Eddy hoped that he could dump the negative Hollywood baggage when he returned to England. England was home and safe. England was where he had started in commercials and television, before landing big roles in Hollywood. His tarnished reputation preceded him back across the Atlantic. He found himself unemployed and unemployable.

Bill Blake said to him, "I set a trap for you, O Babylon, and you were caught before you knew it."[4]

Bill had taken Eddy to his apartment to fetch some clothes and his passport. The only consolation was showering and getting out of his soiled clothes before the flight to Hong Kong.

Eddy tried to be optimistic. His life of late had read like a TV celebrity crash and burn reality show. The public had an insatiable appetite for this kind of thing. All he had to do was record his experiences. These included an arrest for immoral earnings and a

---

[4] Jeremiah 50:24.

beating by Samoans for competing in the LA drug market, and that was just the tip of the iceberg.

Eddy finished his beer. He went back inside the house where the foursome was still sitting around the table. The rattle of mah-jong tiles had died down. They had brought a metal tureen of fish soup from the kitchen. A skinny man with thick black glasses ate with such fervor that he had a fish tailbone dangling from his left nostril.

Eddy was thinking about having another attempt at talking to Fat Pong when the beat of helicopter blades broke through the jungle calm. *At last, some action*, thought Eddy.

Fat Pong leapt up, swilled down the last of his soup, and ran outside. The helicopter set down on a helipad inside the compound. They all followed Fat Pong outside except for the one with the fish-bone up his nose who took the opportunity to grab some more soup.

How does he stay so thin? thought Eddy as he left the building. *I could make a fortune out of his diet—the stuff-yourself-and-stay-a-beanpole plan.*

"Okay. You come now."

Fat Pong was beckoning him.

"Into chopper. Chop chop. Ha-ha-ha, chopper chop chop!"

Eddy's laugh was hollow. "Nice one, dickhead."

He climbed in the rear of the helicopter, taking off his backpack. Fat Pong jumped into the front seat next to the pilot. In seconds they were airborne, rising out of the clearing, the helicopter lights briefly illuminating the jungle below.

As soon as they were in flight, Fat Pong turned and started rummaging around in the space between the two back seats. He grabbed a small bag made of woven plastic fiber with red, white, and blue stripes. Eddy had seen many of these bags in LA, used by Asians and Latinos. The stuff they generally carried was not as hot as the contents of this bag. Fat Pong flashed a grin at Eddy as he opened the bag that was packed with powder-filled condoms, looking like little white pillows.

"For you," said Fat Pong.

They flew for what seemed like an eternity. It was dark outside with nothing to see and noisy in the cabin. The helicopter started its descent, and Eddy spotted the lights of a small airport. After landing, Eddy got out of the chopper. Fat Pong, who carried the plastic bag, followed him. A Learjet was standing on the tarmac in front of an open hangar. It was being attended by several ground crew members and looked civilized and inviting after the day's ordeal.

The rotor wash made speech impossible. Fat Pong took his arm and led him over to the Learjet, stopping at the staircase, pointing to the open cabin door mouthing, "You go." He gave Eddy the bag of heroin and turned back to the helicopter. Eddy trudged up the stairs and into the dimly lit air-conditioned cabin. He collapsed into the nearest seat, threw his backpack and the bag full of heroin onto an adjacent seat, and closed his eyes.

He muttered to himself, "At last. Let's go home."

A familiar voice said, "Poor soul. You homesick?"

Eddy turned in his seat to look at a figure in the shadows at the rear of the cabin. He had just heard the voice of a notorious Hollywood brothel madam. Only the individual reading lights were lit. He could make out the silhouette of a slender woman in the gloomy interior of the Learjet.

"Ahh, poor Eddy, you homesick?"

Eddie squinted into the half-light of the cabin and stood up, banging his head on the cabin roof as he moved to the back of the plane.

Sitting in the cabin rear was the infamous Madam Sin, owner of the Lucky Lotus nightclub, situated off Hollywood's Sunset Boulevard. The Lucky Lotus was a front for a major call girl operation run by Madam Sin. Eddy had worked on commission for her from time to time. He would introduce fellow actors to this flesh market, which led to the arrest for living on immoral earnings.

Eddy spoke in a whisper, "Madam Sin, what are you doing here?"

"Well might you ask, Mr. Relish."

She switched from Chinese pidgin to beautifully modulated English.

"Mr Relish ... Edward, please sit ... yes I know it's a little confusing. My name really is Tzin, Cynthia Tzin, but correctly spelt tee, zed eye, en. Rather amusing don't you think, a bawdy-house keeper that really has sin in her name? How discourteous of me. Would you care for a drink?

"Uh, yeah; I mean yes, please."

He sat down opposite her with a table in-between.

Cynthia Tzin's tone demeanor made Eddy feel like a small boy. He tried to collect his scattered wits.

"I am sure with all that's happened in the past few weeks, you must feel a little dislocated."

Eddy shook his head. "That's an understatement."

"Well, isn't understatement an English characteristic?"

Eddy looked at her.

"No, Mr. Relish, I am Chinese not English, but I was educated in England at Cheltenham Ladies College. I am more familiar with the English language than you would think."

Eddy said, "But what, how, who, I mean what's going on? I only agreed to go along with the Reverend Bill's plan because he threatened not only me but Sharon as well. Since then the whole world has turned upside down, and now I seem to be a prop in the Beijing Opera. I mean, please, what is going on?"

"All in good time Edward. May I call you Edward, I think Mr. Relish is a little too formal, and Eddy sounds rather common. Would you care for a whiskey and soda?"

Cynthia picked up a telephone next to her seat. She uttered a command in Chinese, and the main cabin lights were illuminated. Cynthia rose and fixed the drinks in the aircraft's tiny rear galley. Cynthia gave him an appraising smile.

"You may relax for the time being, Edward; you have been entrusted to my keeping, and I will deliver you to England in good time. As you have probably guessed, my role, as a person living on the earnings of prostitutes, is just a role. I don't think I am telling too many tales out of school if I tell you that I work for Chinese intelligence."

"What? You're a spy."

Cynthia pursed her lips in distaste.

"I prefer intelligence operative. Spy is too crude a word for what I do."

"But surely the Americans ..."

"Know what I am? Of course they do. They let me run my operation in Hollywood because I provide them, as well as Beijing, with a great deal of useful information. The honey trap is the best lubricator of men's tongues."

Cynthia took a sip of her drink.

"Much of what we learn we share with our American colleagues. We frequently pool our resources these days. Los Angeles is the major crossroads of the Pacific. The enemies of China are broadly the same enemies of America and Britain. We tolerate each other's operations in our respective countries as long as we behave ourselves.

"We all have secrets from each other, but the polarized certainties that dominated politics for much of the twentieth century are gone. It is a much more uncertain world. It's better to know who your real friends are, tolerate their peccadilloes, and target our true enemies."

"But why are you here?"

Eddy took another long mouthful of what was an excellent scotch and soda. He felt like his mouth was full of mango flavored marshmallow.

"A bit of luck really, Nancy Liu at the Chinese Embassy in London sent me a routine email intelligence digest, which included your sad tale. Nancy is the cultural attaché at the Embassy. I saw your name and read about your adventures with the Bible-spouting thug and his heroin-filled condom plan.

"This would likely have killed you, by the way. Drug-filled condoms have a nasty habit of rupturing in the stomach. You would absorb enough heroin to keep half the junkies in England 'chasing the dragon' for a month."

She paused to allow Eddy to absorb this information.

"I followed up with our British contacts and with my superiors in Beijing. I heard what was intended for you. I thought, no, I should look after my old chum Eddy Relish, who steered so many of Hollywood's finest to the Lucky Lotus."

"You might have kept the bloody Samoans off my back and got me off that pimping charge," said Eddy.

"Alas, Edward, I was not about to risk one of China's most important intelligence operations over your plight."

"Thank you very much."

"Buck up, Edward, things are not as bad as they seem, and you have more friends than you realize. Now, we are going to get you home, but there has been a change of plan. You are not going straight back to England with that load of heroin."

She glanced at the cheap fiber bag set on a seat at near the plane's cabin door. She picked up the phone beside her seat and spoke again in Chinese. One of the ground crew Eddy had seen outside the aircraft came on board and retrieved the bag.

Cynthia said, "We are going to take a long way round, while I do some business along the way. The Chinese government would not sanction this trip entirely to provide you with transportation home to England. Otherwise, we would send you back on one of our army's military aircraft."

The phone beside Cynthia's seat rang. She listened and then spoke briefly in Chinese. The plane's door raised and shut automatically, and the cabin lights dimmed.

"One more thing, Edward. Under no account must you contact anyone by phone, email, or other means, until I say so. You may be tempted to phone your young lady, Sharon Constable. If you do, I will know, and I will have no option but to rescind our protection. Is that clear?"

Eddy nodded, realizing he had to go along with whatever Cynthia had planned. It would be preferable to being a "pack mule" for a load of heroin-filled condoms.

Eddy sat back in the chair facing Cynthia and blew out his cheeks and wondered if things were beginning to improve. He looked at Cynthia Tzin. In LA, she had looked gaudy, tough, and unsmiling, a lynx-eyed taskmistress in an elaborate wig and heavy makeup, barking commands in bad English.

Her presence was no less formidable here, but her makeup, hair, and clothes were subtle and elegant. The perfume she wore was bewitching. When she moved, her clothes made a gentle susurration that added to her allure.

That last thought surprised him since he had never considered her in the least bit attractive. Now he saw how striking she really was. Her skin was flawlessly smooth like porcelain. Her eyes were dark mysterious pools in which a man could happily drown.

He continued to look Cynthia over while she concentrated on documents. She appeared utterly engrossed in the contents of a folder but spoke with an element of mischief in her voice.

"Are you falling in love with me Edward?"

"Err … what, I mean no."

"Then please stop studying me. Ah, we're ready to depart."

Eddy half turned in his seat to watch the departure preparations. One of the Chinese pilots stepped through from the flight deck to ensure that the cabin door was secure. Satisfied that all was in order, the pilot nodded an informal salute to Cynthia. Cynthia nodded to the pilot, who disappeared into the cockpit. The engines fired up, and the plane began to taxi to its takeoff point. Both Eddy and Cynthia fastened their safety belts.

"Edward, I imagine you'll be feeling sleepy soon; I spiked your drink with a gentle sleep aid."

"Why?" Eddy said in a resigned tone.

"Because you need a good night's sleep, and I have a great deal of work to accomplish. We are going to island hop across the Pacific to several destinations before flying to the United States. You can make your own decisions once we are in LA, but I will be happy to help and advise you.

Eddy felt tired and realized the drug was taking effect. He tightened his seat belt and drifted off to sleep as the plane took off from Hainan.

He awoke several hours later as Cynthia Tzin roused him with a cup of tea.

"Wake up, Edward. Welcome to Brisbane."

CHAPTER 4

SCRAP

Sharon leaned against the kitchen sink, cupping a mug of coffee in both hands. The long sleeves of her thick-knit cardigan acted as mufflers. Sharon had told her best friend Tracey all about Eddy's predicament with Bill and a cast of rogues and law enforcers.

"So, Eddy is in China or somewhere? And it's all top secret?"

"Apparently."

"Then why are you telling me?"

"You're my best friend. I have to confide in someone. If I didn't I'd go crazy. It would be like shouting into an echo chamber."

"Well, I must say, you're taking it very well. If that had happened to my Brian, I'd be beside myself."

"Eddy has nothing to gain from me freaking out. I have had to bail him out of other scrapes. I suspect that this is no different; just a bit more complex than other screwups he's created through his malign genius."

"You know Reverend Bill; he's an absolute nutter. If he finds out you knew about this plan to trap him, he'll find a way of getting to you, even from behind bars."

"I know," sighed Sharon. "Bill says he's got God on his side. But somebody's got to stand up to him."

"So what are you going to do, apart from sit and wait for Eddy to arrive in England and get squirreled away? You know it could all easily backfire. Eddy has no guarantees as far as I can see. They could just as easily lock him up in jail, never mind a safe house. Why should they let him out? Who is going to believe a set-up job that involves him as a police accomplice? Eddy Relish, failed actor and villain, globetrotting with a stash of heroin under the protection of the Chinese secret service. Nobody will buy that."

Sharon sighed at her friend's skepticism, but looked resolute.

"I have my ways. Reverend Bill has aspects of his history that he would prefer to remain outside of the public domain. He has a fierce desire to be a respectable businessman. Mum and Aunty Jan used to take me to his office and warehouse when they were cleaning. He talked to me when I was playing with my dolls on his office floor."

Tracey gasped and then laughed. "No way. Bill wants to go legitimate?"

"He won't give up crime altogether; he enjoys it too much. But he wants to be recognized as a big success, I'm sure it's got something to do with being an orphan. Did you know that he reads the biographies of business moguls like Aristotle Onassis and Donald Trump?

"He'd pick out a book, show me a photo of someone like Rupert Murdoch or Robert Maxwell, and talk to me.

"You know what, young Sharon, I'd never tell this to any of the trash that work for me, but this is where I want to be one day, not scraping a living screwing people in Knockney. Out there in the big world, doing deals on the world stage. What do you think of that, eh; Bill Blake, international financier; Bill Blake, banker."

Tracey burst out laughing again, putting her hand over her mouth.

"My god, Sharon, you're not serious, are you? Reverend Bill wants to be the next Rockefeller?"

Sharon smiled, inclining her head slightly.

"I think I might need your help. Is your brother still in the scrap metal business?"

CHAPTER 5

FISH

Eddy Relish sat on a remote beach in northern Papua New Guinea. He wondered how he came to be in a country he had not heard of, with a group of children with whom he could not communicate. Papua New Guinea was the stepping-off point for the island-hopping itinerary that would bring him to LA. Cynthia had said it was up to him if he wanted to go back to England.

Cynthia said that Chinese intelligence operatives would swing through the Pacific Islands, under the guise of investors looking for business opportunities. They would meet with politicians, government officials, and other local businessmen and amass intelligence information in the process of their discussions.

Many Pacific Islands had small populations of ethnic Chinese running businesses. Cynthia would meet with such people. These Chinese communities had no formal connection with intelligence gathering. Their business connections meant, however, that they were familiar with the communities of which they were a part. Many families were mixed race with family in both the Chinese and indigenous island populations.

After clearing customs and immigration in Port Moresby, the Learjet had continued north and touched down at the town of Kavieng on New Ireland. The two pilots checked them into the only hotel in the small town. Cynthia and Eddy were collected at the airport by a local Chinese businessman and his family. They took Eddy to their store, where he was kitted out for the hot weather in shorts and a T-shirt.

The youngest son, Wyvern, took Eddy out to a beach for a swim. It was evening, about five o'clock. The sun was hanging over the sea, and Eddy could feel the waves of heat, even before sunset. The feeling of helpless bewilderment had reduced him to an almost automaton state.

The young Chinese that had brought him to the beach had been pleasant enough. He asked about England and the English soccer league. Eddy tried to make conversation but was still in a state of shock and disbelief.

Wyvern dropped him at the beach and said he would return in about an hour. He threw Eddy a towel and passed him a small polystyrene cooler of beer. Swimming was far from Eddy's thoughts as he sat on a log looking at the sea, sipping cold beer. He smelled wood-smoke from the forest on either side of the beach clearing. There were people living in huts thrown together from wood, matted palm-leaves, and corrugated iron. He hoped they were friendly.

A large brown man emerged from the trees. He was clad in a sarong, carrying a basket under his arm, from which protruded a machete. He approached Eddy and smiled broadly.

"*Apinun masta*," said the man.

He noticed the man's teeth were stained blood-red, from chewing betel nut. Eddy nodded, and the man kept going down a path parallel with the beach. A group of children trotting behind the man came and examined Eddy. They ranged in skin color from light tan through reddish brown to dark chocolate. They had huge brown eyes and big white-toothed smiles. Several of them had red or blonde hair.

Eddy started to talk to them.

"My name's Eddy. What are you lot called."

They laughed, and then the boldest one said his name was Mathew and pointed round the group naming the others.

Mathew said, "*Yu husat masta?*"

Eddy thought a moment and reckoned they were asking who he was.

"I'm English; my family came from Poland. My second name is Relish, but it's really Relitz. Kids at school, about your age actually, called me Eddy Relish."

Eddy did not know how much the local kids understood, but he plowed on.

"My dad was killed in a road accident; I was eight at the time. I'd worked hard at school up till then. My three sisters are older than me, and they did well at school, even after Dad died. I was depressed for ages and couldn't be bothered anymore. Mum and my sisters used to get upset with me. I got sent home from school and came bottom of the class, I mean, I thought why bother after Dad died."

The local kids continued to stare.

"You want to hear more."

"*Em nau.*"

Eddy understood that to be a yes, and the kids seemed attentive, so he continued.

"The school started acting classes when I was eleven. It was an alternative to sport, which is great if you do not want to freeze in an English winter. There were a lot of girls in the class, which was great. The teacher who took the class had contacts with the theater world in London. Sometimes producers and casting directors would come looking for kids to take background parts or small walk-ons with a few lines. I was thirteen, and I was picked out by a film producer to play the Artful Dodger in a TV production of *Oliver Twist*."

Eddy stopped to draw breath. The kids were still fascinated. Eddy smiled at them and pulled another beer from the cooler.

"I got an agent and adopted the name Eddy Relish. I'm not a big guy so I could play teen parts for several years. I jumped in with both feet. I did modeling, TV, and films. I was supposed to do a few hours a day schooling, but school was over for me. Can you believe that at sixteen I was both a heartthrob and heartbreaker?

"A couple of years later I was shopping on Rodeo Drive for a gift for my girlfriend. I was browsing in a shop, and this girl came up behind me.

"'Can I help you, sir?'

"'I'm looking for something expensive for my girl. Hang on, have we met?'

"'I don't think so, sir.'

"'But I know you; I'm sure of it. You're Jenny Clayton, the English rose. Every boy I know used to have fantasies about you, me included. What are you doing here?'

"'Working.'

"'Yeah? Aren't you still acting?'

"'Please, Mr. Relish, I can't talk to you at work like this. I will lose my job. Are you going to buy something?'

"'Well if I promise to buy something, can I talk to you?'

"'Oy, mate.'"

He shouted at the store supervisor.

"'I'd like to spend an obscene amount of money on birthday gifts for my girlfriend, and I'd like the charming Miss Clayton to help me with my shopping.'

"'Of course, sir, Miss Clayton is at your disposal.'

"'Thanks.'"

The supervisor moved on.

"'So how come you're not still in the business?'

"'Are you really going to buy something? The pay here is only just above minimum wage, and we need the commissions.'

"'Don't worry. You know who I'm going out with, right?'

"'Yes, Lynn Skynn; she shops here from time to time.'

"'I know. She's gone very upmarket since she moved from porn to mainstream. We just wrapped a new film, a high school comedy, about a junior nerdy type, me, who falls for and wins the heart of the head cheerleader. She dropped some unsubtle hints about what she wants for her birthday.'"

"Jenny Clayton relaxed a little."

"'So what are you doing working here?'

"She sighed. 'The parts just dried up, I'm not the only pretty face in Hollywood, or the only young English actor. Half the shop assistants, bus boys, and taxi drivers in this town are aspiring actors. The other half are actors that have had their brief day in the sun.

This place is full of failed Brits who thought they'd make it big in Hollywood.'

"'But Jesus, Jenny, you were a big star, a teen icon. I don't get it.'

"'I grew up, Mr. Relish.'

"She said this without rancor or bitterness.

"'Yeah, but you still look great.'

"'Not as great as when I was thirteen, Mr. Relish. By the time I was eighteen, my career had pretty much ground to a halt. The only options were to find a regular job or go into porno.'

"'You're joking, porno?'

"'Yes, I had some serious offers, but of course I wouldn't stoop that low … Oh, Mr. Relish, I'm so sorry; that didn't come out too well.'

"'It's all right; come on, let's do some shopping.'"

Eddy realized he had been reminiscing in his thoughts. The kids were growing restless and looking around for something else to do.

"'Not much else to add, really. I thought I was on top of the world, and it would never end. I saw some of those *Where Are They Now?* TV shows about teen idols. It was just the same for me—a lot of booze and drugs. I really fell so far I never thought I would get out of the hole. By the time I was twenty-one, I was unemployed and on my arse. I was pimping drugs and girls; well, you don't need to know all the details.'"

The local kids' attention span expired, and they went trotting down the beach path, chattering and laughing. Eddy felt abandoned and forlorn. He gazed out across the green and brown shallows of the fringing reef. Fish with improbable colors darted between the corals.

The huge breakers rose out of the deep blue ocean. They fell on the reef with a slow "kerrump," like the sound of distant artillery. He paddled in the shallows enjoying warm seawater. He disturbed a brown sea cucumber. It squirted out tendrils that stuck to the skin of his feet. A black and white banded sea snake swam by.

Eddy thought this was a suitable moment to retreat to land. The kids returned. One of them found a black sea cucumber and held it to his groin, where it squirted a jet of water. He was pleased to see that Papua New Guineans had an appreciation of toilet humor.

CHAPTER 6

DEAL

B ill licked his finger and turned the page of his Bible. He sat at the tiny desk that constituted the business facilities in his room at the Wanchai Ramada Inn. He was reading again a passage from Exodus. This had always inspired him since the day he ran away from the orphanage.

The thrill of the Bible for Bill was that it established a moral basis for his immoral life. Every action he had ever undertaken could be justified in terms of a biblical rationale. The Bible was the source informing Christian interpretation of God's Word. The Popes were corrupt charlatans; though they were the descendants of Peter and the chosen successor of Jesus. This meant to Bill that he was free to interpret God's Word as he saw fit. What he saw today was an excellent fit.

Bill was in Hong Kong to track down Eddy Relish. He had received a garbled email from his Three Fingers Triad contact. He had inquired about the expected arrival of Eddy Relish from Hong Kong. The email said that Eddy had gone missing from his hotel room—a room in a hotel owned by the Three Fingers Triad. Further inquiries from Bill met first with evasion and then silence.

Bill was going to keep another appointment before dealing with the disappearance of Eddy Relish. He had received an unexpected fax at the Ramada Inn. It came from Eric Dwyer, a Knockney resident and London metal trader. Eric had advised him of a possible business opportunity. Bill was suspicious why Eric would want to do him a good turn. On the other hand, people were always trying to curry favor with Bill, hoping to build up credit.

Bill emerged from a taxi and settled into an armchair in the lounge of the Hong Kong Grand Hyatt. He told the staff that he was expecting a Mr. Silberstein. He would be obliged if they would direct Mr. Silberstein to Bill when he arrived. Bill settled in, browsing through a coffee table book about the hotel.

The book boasted that the same chair pattern adorned the seating at Whites Club in London's Lancaster Gate. Bill relaxed and leaned his head against the antimacassar, crossed his legs, and had a sudden desire to become a cigar smoker. It seemed appropriate.

Bill was about to meet Sol Silberstein of Global Metals and Minerals. He was going to seal the deal that would take him from the Knockney nether world to the stratosphere of international finance. In this world, nobody had heard of orphans, except when paired with widows. Bill felt like a child, about to enter a wonderland of dreamers and schemers.

Bill looked up. Silberstein entered through the revolving doors, pursued by his young assistant. A Hyatt bell captain pointed to where Bill sat. Silberstein moved like a king bull in a herd of bison. He fixed his gaze on the Reverend and made a beeline in his direction. Silberstein looked neither left nor right, expecting all obstructions moved.

The Hyatt bellboys scrambled to move a luggage trolley that barred his path, while other hotel guests gave him a wide berth. Bill rose to meet him, overwhelmed by the man's strong grip, the dynamic force of his personality, and his expensive aftershave.

"Mr. Blake, Bill, pleased to meet you!"

Silberstein's accent mixed American English with eastern European and Lebanese influences. He had a smooth, domed forehead, engorged upper lip, and permanent five o'clock shadow. He sat down and snapped his fingers—ordered sandwiches, coffee, and whiskey—lit a large Cuban cigar, and contemplated Bill.

"So, my gangster friend, what I can do for you?"

Bill was off balance. The Silberstein portrayed in an online *Newsweek* article was a smooth but ruthlessly focused wheeler-dealer. He had taken a phone call from his operations manager in the Congo during his wedding ceremony. His hallmark was supposedly a total lack of joviality. Silberstein's staff had done some research on Bill Blake. They knew about his less than savory reputation.

Bill's instinct was to plan Sol's immediate demise. Sadly, he could not afford to obey his instincts. There were five hundred thousand reasons why he needed to do a deal with Sol. Half a million pounds worth of revenues needed laundering and repatriation to England. Eric Dwyer's fax was too good to ignore. Dwyer said that Sol Silberstein was desperate to find a buyer for a shipment of scrap from ex-Soviet Central Asia. It happened that Sol was in Hong Kong.

"Gangster?" said Bill. "Shall we just say that I have long had aspirations to practice my craft in a more sophisticated milieu? I feel I have achieved all I can as an artisan, and I seek gainful new employment among the commodity markets."

Sol said, "Excuse me? Please. I do not know what the fuck you are talking about. I was told we can do business. I do not have a lot of time, so shut the fuck up and listen. If you think we can deal, then let's deal. If not, bugger off, I am very busy. I have a meeting with my Hong Kong lawyers at half past four, so that gives us, let's see ..."

Sol looked down at the Piaget watch he wore on his right wrist.

"Twenty-six minutes."

Bill grimaced and swore to himself. He was unaware that this was the Silberstein style—to ensure that everybody he encountered should feel ill at ease and discomfited. Bill had not felt this humiliated in years but had no choice other than to play along.

He said, "Okay, let's cut the crap and—"

Sol said, "I loathe that cliché, 'cut the crap'; it's so trite, unamusing, and faintly disgusting. Do you have an alternative you can offer me?"

"No, Mr. Silberstein, I don't. Enough of this already, please! Tell me what the business entails."

Bill's self-control teetered on a knife-edge, but he had to hear this through. He gripped the arms of the chair until his hands blenched.

"Okay. Here is where things stand. My brother has decided that we at Global need to cut our exposure in Kazakhstan. And I agree with my brother."

He paused and clasped his hands together in front of him.

"We have been moving four thousand tons of Kazakh nonferrous scrap every month for the last year—proceeds from the dismantling of Stalin-era public housing. They were built like brick shithouses but with plenty of lead, zinc, and copper piping and wiring. Anyway, my brother says our country risk exposure is at unsustainable levels.

"What he means is we are up to our fucking eyeballs in Kazakh sewage, and we need to start breathing again. So where you come in is I am told you have financing capacity for some of this stuff."

Bill said, "Yes, it's true; I do have access to liquid funds. How much are we talking about?"

"Upward of two mil, maybe three; it really depends on … excuse me."

Sol looked behind Bill as a young man walked up to the table. The young man had the prominent Adam's apple of the adolescent and a half-open mouth.

Sol said, "Thomas. What do you want?"

"I couldn't place the order for July copper, Mr. Silberstein."

"And why, pray fucking tell, is that, Thomas?"

"The broker wanted you to authorise the order personally, Mr. Silberstein."

"Jesus, it is within your weasel limit, for fuck's sake. All you have to do is give him the order, and if he refuses to place it, then he is refusing to do business with Global Metals and Minerals. Then goodbye Mr. Fucking Scumbag Broker; he can move to a trailer park in Arizona, get a real estate license and a fat-arsed wife, and see how he likes that, the fucker."

"I hear what you're saying, Mr. Silberstein, but—"

"Your hearing what I say is not enough, Thomas. What is required is that you listen to what I am fucking saying; you know what I'm saying? Then, you process it in your tiny teenage brain and execute it. Do you hear me?"

"Not only do I hear it; I'm listening," said Thomas.

"Good boy; now, scarper, double the order. We want one thousand tons, July delivery, and tell that broker, whoever it was, you tell that broker this: if he has a problem, then I have a problem with him. Where is that fucking drink?"

Sol twisted in his seat.

"Hey, you. Chocolate teapot. Yes, you; I placed my order forty minutes ago. Where is it?"

The bell captain was already three quarters of the way to Sol's seat before Silberstein had finished the question.

"I am sorry, Mr. Silberstein. Can I ask what it was you ordered again? And with whom did you place your order?"

"I don't even remember; it was in my dim and distant past, when I was young and carefree. Maybe it was a scotch, a cucumber sandwich, and a coffee."

He pointed at a thin bespectacled waiter that was passing by.

"That fuckwit, he took my order. I don't want to see him again, thank you. Please arrange that he not serve my table, ever; I would be much obliged. Thank you."

He turned to Bill, his face red and flushed with anger. In the next instant, his face was calm, composed, and wearing a charming smile.

"Bill, where were we? Ah yes, the scrap shipment; it would be worth a couple of million."

"I don't know that I want to commit to that. I mean this is our first date, and we haven't even danced yet."

"Of course. I would not expect you to trust Sol Silberstein with your last $2 million. Why not start small?"

"Like … half a mill?"

Bill was learning some of the vernacular.

"We could do that. I understand there is a mixed shipment of buzz berry and armature wire that's paperwork ready. I think my Kazakh friends would take whatever you're offering for that, as long as you can deliver the funds."

Silberstein paused and winked. "You know how to deliver funds, don't you?"

Bill nodded.

"Real pleasure doing business with you, Bill. I will have Thomas give you the contact details, and you can take it from there. Thomas is a good man; he's only nineteen but he has the makings of a fine trader. He's family—the younger brother of my brother's wife—don't know what the fuck that is, my brother's brother-in-law?"

The drinks and sandwiches had arrived. Sol had taken one bite from the sandwich and one sip of the whiskey when a cell phone in his pocket started beeping manically.

"Bill, I have to go now; such sweet sorrow, my friend."

Bill replied, "The appointed time has come. You will arise and have compassion on Zion, for it is time to show favor to her—"

"For her stones are dear to your servants; her very dust moves them to pity."[5]

Bill had never experienced anything like it; Sol had completed his Bible quote!

Sol stood up, shook hands with Bill, and left. Thomas and a tall blonde woman, with a tiny waist and large breasts, trailed after him.

---

[5] Psalms 102:13–14.

CHAPTER 7

ROCK

Eddie Relish continued his journey. He jotted down on a piece of paper the islands they had visited after Papua New Guinea. These included: Solomon Islands, Vanuatu, Fiji, Tonga, Samoa, Cook Islands, and French Polynesia. In Tahiti, Cynthia spoke fluent French, as if she had spent her entire life in Paris.

Each visit fell into the same routine. They would land, check into a hotel, with the two Learjet pilots. Chinese families living on each island group met Cynthia. Eddy would be stared at and then driven off to a beach to amuse himself. He would spend the night, dining alone in the hotel, and then be collected by the aircrew in the morning.

They were now on the big long haul to Los Angeles, from Papeete. The Learjet would need to touch down in Hawaii to refuel. He was experiencing a journey across the Pacific Islands in style. However, he was lonely and out of his depth. He had occasionally tried to engage Cynthia in conversation during flights, but she had been preoccupied with work. She spent long periods on her laptop computer or reading printed documents brought to her by one of the pilots.

He brought her a glass of ice water from the small galley on the plane and placed it in front of her. She was dealing with a sheaf of reports, all in Chinese characters.

"Edward, thank you; how thoughtful. I am sorry we have not had a chance to talk in depth, but my masters in Beijing demanded their pound of flesh for this trip. I had better not disappoint them. I know I should be a better hostess. I promise we shall have more time to talk about your future when we arrive in Los Angeles."

Eddy usually sat farther up the plane so as not to disturb Cynthia. He mused on his Hollywood days. Even when famous, he still missed much about England. One of his best friends was Malcolm Bolsum, a camera technician also from Knockney. Malcom had introduced Eddy to other English expatriates. Among these were Pete and Peg Micklethwaite. They owned Head-Strong, a Santa Monica store selling secondhand books, records, and hippie paraphernalia. Pete and Peg were relics from the 1960s who had followed the counterculture siren call to California.

Eddy spent many weekends at the beach in Santa Monica. He made a habit of dropping by Pete and Peg's shop for a decent cup of tea. On one visit Pete was sick with pneumonia, which had developed from flu. Peg minded the store while Eddy made a pot of tea and brought it to Pete.

Between coughs and sneezes, Pete had told Eddy his ideas.

"Yeah, my man, it just came to me while I was cataloging this bunch of old rock magazines," said Pete.

He indicated the yellowing piles.

"Here, look at these," said Pete, pulling three separate articles together and laying them on a coffee table. They were obituaries for Brian Jones of the Rolling Stones, singer-songwriter Nick Drake, and Syd Barrett, the founder of Pink Floyd.

"What's so special about these three?" asked Eddy.

"To be honest I was not really sure at first," said Pete. "But they all came from English middle-class families and came to pop music by an initial interest in American blues music. They had talent and good looks in abundance—talk about gilded youth. Look what happened to them.

"What did happen to them?" asked Eddy.

"Jones and Barrett had spectacular success for a few years and then just blew it. Both were forced out of their bands for becoming more and more unstable. Jones died in his swimming pool; no one knows if it was an accident or murder. Barrett died after living in seclusion for decades in Cambridge. Nick Drake made three amazing records but wouldn't do any tours. He became more and more depressed and committed suicide."

"Sounds like they might make a good story for a documentary," said Eddy.

"Already been done," said Pete. "There's been a few docos on TV and radio about all three."

"All right then, how about a biopic? You could call it *The Lost Boys.*"

"I was thinking *Dear Mister Fantasy,* after first album by Traffic."

"I like it," said Eddy. "Let me speak to some folks and see if we can get this project moving."

"My goodness, Edward, you do look miserable," said Cynthia.

Eddy was startled out of his reverie and looked about him awkwardly.

"Oh, you know, it's just we're getting closer to LA and Hollywood. It's bringing back a lot of bad memories. I was just thinking about my film project that got made without me."

Eddy expected Cynthia to go back to her work on her laptop. Instead, she yawned, stretched her neck, and delicately arched her back.

"Would you rub some Tiger Balm into my neck? It's become rather stiff, and you can tell me all about your film project."

Cynthia reached down and took a small jar from her handbag and handed it to Eddy. She turned and bent her head. Eddy found himself mesmerized by the sensual curve of Cynthia's sculpted neck.

"Please tell me about your film, Edward," said Cynthia.

Cynthia's voice broke the spell. Eddy massaged some of the exotic ointment into Cynthia's skin.

"Oh, right; well I was still on top of my game in Hollywood. I had access to a lot of top producers and directors. A friend in Santa Monica suggested a biopic about three dead rock stars."

"Who were they?"

"Brian Jones of the Rolling Stones, you've probably heard of him."

"Yes, of course, and the others?"

"Syd Barret of Pink Floyd and Nick Drake, he was—"

"A singer and songwriter; yes, I have heard of him. I once danced with Syd at the UFO Club."

"Really?"

"Have you seen his first solo record? Who do you think the naked girl on the cover is?"

Eddy stopped massaging Cynthia, stunned by her revelation.

"I told you I was schooled in England. I was rather a wild girl in my younger days. Tell me more about your film."

"You do know you're an urban legend?"

"I have heard; now, enough about me."

"Yeah, it was really hard going; I remember one conversation that more or less ended with this producer saying, 'Lemme get this right, kid. You wanna make a film about three Brits from the 1960s, who are now all dead, who were famous for about fifteen minutes. Am I getting this right?'"

Cynthia laughed and said, "But you persisted."

"Yeah, I put some money into commissioning a film outline from a UCLA film school graduate, to help me pitch my arguments. Many rock stars cite these three as influences. The film couldn't miss if it had the right cast."

"Which it did, except there was no part for poor Eddy Relish. How did that happen?"

Eddy paused, his eyes coming back into focus again onto Cynthia's neck. The painful memories flooded back.

Cynthia said, "Could you rub a little harder at the top of my neck? There's a nasty little knot there. Anyway, you were saying?"

"Well, yeah, it was a winner; the project was picked up by MegaTool Productions. Cy Sly, MegaTool's executive producer, actually advanced me additional funding for the development of the screenplay. Like an idiot, I was too excited to read the small print. The advance meant that the concept then became the property of

MegaTool. I just figured he'd green lighted the project, and I'd get a starring role."

"Which you did not," said Cynthia.

"No."

There was a pause while Eddy gathered his thoughts.

"When the first casting call went out, I couldn't believe it. I reread the list, thinking there had been a mistake. I was offered a minor role as a roadie, with only a few lines of dialog, not even as a supporting musician in one of the bands. I thought there must be a mistake."

Eddy began rubbing Cynthia's neck again, feeling the knotted muscle beneath the edge of the skull where it joined the neck.

Eddy said, "I had a real shouting match with Cy Sly, who kept me waiting for hours to see him. He told me that I wasn't so hot anymore, and the film was a big risk. I should have kept my cool, but I totally lost it, saying five minutes of screen time was unacceptable. He said this was a film about three obscure Brits.

"The film needed stars that were still going to be hot in a year's time. Otherwise, it would just be an art-house film playing in universities, obscure film festivals, and little theaters off Broadway. He offered to build the part up a little, but I was too stupid to see what was going on, so I told him to fuck off; oh, sorry."

"I think your profanity can be forgiven," said Cynthia.

There was a silence while Eddy kept massaging Cynthia's neck. The combination of the Tiger Balm and Eddy's fingers had made the pale eggshell porcelain color of Cynthia's skin flush pink. Eddy marveled at the silkiness of her hair and the delicate fluted whorls of her ears, as he moved her head slightly back and forth.

He wiped his hands on a paper napkin, and then putting his hands on Cynthia's shoulders, he began to knead her shoulder muscles.

He said, "You know what the worst of it all was? I called Pete to tell him what had happened about his idea, how I had totally screwed things. Peg answered the phone and told me that Pete had died that morning, just flopped down in an armchair, took a last drag on his cigarette, stubbed it in the ashtray, and stopped breathing.

"*Dear Mr. Fantasy* went on to win a truckload of Golden Globes,

Oscars, and film festival prizes. Its soundtrack was one of the bestselling soundtrack albums of all time. Pete died in obscurity not knowing his idea was such a success. MegaTool tracked down a whole load of pop stars from that period and invited them to the London premier."

Eddy sat back in his seat. Cynthia moved her head back and forth and made small adjustments to her blouse.

"Thank you, Edward. I feel much better. I think you have magic fingers."

"What? Oh, you're welcome," said Eddy.

Cynthia went to the rear of the plane and returned with two large whiskey and sodas. "Here we go, Edward; this will help banish the blues until we get to Hawaii."

CHAPTER 8

WEED

Inspector Clore sat in Knockney's central police station facing a glowering Rastafarian. The young rebel went by the name of Rasta-Blasta, a local deejay on Knockney's Radio Caribe and in various Knockney venues. He wrote newspaper and magazine columns that raged against the oppressive and racist policies of the UK government.

Clore reviewed the file in front of him. Rasta-Blasta's real name was Nigel Owen. His father was a London-based Barbados barrister and privy counselor. He had married an English QC, and their union was blessed with Nigel.

Clore said, "Nigel, you were found carrying twenty pounds of marijuana. Even with our more relaxed approach to the drug, this is a serious offense."

"I don't know nothing about this, and my name is Rasta-Blasta, not fucking poncey name Nigel no more. Another thing, herb should not be a crime. It is a blessed herb for all Rastaman."

Clore reached across the table and slapped him across the face. In place of the Rastafarian was a very aggrieved Englishman.

"Bloody hell, Inspector, what the fuck are you playing at? I'll have your badge for this outrage."

Clore looked on with a sour grin on his face.

Clore said, "I dare say you could, Nigel, but now we're both speaking like adults, can I continue?"

Confusion rippled over Nigel's face, and he continued in his normal voice.

"If you know who I am, then you know who my father is, and what he'll do to you for hitting me."

Clore looked back with indignation.

"Hit you, who me? Do you see any other police officers in the room? Is the recording equipment switched on? Is your lawyer present? This isn't a formal interview; we're having a friendly chat."

Nigel stared around the room. He noticed the cassette recorder was not operating, and the CCTV camera light was not glowing red.

Clore said. "Nigel, I spoke with your father about thirty minutes ago; his exact words to me were, 'Please, Inspector, knock some sense into the boy,' so I don't feel that I have anything to fear from him or your mum.

"Now, Nigel, from whom did you acquire twenty pounds of marijuana? Why are you holding this load of herb for the Reverend Bill? I know that our political masters seem hell bent on decriminalizing marijuana, but even they would not turn a blind eye to this one, even if it was perpetrated by a genuine Rastafarian."

Nigel sighed. "Inspector, how much trouble am I really in, I mean if I tell you the truth, what am I looking at?"

Clore leaned back in his chair and looked at the young man in front of him.

"Well, I won't bullshit you and tell you you'll walk free from this one. Like it or not, we found you with twenty pounds of wacky-baccy in your possession. If there are extenuating circumstances, and with the Reverend Bill I can believe there will be, then you probably won't be doing any jail time. If we put in a good word with the Crown Prosecution Service, then you'll probably get off with a slap on the wrist and a fine—probably more than a few quid but easily within your income bracket."

Clore paused.

"But, if you play silly buggers, then we won't put in a good word with the CPS. We'll paint you as a drug fiend, preying on the innocent waifs of Knockney. We will demand they lock you away for a long stretch. A long stretch is what your little bottom is likely to experience when the prison queens get hold of you. I mean a pretty mixed-race lad like you will drive them wild. I can see them scratching each other's eyes out over who gets to pop your cherry."

"Fuck me, Inspector."

"Not me you have to worry about, son. I know what side my bread's buttered."

"Oh, fuck, you know what I mean. Look, Reverend Bill asked me to look after the fucking stuff, and you do not say no to Reverend Bill. I mean even the Yardies are scared of Bill, and they are not scared of anyone. The man is a fucking psycho. He nailed his dentist to his own chair, just because of the swelling from work he did on Bill's lower jaw.

"The dentist was stuck to his chair by his ears all night, until his dental nurse came back in the next day. He could have got himself free, but Bill told him to stay where he was and contemplate his punishment. I know the dental nurse, and she told me that Bill had sent her home. Bill said to her, 'He hath also broken my teeth with gravel stones, he hath covered me with ashes.'[6]

"I told you the Yardies are frightened of him. Do you know why?"

"I heard rumors and stories, something about one of them trying to kill Bill, not being very successful, and Bill exacting revenge with a soldering iron."

"Do you know they actually shot the Bill six times, but he wouldn't die? Those Yardie gangsters are hard men, but they come from Jamaica and are superstitious. They're in awe of the bastard."

"Like I said, I heard the rumors. What happened?"

"They ambushed him coming out of a pub on Thabo Mbeki Street, after they reckoned he had 'dissed' one of their members in the Pig and Whistle. I mean until then their paths had never really crossed. In fact, they might even have worked together under other circumstances. They weren't stepping on each other toes, just drinking in the same bloody pub."

---

[6] Lamentations 3:15–17.

"So what happened?"

"Bill gets himself a soft drink at the bar and was heading back to his table, when he bumps into head Yardie, Winston Jackson. Bill knows who this is, and I think he was feeling charitable in that psycho way of his. He just makes an innocent crack—knowing Bill, probably a biblical quote."

"Jesus, he got off lightly, I would say; he must have been in a good mood, but presumably Brother Winston was offended."

"You know the Yardies, Inspector. For a bunch of well-hard bastards, they're real prima donnas. Winston goes back to his table all affronted and relates what's just happened. A few of the crew's saner souls suggest leaving well enough alone. Winston's not happy with this, reckons that he had been disrespected.

"So, the boys wait for Bill to come out of the pub. When he does, a couple of them open fire. They hit him about six times. Bill roars in defiance, grabs the nearest bloke, and breaks his neck. The Yardies cannot believe what they are seeing; they're too shocked to open fire again. Bill had not gone to meet his maker but has killed one of their number and grabs another. The lads cut and run leaving behind one dead and one guy in Bill's clutches."

"Do you mind if I make some notes? We've reports of so many incidents with the Yardies but no accounts."

"Okay, but keep my name out of it, and I'm not agreeing to anything except the possession charge."

Clore said, "Agreed. Carry on."

"Despite leaking blood like a sieve, Bill knocks this guy out, drags him to his car, and chucks him in the boot. He drives around to Doc Patel's late-night surgery. He walks in and asks the patients if he can jump the crew. You can imagine, all six foot four inches of Bill standing in the doorway grinning and dripping blood. He clears the surgery, barges in on Doc Patel, and dismisses the poor bastard who's spread-eagled over the couch for a prostate exam ..."

"Come on, how come you know all this much detail?" said Clore.

"Because the poor bastard getting his prostate examined was our studio engineer."

"Oh, okay then, fair enough."

"Bill drags in the doc's receptionist so she can't phone the police and tells our sound engineer to take a seat and keep his gob shut. Bill makes Patel get to work cutting out the bullets. Poor old guy; he knows Bill by reputation from patching up the results of the Reverend's nail-gun jobs.

"It turns out that all six bullets are in shallow wounds. They lodged in his ribcage and chest—no mortal wounds to main arteries, nothing requiring more than basic surgery. Bill wears a stiff leather waistcoat that slowed down the bullets. At most, he had a sore torso for a couple of weeks. After getting a patch-up job, Bill explains what he will do to Doc Patel and family should he breathe one word of this to anyone."

"Well, fascinating as this is, Nigel, when are we going to get to your story?"

"I'm coming to that. Anyway, Bill still has this other Yardie in his car boot, so after getting patched up and filled with painkillers, he motors around to his place by the river.

Clore said, "That old lock-up under the railway arches; yeah, we know it. We call it Bill's torture chamber. That reminds me, I remember the shooting incident because eventually someone called the police, but no one would say a word about it when we got there. In fact, we thought it was just another Yardie gang fight, resulting in one dead soldier. Now you tell me the Reverend was involved, the curtain of silence makes a lot more sense. Anyway, go on."

"Bill takes the car inside and gets out the still unconscious Yardie, or at least I figure that's what happened. All I know is that he stapled the poor bastard to a sheet of plywood and then began to compose a message on the guy's chest and stomach, using a soldering iron. Of course, being Bill, the message was a Bible quotation: 'Let them be turned backward, and put to confusion that desire my hurt'[7]."

"How do you know what it said?" asked Clore.

"I read it. Bill found out where Winston lives and actually

---

[7] Psalm 70:2–3.

dropped off the bloke. He says to Winston, 'Now we've both shed a bit of blood, let's call this quits.' The upshot of this is that poor old Doc Patel is dragged out of his house to make a house call and patch a sore Yardie with the usual dire threats to life and limb.

"The Yardies and Winston take stock. They have just taken possession of some poor moaning comrade on a sheet of half-inch plywood. They figure there's not much mileage in pursuing this further. What's more, Bill is all smiles, admires Winston and says that they should work together. He knows Winston and his boys are fond of 'weed,' and he can put some good Turkish product their way. I found out all this from Winston himself."

"I didn't know you were on speaking terms with the local wildlife."

"Ha-ha, very funny, Inspector. I know many of these guys from my deejaying in clubs and parties. It is always sensible to keep on the right side of them. Anyway, I get a call from Winston to go round and see him in his flat."

"What, at Forbes Burnham Mansions?" said Clore.

"Yeah, you know it then."

"Well you couldn't bloody miss it could you, with the ANC and Rastafarian flags painted on the side of the building, plus the large sign saying, 'Whitey Pigs Fuck Off' nailed up at the entrance," said Clore.

"I go to Winston's place, and his mate is still recovering. I could read the inscription branded on his flesh when they changed the bandages. Winston then tells me that I have to go and see Bill to pick up a package. Bill is still a little bit suspicious of being approached by a black guy. They both agreed that I was ... shall we say ... harmless. I was not overenthusiastic about being a go-between for a Yardie and a madman, but I knew I had no choice.

"That is how I came to be in possession of over twenty pounds of best imported Turkish marijuana. Bill and Winston agreed this would be sold by the Yardies and split 60/40 with Bill."

"Bill takes a smaller cut?"

"Yeah, he figured the Jamaican boys had to do most of the

legwork and so was willing to be magnanimous. It is never about the money with Bill, as long as he is enjoying himself. I picked up the bag full of dope from Bill and stashed it at home, ready to take around to Winston. The next thing I know, your colleagues come charging through my front door."

Clore leaned back in his chair and rubbed his eyes.

"All right Nigel, I don't suppose you are prepared to go in the dock with that story. Your life expectancy will be marginal if you do. I suppose you will have a good lawyer who might argue that our search and seizure at your place was very iffy. Still, at least we know a lot more than we did. We'll do what the Yanks call plea bargain for you. You'll get a fine and community service. I imagine that this little escapade will boost your image among the local youth."

Nigel looked relieved and relaxed for the first time since his arrest. As Clore was getting up to go, Nigel spoke again.

"Inspector, when I went round to one of Bill's places to pick up the weed, a little strip club in Knockney's China Town, he asked me if I'd seen that out-of-work actor, Eddy Relish? I hardly know the guy. I know who he is, of course, and seen him about Knockney, trying to scratch a living. Is he in trouble with Bill?"

Clore said, "Let's just say that Eddy is on a lot of people's shit list at the moment."

CHAPTER 9

ALOHA

E ddy Relish surveyed the mean looks he was attracting in a dank Hotel Street bar. Tourists did not frequent this part of Honolulu. The great trip across the Pacific was nearing its conclusion. After Hawaii, he and Cynthia would complete the journey in Los Angeles. He thought the stop in Honolulu would be only to refuel.

"Well, Edward, we may have more time in Honolulu than I had at first anticipated, so you will be able to explore for a couple of days. I have arranged for us to stay in Waikiki. You'll have to look after yourself, I'm afraid, while I am occupied with my intrigues."

The Learjet landed at Honolulu International Airport. The US Border Patrol processed Cynthia and Eddy in a VIP lounge. Several quiet burly men accompanied the immigration officials and talked softly with Cynthia, who gestured toward Eddy.

A uniformed immigration official detached himself from the group around Cynthia and looked at Eddy's passport.

The official asked, "Mr. Relish, you are a British citizen?"

"Er, yes I am," said Eddy.

"Real name Edvard Relitz."

"Yes, that's right; Eddy Relish is my stage name."

"So you're an actor?"

"Yes, only I'm resting at the moment."

"Why, are you ill?"

"No, it's an English theatrical term. It means I haven't got any work."

"Are you planning to work in the USA?"

"Well, I did actually work here, in Hollywood, when I was younger. I wouldn't mind working here again if I was offered work."

"So you're planning to work here?"

"No, I'm just passing through with my friend Cynthia; I am going to LA and then back to England, I guess. I suspect it depends though on what Cynthia's got planned for me."

"Is she your wife?"

"Er ... no."

"Are you related to Miss Tzin?"

"No, look at her. She's Chinese; I'm a Brit of Polish extraction."

The man stared long and hard without saying anything and then spoke again.

"Would you like to work in the US?"

"Well, yes, if anyone would employ me, but I've had no offers of work in a long time, and my visas are no longer current," said Eddy.

"So you are planning to work illegally in the US."

"Hey? No, of course not. I told you I'm just passing through the United States on the way to England."

There was another pregnant silence as the official stared at Eddy.

He said, "I just asked you if you'd like to work in the United States. You said yes; you then admitted that you don't have the requisite visas to work as a legal alien in the United States."

"What! No, I did not; well, yes, I did, but I was only being polite. Look, I am traveling with Miss Tzin, who offered me a lift from China to LA and to help me on my way to England."

"What were you doing in China, Mr. Relitz?"

"Err ... I was on holiday in Hong Kong."

He had had to check himself from mentioning his real reason for being in Hong Kong.

"This flight originated from a military base on Hainan Island, which is a restricted area to foreigners. So, you are looking for work in the United States, without the appropriate documents, and you boarded a private flight from a part of China restricted to foreigners."

Eddy's vision began to lose focus as he tried to deal with the robotic mentality of the immigration official. He felt like bursting into tears.

"No, I am not looking for work in the United States. I was an actor here and—"

He broke off realizing he was digging a deeper pit. He looked up and saw Cynthia detach herself from the main group of men. A man in a lightweight tropical linen suit and dark glasses followed her.

Cynthia looked at the immigration official, seeing his name on an ID card pinned to his shirt.

"Can I perhaps be of assistance, Officer ... O'Brien?"

"No, ma'am, I think I can take care of this," replied O'Brien.

"Nevertheless Officer O'Brien, my good friend Edward has informed you that he is passing though the United States for a few weeks holiday, on his way back to England. I arranged for him to spend time in Hainan after his visit to Hong Kong, and, yes, I know that parts of Hainan are restricted, but not to me."

Officer O'Brien took a breath and raised himself up to his full height. Before he could speak, Cynthia put her hand lightly on his forearm.

She said, "Officer O'Brien, you've heard Mr. Relish's responses to your questions. You do not appear to be an unintelligent man, but you appear to be willfully misinterpreting poor Edward's statements. It may be that you think his arrival in America with me is somewhat suspicious. However, you will note that other representatives of your government have not afforded me the same discourtesy. Mr. O'Brien, I want you to think about this before you utter one more word."

Cynthia paused for a second. It was very quiet in the VIP lounge.

"You could continue to torment my poor friend with your willful attitude. However, I assure you, this would result in your transfer to one of the more remote US Arctic islands. You will dream of the balmy climate in Honolulu when you go to empty out the trash, hoping there are no lurking polar bears. Or you could simply stamp Edward's passport, welcome him to America, and send us on our way."

Cynthia's speech made O'Brien go pale. The man in the linen suit and his companions, were all staring at O'Brien. One of them mimed cutting his throat to the amusement of the others.

Eddy could sense O'Brien teetering in the balance for a second or two longer, and then he stamped Eddy's passport.

"Welcome to the United States, sir."

Eddy mulled these memories over in the Hotel Street bar. He had enjoyed the way the immigration official had wilted under the steel of Cynthia's glare and the smirks of the spooks.

Being a street creature by habit, he had forsaken the sterile precincts of Waikiki and the luxury beach hotel. Eddy mooched around Waikiki during the day, but there was not much else to do, apart from lying on the beach. The shopkeepers of Waikiki had lobbied to keep the streets clear of street performers, unlike other similar great maritime cities such as Sydney or San Francisco.

Noisy tourists packed the Waikiki bars. Eddy wanted dark dingy surroundings with people who showed life's scars and body blows. Eddy found what he wanted on Chinatown's Hotel Street. Grocery stores, traditional medicine shops, and restaurants stood next to bars and strip joints. He prowled the streets between Fort Street and River Street. It looked to Eddy more cheerful than Knockney's red-light district. This comprised Bell End Lane but renamed Patrice Lumumba Lane by the puritanical left-wing council.

He encountered a large number of homeless vagrants and derelicts on the downtown streets. As twilight fell, more of these creatures emerged, followed by drug dealers and hookers. Eddy retreated into a bar where the people inside looked worse than those on the street.

CHAPTER 10

GNOME

Sharon had arranged to meet Eric Dwyer in Knockney's Grey Park during her lunch hour. Eric had confirmed that he had sent a fax to Bill about a potential deal with Global Metal and Minerals. The park was a memorial to a Victorian colonial secretary. Knockney Council had rechristened it Jean-Bertrand Aristide Park.

Sharon sat on a bench overlooking the duck pond, a large puddle that was the centerpiece of the memorial. She was reading Noam Chomsky's *Failed States*.

"Hey, Sharon, what's so funny?" It was Eric.

"Hello, Eric, I was just reading some Noam Chomsky. It's brilliant; pure comedy."

"What, he's called Gnome, like a garden gnome."

"No, you twit, N O A M; you should read this stuff."

"I think I'll stick with the tabloids; anyway, have you heard what happened with Bill?"

"No, tell me, tell me. Did he take the bait?"

"It worked like a charm. You were right; he could not resist trying to go semilegit. I do not get involved in that kind of stuff; it's very dodgy. One of the brokers I know is seriously into larceny in the emerging markets. He put me on to Global Metals. Dealing with Global is like wrestling with a pig while rolling in shit. You think it's a disgusting, degrading experience, and then you realize the pig really enjoys it. That's Global, and Silberstein is the dominant boar."

"So what's the scam?"

"It's diabolical, really. There were these nuclear power plants in ex-Soviet Central Asia that the authorities have wanted to dismantle. They are toxic; I mean very toxic. We are talking about plant designs that were rejects from the Chernobyl tender. You cannot demolish them legitimately; licensed demolition teams will not go near them. The authorities turned to the Chechen black market; you pay five bucks per man to go in and demolish anything. Those communists couldn't build shit, but they sure know how to destroy it. That's what they've done. They've converted it to scrap and passed it off as plumbing and wiring from decrepit housing projects."

"From the same place, right?" asked Sharon.

"Yeah, this stuff is in Kazakhstan. Anybody in the market knows this stuff is nasty and will not go near it. You have to understand the central tenets of commodity trading. The only way to turn a profit is to exploit your counterparty's ignorance. Shaft your customer; that is how it works. Bill is about to become the proud owner of five hundred tons of toxic scrap metal. When he tries to unload this stuff, the combined forces of the CIA, the IAEA, and the Kazakh government will be queuing up to respond."

Eric lit a cigarette.

"So all I had to do was alert Bill to the opportunity and the rest was—"

Sharon interrupted him. She had not realized Eric would get himself so personally involved when she asked for his help.

"Hang on. Why would you take such a risk?"

"I'm only ever going to get one chance to shaft that bastard, and I thought this was it. He's had it coming, after what he did to Uncle Sam."

"Uncle Sam? What's he ever done to the US government?"

"Not that Uncle Sam, my uncle, Sam Scully, the landlord of the Fork and Knife. Bill really hurt him badly."

"Fair enough," said Sharon. "We can only hope this ends the way it's meant to end."

"It will; don't you fret. Come on; I'll buy you a drink."

"That's all right Eric; I've got to go see the bank about a mortgage on my new flat. I don't want to go in smelling like a wino."

Eric planted a kiss on her cheek.

"You're a sweetheart."

He was about to walk away when he remembered. "Oh, any news of Eddy?"

"No, but Inspector Clore left a message on my voice mail this morning. He asked me to call him back. He didn't say what it was, and I've not been able to get hold of him."

"Well, let me know if you hear anything, okay?"

CHAPTER 11

SANDMAN

Eddy Relish leaned back in his Learjet armchair and reflected on the past few days in Honolulu. He met men and women with defeat etched in their faces. Eddy noticed a man in a bar endlessly scratching and picking at scabs. The bartender followed his stare.

When Eddy ordered another beer, the bartender leaned close and talked in a low voice.

"Don't go staring at that guy. He's a tweeker—an ice addict. They go days without sleep and get beyond paranoid."

Eddy looked into the mirror behind the bar so he could observe the man.

The bartender said, "His mistress got him into the drug for marathon sex sessions. He was a big shot at the local phone company. No one knew at first. Then he totally lost it on a business trip. He was in business class, with the fancy food and drink. When the flight attendant gave him his dinner, he crammed it into his mouth with bare hands and started screaming for more food. They had to restrain him on the plane, which turned back to Honolulu."

On the penultimate night in Honolulu, Eddy climbed into bed about midnight. He had drunk too much in Chinatown and soon fell asleep.

He awoke in the small hours with a headache. As his eyes focused, he saw a silhouette—someone seated in the room's armchair.

Hey, uhh, what, who?"

"Ssshh, Edward, go back to sleep," said Cynthia.

"But what the hell are you doing?"

"I'm watching, to make sure the Sandman doesn't steal you away. Now go back to sleep."

"Oh … I've got a headache."

"Don't put on the lights; just feel on the dresser next to you, there's a glass of water and two aspirin. Take them and go back to sleep."

He drank the water and swallowed the medicine. He soon drifted off to sleep despite wanting to stay awake and watch what she did next. In the morning there was no sign of her. There was a slight trace of her expensive perfume. He tapped on Cynthia's adjoining door, but there was no response.

That day he toured the island of Oahu on the regular bus service. He lunched out at the Hilton Hotel in Turtle Bay and enjoyed being a tourist. He did not prowl the bars of Chinatown but wandered around Waikiki in the evening.

Eddy woke again in the small hours, without the headache and without a silhouette in the armchair. He sighed with relief. Eddy turned over in the bed to go back to sleep and realized that Cynthia was sitting next to him. She sat above the bed covers, propped up on two pillows. He felt her hand on his forehead.

"Good night, sweet prince, and flights of angels sing thee to thy rest," said Cynthia.

"Jesus, you're going to give me a heart attack doing this. What are you doing?"

"I told you, I am looking out for you, guarding you from the Sandman, so he doesn't steal you away in your dreams. Now relax, and go back to sleep."

Jesus, he thought, *how can I sleep with her not twelve inches away. What if I fart?* This made him giggle. He took a few deep breaths, calmed down, and fell asleep. In the morning, there was no sign of her again except the trace of perfume. There was a note on the table beside his room key. It told him not to leave the hotel.

The bell desk called him that a limousine would take him to

the airport. The car picked him up at a little before midnight. The limousine took him to Honolulu airport and directly to the Learjet. Cynthia was waiting for him on the plane, working at her usual table. She smiled, told him to prepare for takeoff, and returned to her work. Eddy wanted to ask Cynthia about the past two nights and wondered how to broach the topic.

He also wondered how he was going to explain this to Sharon.

"So, toward the end of your epic journey around the Far East and Pacific islands, you end up in Honolulu with a cross between Suzie Wong and Mrs. Robinson, who spends two nights with you, one of them actually on but not in your bed?"

"Uh, yeah, that's about right."

"This is my Eddy Relish we are talking about—the human gland, the man whose brains reside at the end of his willie. The man who can hardly resist the advances of any woman, let alone the proprietress of a high-class LA knocking shop. Someone though advanced in years still makes men go weak at the knees and women extremely jealous and insecure."

"Well, I don't know about the women …"

"Well, you bloody well should, because that's exactly how I feel!"

No matter how honestly he told the story, he would always sound guilty. He glanced over at Cynthia who, despite the early-morning hour, was absorbed in documents and emails. She would not want to be disturbed. Eddy looked at his watch—four more hours to LA. He closed his eyes and slept.

CHAPTER 12
PASSPORT

Abdul Madbul sat on a mattress in a Southall townhouse built for a Victorian family but housing over forty migrants. It was the safest place to lie low. He had hoped to start a terror cell in the Chumleigh mosque, a fertile breeding ground, given the high unemployment among young Asians in the area.

Despite his wariness, he must have fallen asleep. A man was gently shaking his shoulder.

"Hey, bruv, not met you before. I sleep in here too. I'm Fahad."

Madbul thought the man had said Fa'aht. He realized his mistake. "I'm Abdul."

"Where you from, bruv?"

"Albania. What about you?"

"From Pakistan, bruv; from Karachi. You looking for work?"

Madbul looked into Fahad's eyes, which were green and without guile. Madbul suspected he was simple and an unneeded mouth to feed; send him to England, problem solved.

"Yeah, I'm looking for work."

"Tell me about yourself, bruv."

"I was born in Albania."

"Where's that, bruv."

"Next to Greece."

"Oh, right."

Madbul saw there was no point in explaining further. Fahad's geography outside of Karachi was limited to England.

"My parents were Muslims."

"Best kind, bruv."

"Yeah, but they were killed when I was seven."

"Oh no, bruv; it must have been written, inshallah. Tell me more; they threw me out from the telly room. They said I talk too much."

Madbul guessed Fahad was in his early twenties. He wore a Pakistani salwar kameez.

"You do talk too much, but I don't mind."

"You're a good man, bruv. Can you speak Arabic?"

"Some, but I'm still not fluent. How about you?"

"No, well some, but I can't read, and I have a hard time remembering things. Tell me more, bruv."

"After my parents died, I was put in an orphanage. Then I went into the army. Can I trust you?"

"Yeah bruv, we're all brothers here."

Madbul knew he was taking a big risk but this simpleton might prove useful.

"I was recruited from the army into the Albanian security services. I trained in China and North Korea. I became an assassin, killing enemies of the state."

"No, you're teasing me."

"I would not lie to a brother."

"What was China like, and North Korea?"

"Didn't see much; we trained in camps away from any towns.

Madbul was caught up in his own memories.

"Then everything went wrong. It was like Communism became a dirty word; our great teacher Hoxa was despised and ridiculed."

Madbul stopped speaking, and Fahad became nervous.

"What happened next bruv?" said Fahad.

Madbul looked at him. Fahad recoiled from the ferocity in Madbul's eyes. He made to get up and leave, but Madbul grabbed his arm.

"Sorry, bad memories."

"Yeah, okay, bruv; you scared me. I thought you'd kill me."
Fahad gave a nervous giggle.

"I ended up in Paris. I worked across Europe—seasonal work on farms and in factories where you take cash for wages. I heard Albanian spoken by a group of men one evening. They were Albanian exiles from Kosovo. They were going to a local mosque, so they took me with them."

"Good place to go, bruv."
Madbul shook his head at the memory.

"I had not spoken or read Arabic since I was a young boy. I had to relearn the Koran and other sacred writings."

"Wish I could learn them."

"You can speak English."

"Yeah, but it's on telly and the radio, and everything's in English, so it's easy to remember. Go on though, bruv."

"We were walking home one night when a Moroccan gang attacked on us. They had knives and chains. My friends were frightened, but I was not. Their ringleader was easy to spot, so I grabbed him and broke his arm."

"Wow, you're a lion, bruv."

"My new friends said that. I asked them not to say anything about the attack, but people talk. Like you.

Fahad laughed. A bearded man put his head around the door.

"Is this idiot bothering you?"

"No, it's okay," said Madbul.

"Hit him if he won't shut up. We're watching the football downstairs. Good game."

"Thanks. I'm a bit tired; Fahad and I are just talking."

The man nodded and withdrew.

"Thanks, bruv, they're always hitting me or kicking me. That was my brother; he hates looking after me. So what happened next?"

"I met these Algerians at the mosque, after evening prayers. They talked about the decadence and corruption of the West."

"Yeah, bruv, it's awful, but I like looking at the girls. Is that wrong?"

"It's not your fault. It is the fault of women; they awaken a sickness in men's hearts by their impure ways. The men I met were part of a group called Fa'aht."

Fahad laughed and said, "Sounds like fart; oh, sorry, bruv."

"It's a contraction of old Arabic phrase for silent but deadly. Fa'aht has no vision of a global caliphate. Our mission is to rid the world of all the vile and filthy kufars. Only Fa'aht members would survive.

"That's a bit harsh, bruv."

"Harsh but not without logic; our founder is known as the Mahdi. He teaches that Islam arose in the tropical deserts. Those farthest from the holy places and shrines are thus the most damned of the kufars. The most damned are the Eskimos."

"Okay, bruv, so are you making jihad on the Eskimos?"

Madbul stirred and looked embarrassed.

He said in a stiff voice, "Exacting punishment on the ice dwellers of the Arctic is hard. We've so far been limited to sending letters to Greenland and Alaska, telling the Eskimos to repent their sins and join Fa'aht."

"But you got skills, bruv."

"Yes, I was sent to England to begin a campaign here. It's not the Arctic, but it's a start, and these people are as damned as the ice dwellers."

"How did you get here, bruv? I'm legal; I got a visa in my passport, but lots of people in here sneaked in from France."

"I've got a passport. I took it from another Albanian called Globtic. He married a French woman and became a French citizen. He made the mistake of telling me."

"Whoa, bruv, you mean—"

"It was not difficult to alter the passport."

"So was Southall the first place you came too?"

"No, I'd met a man in Paris called Eddy Relish."

"What, the same as that movie star? I saw some of his movies on video back home."

"He told me he lived in Knockney. It was not hard to find him.

People in this country will tell you anything. Relish took me to the Chumleigh mosque, where I was going to begin recruiting people to Fa'aht. But I found out at the mosque that I was being pursued by British intelligence."

"How?"

"I overheard two African men speaking in French. Globtic's body had been found in the Seine. It was then I realized that this absurd Relish could identify me. No one knows what I look like, but they know Relish, even though he is a fallen star."

"So did you find him again and, you know …"

"Kill him, no. I was hunting him in Knockney. I dressed as a beggar—not hard in London. I saw him enter a bar, what the English call a public house."

"Oh, yeah, we sometimes go to the pub. We're not supposed to drink, but my brother says beer is okay, but not strong drink like whiskey. Sorry, bruv, can't stop talking."

"A man who looked like Relish drove past me."

Fahad screwed up his eyes, trying to make sense of this.

"So someone was up to monkey business," said Fahad.

"Monkey business? Yes, monkey business. There were watchers everywhere. You would not see them, but I could. There were even Chinese watchers—an old man and a woman keeping watch. I thought I would follow him and kill him when he came out of the pub. He left the bar but was with another man—a man who looked like one of Shaitan's minions.

"So what are you going to do now, bruv?"

"I wanted to take Relish's whore to find out where he had gone. I still want to slit her throat, but with watchers everywhere, I knew I would be caught. I think I'll go somewhere else, somewhere in Central Asia, where I can start again."

"Wow, bruv, you're like a Muslim James Bond."

"Where's your passport, Fahad? Can I see it?"

Fahad scrabbled under a nearby mattress and extracted a Pakistani passport.

"Here it is, bruv; see, here's my English visa."

Fahad flicked the passport open to the page with the visa. Madbul noticed the absence of other visas or entry and exit stamps.

"Do you long for paradise, my brother?" said Madbul.

CHAPTER 13

FOLKSONG

Eddy awoke from a short sleep. LA was drawing near. The sky was taking on the familiar yellow hue. Vague skeletal shapes such as TV towers and tall buildings punctured the ochre mist as they came in to land at Santa Monica airport.

Cynthia donned a hat with a gauze veil and left the plane ahead of Eddy. Baggage personnel placed their luggage onto a trolley. Cynthia turned around to check that Eddy was in tow.

"Come along, Edward; don't slouch."

Eddy was depressed. This was not how his LA arrival had worked in the past.

Cynthia continued brightly "Edward, let us enjoy ourselves here. We shall be staying at the Ocean Suites. Doesn't that cheer you up?"

Eddy remembered it well—a beautiful two-story stucco hotel overlooking Santa Monica beach. They took a taxi from the airport. It was a short drive down the last couple of miles of the Santa Monica Freeway. They emerged onto Ocean Boulevard. Eddy saw the Ferris wheel and roller coaster and smiled.

Cynthia noticed the change in Eddy's demeanor.

"That's the spirit, Edward. We'll check in, and then we can take a stroll on the beach. I want you to enjoy yourself for a change."

They walked to Venice Beach, where Cynthia suggested they stop for a drink. They sat down in one of the beachfront bars.

The drinks arrived, and Cynthia said, "Edward, you are probably curious about my behavior at the hotel."

"Yes, curious would describe it fairly well."

"Well, let me explain …"

Cynthia paused for a second to let a waiter move away from them and then continued.

"I spent last night and the previous one maintaining a vigil so that you would come to no harm. Your nemesis, Bill Blake, has taken an extreme dislike to you. He failed to find you in Hong Kong, and the Three Fingers Triad was very opaque in response to his questions. They seemed to imply that you had disappeared of your own accord. He was hoping to finance part of his new venture into scrap metals by having you do your rather risky heroin in the condom caper.

"When your absence was revealed, he was quite beside himself with rage. More than one Triad member found himself stapled to various pieces of wood. They managed to convince Bill that they frowned on this type of behavior. Indeed, according to Nancy Liu, the Three Fingers Triad was relieved to get Bill onto a plane and be rid of him.

Eddy laughed. "Yeah, that sounds like Bill; you've got to admire his disregard for all human life, including his own."

"To cut a long story short, various hit men were engaged worldwide to kill you. We had not realized that Bill's contacts were so resourceful. They managed to track you down in Honolulu. Of course, you made it rather easy for them, wandering about in Chinatown. Fortunately, I had our Honolulu consulate keeping an eye on you, so when we heard about Bill's plan, we tightened up security around you."

"Who were they, the people, the minders? Did I speak to any of them; I mean, were any of the crazies and loons I talked to part of the crew?"

"No, those were genuine unfortunates. Our people noted a few suspicious characters scrutinizing you, but an attack on you in broad daylight seemed unlikely. We expected an attempt on your life during the night. This was why I spent my nights playing your bodyguard.

I did not want to let on until we were out of Honolulu. It's easier to protect the innocent when the innocent is not looking nervously over his shoulder all the time."

"Hang about, what about now? Here on the mainland, in LA?" asked Eddy with a tremor in his voice.

"When Bill landed in London back from China, he was immediately taken into custody on our request. His arrest and detention was not, shall we say, smooth. There are several police and security officers nursing headaches and broken bones. Mr. Blake was detained in a discreet high-security facility at Heathrow Airport, which technically is not on British soil, and so legal niceties such as habeas corpus do not apply. Nancy Liu—"

"Er … the cultural attaché, right?"

"Quite; Nancy Liu paid Bill a visit in this facility and explained to him that his freedom was contingent on calling off the contract on your life. Mr. Blake had committed no crime, you see; well, none that for which he could be charged. It was arranged to incarcerate him 'outside England,' as it were, so he could be persuaded by the threat of indefinite imprisonment.

According to Nancy, Bill explained in detail what he would like to do to her were he not bound in chains. She would receive piercings in discreet parts of her anatomy. Eventually, a phone was brought for Bill. He made monitored calls that called off any assassination attempt and arranged payments for various individuals for their troubles."

Eddy nodded; he was still trying to understand everything that Cynthia had told him.

"Nancy reports that when Bill was calmer she told him that he should understand that he was now under the protection of elements of the government of China. Should Bill or his minions harm a single hair on your head, China would not forget or forgive such impudence. We would avenge any hurt on you despite his fearsome reputation. Even a psychopath like Bill understands that he is mortal. With one billion people at our disposal, we could exact our revenge at our leisure. I was not fixated with the need for your company in

Honolulu, merely playing bodyguard in case a bogeyman came in the night."

"Thank you very much; really, I mean it, although I don't know what I have done to deserve such special treatment."

"All in good time, Edward."

They finished their drinks and along they strolled back to Ocean Suites. Cynthia linked her arm through Eddy's. This surprised Eddy, who was more used to Cynthia's imperious and condescending manner.

At the hotel, they collected their keys and went up to their adjoining rooms. Cynthia asked if Eddy would like a nightcap. Since it was only 10:00 p.m., he acquiesced and joined her in her room. Without asking, she fixed two large scotch and sodas, with plenty of ice. She carried them over to a sofa and beckoned Eddy to sit down beside her. As he sat, she undid the pins and clips that held her hair in place and shook it out. Seeing the mane of jet-black hair fall across Cynthia's pale cheek and shoulders was mesmerizing.

"Edward, are you falling in love with me?"

He remembered that she had asked him this question before as he had stared at her on the plane.

"Er … no; I mean, well, errr … no."

He gulped down his drink and made pretense of looking at his watch and going through the motions of being sleepy.

"Good night then, Edward."

Back in his room, he considered his fate and wondered what he should do. It was going to be hard explaining to Sharon why Cynthia was in his Honolulu hotel room. He also knew that he would have no chance concealing the fact that he had become strongly attracted to Cynthia, who was teasing this infatuation.

He cast his mind back to the Tzin he knew in LA after his fall. That woman was a hard-faced harridan, every inch the oriental mama-san, barking orders in broken English, with her elaborate wig and makeup. The real woman was a million miles removed from that ghastly creature. He yawned and realized he really was tired and so went quickly to bed.

He awoke to the sensation of a moist tongue in his ear and a weight on his chest. As he struggled awake he inhaled Cynthia's perfume. She was astride his chest licking his ear.

"Ah, Edward, you've woken up. It's Naughty Madam Tzin, or should that be S I N. What do you think, Edward?"

He found his voice as realization suddenly dawned on him

"That was more than just whiskey you gave me, wasn't it?"

She broke off from nibbling his ear lobes and sat up in the dark, outlined in silhouette.

"A little herbal remedy to make you sleepy and relaxed; something else to put a little starch in you."

Eddy realized that it felt as if he had a giant redwood emerging from his groin. Without warning, Cynthia pulled back the bed sheets, opened her gown, and after a few delicate movements, set to with considerable enthusiasm.

Eddy's main emotion was surprise at Cynthia's speed and strength. He ran his hands over her body inside her gown and felt the warm suppleness of her skin and the strength in her finely toned muscles.

She rocked back and forth singing, "Ride a cock horse to Banbury Cross, to see a fine lady on a white horse."

On and on she went, reciting a litany of English folk songs.

"When sweet Polly Oliver lay musing in bed, a sudden strange fancy came into her head, to follow her true love …"

This went on for several hours through the night. After each climactic moment, Cynthia would rest, humming what appeared to be an endless repertoire of English songs. She would lay sprawled on his chest for about fifteen minutes until drugs revitalized him. She would set to with a renewed vigor.

"One misty moisty morning when cloudy was the weather, I spied an old man a clothed all in leather …"

CHAPTER 14

MISTAKES

"**Y**ou idiot, you incompetent fool. How could you let him get away?"

Clore stared back at himself from the mirror as he spoke. The weeks of patient surveillance had finally paid off. The man greeted by the imam of the Chumleigh mosque was the Abdul Madbul suspect arriving for morning prayers.

Clore had parked his 1967 racing green Austin Healey 3000 at an ideal vantage point. He could monitor the only exits from the mosque complex and be ready to pounce on Madbul. The security team had investigated the backgrounds of everyone entering and leaving the mosque.

The team had narrowed down the search to two individuals. They had divided the team into two squads so they could watch them around the clock. Clore was assigned to his squad's morning shift at the mosque. Before he went on duty, he received a call from a Special Branch colleague.

The officer said, "The other squad have cleared the second suspect. He really is a pharmacist's assistant, albeit very devout. Nothing wrong with that; so is my wife. So now, I need you to be extra vigilant, okay? Stop pretending to be Inspector-fucking Morse and don't get lost in that horseshit opera."

He knew it might be a long wait, so he had come prepared with his CDs. These included Puccini's *Turandot*. After about an hour of waiting, the opera had reached his favorite part. Clore mouthed the words and closed his eyes. The soaring melody tore at his heartstrings. He opened his eyes again and blinked, seeing a car drive off. There was a familiar figure at the wheel; the Madbul suspect had left the mosque.

The Madbul suspect had arrived in a white van, but this was a red Toyota pickup. Clore thought he must be switching cars. Clore started the engine and tailed the car. He followed it along Chumleigh High Street, until they hit a red light. Clore drew level with the car, looked into the window through the corner of his eye. The man behind the wheel was not the Madbul suspect. He did a U-turn and went straight back to the mosque to find people streaming out. Worship was over, and the Madbul suspect was nowhere in sight.

He reluctantly got on the phone to the Special Branch agent. There was an icy silence after Clore had explained what had happened.

The Special Branch officer said, "When you were at Police College, did you ever hear of the concept of calling for backup?"

"Yes, of course, it's just—"

"What were you doing before you gave chase?"

Clore said, "I was watching the exits, as ordered."

"That's it, just sitting there watching the exits, nothing else, all senses focused on watching for Madbul; nothing on the radio, no CDs playing?"

"Er … I had some music playing," said Clore.

"What music?"

"Puccini's *Turandot*."

"Christ, what did I fucking tell you? Did you at least get the registration of the white van?

Clore recited the registration number.

"Okay, so he's probably left in the same vehicle, which you would probably have seen if you weren't so fucking distracted. Hang up and go home."

Clore was inclined to interpret this as go home and hang himself. He was still seething about his own stupidity when the Special Branch officer called.

"Luckily for you, you're not a complete idiot. We were able to use CCTV to track the van to Heathrow. The images are too poor to get a great facial image, but it was definitely the driver based on what he wore. He went to Aeroflot and got on a Moscow flight, connecting to Kazakhstan. We crosschecked the time the Madbul suspect checked in with the Aeroflot agent. Turns out she had assigned a seat to a Pakistani passport holder by the name of Fahad Kahn."

CHAPTER 15

BREAKFAST

Dawn appeared as a gray smudge. Cynthia relented and rolled off Eddy's exhausted body, lying beside him. He half expected her to steal out of the room or be gone when he awoke. She had rolled onto her side with her black hair drawn back from her face. Despite the lack of makeup, she looked remarkable for her age.

He saw a star-shaped wound on her shoulder, which he guessed was from a bullet. Gazing beneath the covers along the curve of her spine, she bore other scars. He dredged the relicts of his memory. He wondered if Cynthia had been a Red Guard or had been on the receiving end of the Red Guard's temper tantrums.

She caught him off balance without looking at him.

"When you've finished inspecting this old bird's carcass, perhaps you will ring and arrange some breakfast," said Cynthia.

Eddy started, not so much from her voice but because he felt awkward about what to say.

"Oh, right; um, good morning err ... sweetheart."

Cynthia hooted with laughter, rolled over, and playfully bit his nose, making him yelp.

"Oh, the lead-footed subtlety of the English; guarding you, Edward, and dealing with every Chinese agent and contact between Hainan and Honolulu has been a stressful experience. A vigorous bout of sexual intercourse was required to clear my head and ease the kinks in my muscles. I am so glad you could oblige. Now, order breakfast while I have a bath to complete my therapy."

She kissed his cheek. In a fluid motion she rose, donned her silk kimono, and disappeared into Eddy's bathroom.

Bugger, he thought. *Bugger, bugger, bugger.*

A spectrum of conflicting thoughts played through his mind. He had cheated on Sharon before but this felt different. Eddy had grown used to Cynthia and developed a strong affection for her. He knew they would soon part company. This made him feel sad and afraid, and feel even guiltier about Sharon.

Cynthia had locked the bathroom door so Eddie went downstairs and used the lobby toilet. He came out and thought about ordering breakfast in the restaurant. There was a sign on the restaurant doors that it was closed for renovations.

He wandered along Ocean Boulevard and recognized an old haunt. He had often sloped off from the endless bingeing and sex at the Ocean to the indifferent service that was Moggio's hallmark. He found a table, and a surly waitress took his order.

"I'll have a bagel," said Eddy. "Toasted, with cheese, and a fruit salad to go."

He tossed the menu onto the table. The couple at the next table were talking loudly—commonplace in America. There was a man in his late twenties with Brillo-pad hair and an attractively plump woman who bore a resemblance Monica Lewinsky.

"I don't quite follow. Are you still with RAND or not?" said the Monica Lewinski look-alike.

"Well, yes and no. I am on the payroll, but I don't dare go in."

"Uh, okay. You don't dare go in. I don't get that. Why don't you dare go in? I mean, help me here. Hello?"

"It's my subordinates. They don't respect me. I ... I ..."

"Please, what is this?"

"I know, I know."

"Okay, here's what we'll do."

"We will?"

"Excuse me. Why are you staring at my tits?"

Eddy suddenly realized the Monica character was talking to him, not Mr. Brillo-pad.

Eddy replied, "I'm sorry; don't mind me. I'm just waiting for my bagel."

Monica ignored him and continued, "So, back to basics. Psychology 101. Why do you think they don't respect you?"

"It's the way they respond to everything I say. Any idea I have, they all want to knock it. I can tell. They think I'm past it; it's so disheartening. Okay, I'll give you an example that, like, illustrates my point. I was walking past the water cooler the other day, and I heard one of the guys whisper to his coworker, 'There goes Eddy Relish.' Man, that hurt. I mean, that really hurt."

Monica pursed her lips, and her eyes rolled upward before her lids closed.

"Eddy Relish? I'm sorry, why did that hurt?"

"Eddy Relish was the ultimate fizzle-and-burn loser in Hollywood. He was a byword for failure back in the nineties. My brother was in the movies and knew him. For a while, any wannabe who's now a has-been was an 'Eddy Relish.' I think the term lasted about seven or eight months. Then it burned out, but these guys at the water cooler were talking about me. I know it. I was the youngest nanoeconomics research fellow at the institute; I was published across Western civilization; I was big, you know, big, and now I get this alienation treatment; it's just so …"

Eddy had stopped listening, and he felt a strange rush. He remembered his thoughts while stuck in China. He was still somebody in this town. His becoming a nobody after being a somebody represented a potential advantage. Reality shows and scripts started running through his head.

The bagel and fruit salad arrived. He picked them up and left, and as he stood, he blew a kiss to the couple.

"Brillo, Monica; I love you," said Eddy.

"Who is that guy? Is he nuts or what? What is it about this town?" said Monica.

Her voice trailed off.

CHAPTER 16

MEDITATION

B ill was sitting on the Moscow-bound plane on the runway at Heathrow looking out of the window. He realized he had a window seat when he boarded the plane. The aisle seat was occupied by what looked like a Pakistani man, judging from his clothes. The man was reading the Koran and shuffling prayer beads with his fingers.

"Excuse me, could we switch seats? I'm a big bloke, and I'll be cramped by the window."

The man looked up; his eyes flicked over Bill. He said nothing but lifted the chair arm and slid over to the window seat.

"Thanks, mate," said Bill.

Despite the man switching seats, Bill was brimming with an unquenchable rage. Since when did people get off on insulting him and threatening him?

Twice now in as many weeks, he had been subject to personal abuse. There was the business with the Jewish metal trader, followed by being warned off Eddy Relish by some Chinese bint. He remembered King Saul telling David that the dowry for his daughter Michal is a hundred Philistine foreskins.[8]

"I'll take more than a hundred of them," muttered Bill. "I'll string them together into the biggest fucking necklace you've ever seen and hang it around the Post Office Tower."

His neighbor glanced at him and then back to the Koran.

---

[8] Samuel 1:18–25.

Bill paused in his thoughts and carried on.

"Actually, that's not a bad idea, I think I'll try that; you could remove the slime from entrails and knock up a decent elastic band."

He pulled out his electronic memo recorder and spoke into it:

"Business idea: products from intestines, binding, elasticity properties."

A wave of dark despair passed over Bill. This was happening with greater frequency. He recognized he was sliding into greater mental instability. He had bullied prescriptions for powerful antidepressants and mood-altering drugs from various Knockney doctors, including the hapless Dr. Patel. He shook a few of his pills out of a medicine bottle and crunched them up, swallowing them with a gulp of bottled water.

To Bill all the people he perceived as enemies were grouped as "Them," a set of conspiring bastards that he pictured in league with each other. Silberstein and his family, Nancy Liu and the staff of the Chinese embassy, and for good measure all the bastard friends of Eddy Relish. The little shit, thinking he could shelter under the protection of the Fu Manchus. Relish was not going to get away with it.

"It is mine to avenge; I will repay,"[9] he muttered.

The bouts of paranoiac depression had become more frequent after his return from Hong Kong. The promises about not harming Eddy Relish were worthless, but canceling the hits on Relish negated the one ace card he thought he held. *Every cloud has a silver lining*, thought Bill, who was surprised when Nancy Liu's manner thawed.

"Thank you, Mr. Blake," said Nancy Liu. "Now we can have a much more civilized conversation. I understand you have had dealings with a friend of my husband."

Bill said, "Do you mean Mr. Silberstein."

"Yes, my husband, Zhang Xing Liao, is vice president of the Chinese Recycling Council or CRC. He supervises China's supply and purchasing of scrap metal on a global basis. Did you know everybody

---

[9] Deuteronomy 32:35.

in the metal trading world refers to my husband as 'Magnesio'? He cornered the magnesium market in the early nineties. Prices rose to unprecedented levels; he then drip-fed his accumulated supply onto the market. He made great fortunes for himself and other leading party members."

Bill said, "Mr. Silberstein's assistant, Thomas, told me a little about Mr. Zhang, and the Magnesio legend. Thomas told me that Mr. Silberstein had just met with Mr. Zhang and told me the story. Please accept my sincerest apologies. Had I known you were married to Mr. Zhang I would not have been so rude. My musings on the virtues of body piercing were just a tasteless joke. Let me apologize again."

Nancy said, "My husband always welcomes the opportunity to listen to business proposals that might benefit the CRC; I would be very happy to arrange an introduction. Here is his card. Now you are free to leave."

The following day, Bill entered Zhang's modestly furnished office in Centre Point, Tottenham Court Road. Zhang was a stocky Chinese man with a ruddy complexioned, weather-beaten face. He asked Bill to take a seat and sat down behind his metal desk.

His English was almost free of any accent.

"Mr. Blake, I'm glad to meet you. My wife told me that she thought we should meet; I understand we are in the same business."

"Well, I wouldn't put it that way. I have investments in a number of fields, but it so happens that I have recently diversified into metal trading. I have a load of scrap metal from Kazakhstan on my hands. My reason for wanting to speak to you is to see if you would be interested in helping with distribution. I will be frank with you; I have no expertise or knowledge about sales channels for scrap metal. But my source, Global Metals, is one with a sound regular supply, and I think we are looking at a long-term contract here."

"Is this shipment export or domestic?"

"I have no idea. What do you mean?"

"I mean, is the license for export only, or can it be resold within Kazakhstan itself."

"Good question. I don't know. I tell you what, I'll send you the documentation, and maybe you can advise me on it."

Bill felt that his ignorance was actually an advantage. All he wanted to do was unload the cargo, get funds remitted to his bank in the Cayman Islands, and move on to the next adventure, or maybe take a little time off to tend his garden.

Zhang replied: "That sounds like a fine plan. Please send me the information. Meanwhile, I think the best thing would be for you to speak to our country manager in Kazakhstan. I will brief him on our conversation. You should make his acquaintance."

Zhang reached into a drawer in his desk

"I think you already have my card, but here is a spare, and here is another with contact details for the Kazakhstan CRC country manager."

A few days later, Bill found himself at Heathrow, waiting for takeoff on his plane to Moscow, from where he would fly to Astana. He had a productive conversation with the CRC representative on the phone. He was now looking forward to a few days break in a strange foreign land, diversifying his risk portfolio in the company of ruthless bandits like himself.

His antidepressant drugs kicked in and calmed his frenzied mind. Bill settled into his seat on the plane. He pulled out his Bible, paying no heed to the passenger seated next to him, who continued to finger his prayer beads and read the Koran.

CHAPTER 17

FRUIT

Eddy knocked on Cynthia's door in the Ocean Suites. It was 9:00 a.m. He had followed his breakfast at Moggio's by sitting by the beach and reading *Variety* and other movie papers. Cynthia opened the door and bade him to come in. She was all business again, attired in silk, with immaculate hair and makeup. She ate the fruit salad that Eddy had brought for her, while speaking to him between morsels.

"Edward, I will be leaving you today. I must get back to my house of ill repute and let Madam Sin loose again. You may spend one more night here if you wish, but after that you are on your own."

"Bloody hell, what am I supposed to do? I don't have any money or a way home to England."

Cynthia smiled and gave him an envelope.

"There's $5,000 and an open e-ticket on a flight from Los Angeles to London. You may now contact whomever you wish; here, take this cell phone; the charger is there on the table."

"Oh, errr … thanks. This is great, but umm …"

"Come and see me at the Lucky Lotus club before you return to England and bring the phone back to me. Call me at the Lucky Lotus; the number is already in the contact list. When you come and see me I will tell you more about what has been happening in the world that still makes you important to me and my masters."

"Can't I stay with you at the Lotus?" asked Eddy.

"No, that would be inappropriate. But I suggest you try contacting some of your old friends from your Hollywood days."

"What fucking friends?"

Cynthia raised an eyebrow.

"Oh, sorry," said Eddy.

"I believe you never fell out with Malcolm Bolsum."

"Eh? How do you know about Malcolm?"

"Just give him a call, and give my fondest regards to your girlfriend, Sharon. I expect you'll want to explore a few of your old Hollywood haunts before you return to England."

There was a knock at her door, which she opened to admit the porter, who loaded her luggage on a trolley. Cynthia put her hand on his arm and kissed his cheek gently and then was gone without a backward glance.

Eddy felt weak and lost, like a rudderless ship at sea. He sat on her bed for a minute, coming to terms with Cynthia's departure. It was a cruel wrench, particularly since last night. His thoughts about Cynthia led to thinking about Sharon.

He picked up the cell phone and charger and returned to his own room. He tried Sharon's home phone and got through to her answering machine. He looked at the time—9:30 a.m.—so it would be 5:30 p.m. in Knockney. *She is still coming home from work*, he thought. He tried her cell phone, but it went straight to voicemail. He knew she often had it switched off. He redialed her home number again and left a brief message.

"Sharon, it's Eddy. Look, I can be reached in LA at the following number …"

A piece of paper was taped to the base of the charger unit with the area code and number on it. He read out the number and continued.

"I am just going to look up an old mate of mine who works in the film trade here—Malcolm, you know Malcolm Bolsum. I told you about him, I think. Anyway, I'll let you know where I'm staying when I get settled. Right now I have to leave this hotel after tonight, but I'll probably check out today if I can get in touch with Malcolm. Call me as soon as you can."

He used the cell phone browser to look up Malcolm's number in the LA White Pages. He called but went directly to an answering machine. He began to leave a message, but as soon as he mentioned his name, the phone was picked up.

"Bloody hell, is that Eddy Relish? There is a rumor that you are back in town. Someone spotted you at Santa Monica yesterday, in the company of some expensive oriental crumpet. It caused something of a ripple in la-la land."

Malcolm's English accent mixed southern English, Australian, and American inflections.

"Malcolm, good to talk to you, mate. How you doing?" said Eddy. "Where are you now?"

I'm at the Occan Suites in Santa Monica. I have another night prepaid here, but I was hoping I could stay with you for a spell. I know it's been a long time; well, ten years to be exact, but ..."

"No problem, come on over. You got the address?"

CHAPTER 18

REUNION

Two hours later Eddy emerged from a $50 taxi ride, having packed his small bag and checked out of the hotel. Malcolm saw him arrive and came down to meet him.

Malcolm Bolsum was in his early sixties; tall and thin with a full head of gray hair parted in the middle and tied back in a ponytail. Eddy knew that Malcolm had been a member of one of the midsixties pop groups, known in the United States as the "British Invasion."

He helped Eddy into the apartment. The spare bedroom was the storage overflow, and boxes of electronic equipment, other computer equipment, and guitars were propped against the wall. Eddy flung his bag on the bed and joined Malcolm in the front room.

On the wall was a large framed photograph of Malcom and bandmates in 1965; six mop-topped English youths with terrible teeth and cheap suits. It showed them gathered around their instruments and equipment; a modest collection of amplifiers and guitars.

Eddy glanced at the picture, and Malcolm followed his gaze.

"The Logic Sound, did you know that we were considering calling the group Malcolm Bolsum and the Wholesome Sound, but saner counsel prevailed. Jeff Sodgewick and the Logic Sound hardly set the world alight did it? In any case, the Yanks pronounced it Sodge-wick, pronouncing the w. So the name never made any sense over here."

"Do you ever hear from any of the group?" asked Eddy.

"Actually, I saw them just last week; well, some of them anyway.

They still tour the United States and Australia, playing the cocktail and cabaret circuits in hotels—the land of the living dead—but it's a living of sorts, I guess."

Eddy asked, "What about you? What are you up to these days? Still moonlighting in the skin trade?"

Malcolm laughed. "Mate, the skin trade is huge these days. It is the mainstream."

"What about regular work?" asked Eddy.

"It is regular work, you silly bugger. Yes, I still work in the regular film industry, but the skin work pays the bills more regularly. So what about you? What are you doing here?"

"Well, you're not going to believe this, but anyway here goes ..."

Eddy poured out the whole story. By the time he had finished, it was early evening. Eddy had been talking for about two hours, with only slight interruptions from Malcolm. Eddy left nothing out, including waking to find Cynthia astride his body.

"Mate, I'd say I have just heard the biggest load of shit ever dreamed up."

Eddy looked crestfallen, but Malcolm continued.

"However, I suspect it's all true, because Cythnia Tzin called me yesterday and told me to expect a call from an old friend; she wouldn't say who, but she just told me to be patient, and that patience would be rewarded."

"So you knew who the oriental crumpet was, then. You know the rumor that was going around about me?"

"Yeah; well, I heard the rumor first and didn't know who it was when I was at Fox yesterday. Then I got a call from Cynthia herself on my cell and put two and two together."

Eddy was silent a minute, then spoke again.

"So you know Cynthia—Madam Sin—then?"

"Sure do mate; she contracts me occasionally to do electrical and computer work for her."

Just then, Eddy's phone rang. He jumped, startled by the high-pitched sound of the ringer tone.

"Hello, this is Eddy Relish."

A woman's voice said, "Eddy Relish, where the hell have you been?" It was Sharon.

"Erm," said Eddy.

"Well, I love you too," sneered Sharon.

"Sharon, my sweet. I'm so sorry. It's been a nightmare. I don't know where to begin."

"Well, how about we start at the bit where you decided you'd had enough meat and potato pie and wanted a bit of chop-suey instead? The last thing I heard you say before you disappeared was, I'm off out for a Chinese. You weren't fucking joking, were you?"

Eddy swallowed. "Okay, okay, the game's up. How did you know?"

"Well, for a start, you call me and then leave me a message telling me to call you back on this number: 310-555-3432. There is no such number. So, I conclude that for some reason, you intended to keep me as much in the dark as possible. Fortunately, I've installed a net-based caller ID feature. I think to myself, *Rather than calling him back straight away, I can ...* Sorry, Eddy, this isn't leading anywhere, is it? It's not plausible, the bit about the number, the net-based caller ID. It is all too contrived, like one of those thrillers turning on some innocuous observation or dialog you have to go back and reread.

"Yeah, it feels wrong," said Eddy.

"We have to come up with some other way that the Sharon character finds out about Eddy and Madam Sin," said Sharon.

"You're right. I was wondering if instead of it being a wrong number, it's a real number, and when you call it, Madam Sin picks up the phone."

"Isn't that too direct?"

"Yeah, I think so. We need to work on it some more. Anyway, sweetheart, can I call you back later? I'm at Malcolm's at the moment; it's late, and I'm knackered. Will you be around this evening your time or what? Can I call you in the morning my time?"

Sharon said, "Okay, I'll be home tonight. Call me after eight my time."

"Oh, right. Will do."

They talked for another ten minutes as Sharon brought him up to date with things in her life and happenings in Knockney and then rang off.

See you, Shaz."

"See you."

Eddy turned to Malcolm. "That was Sharon."

"I guessed as much. I like your style. You were doing all right there, mate. Sounds like you still got your acting chops. So what are you cooking up?"

"I've been thinking how to get back into showbiz since I knew I was coming back to LA. The idea of something based on my decline and fall seemed promising. What I heard in Moggio's this morning was like divine providence. I was so excited I had to call Sharon. I figured what is the worst that can happen? I'm back in America again.

"I called from a beachside pay phone so there was no phone call on the hotel bill. I knew Cynthia would scrutinize it like a hawk. I explained to Sharon why I had dropped out of sight, but you know how it is. I had the usual female inquisition and why had I not called sooner.

"Eventually, I was able to get on this career rethink and getting back into the movie business. I pitched her the idea for a story based on my recent escapades. I sketched the plot out and asked her to help develop a script outline and screenplay. She's smarter than me."

"What about you and Cynthia?"

"Here's the clever bit; I said we should spice it with a scene where the Chinese spy does exactly what Cynthia Tzin did last night. Eventually, his girlfriend back in England gets to find out about it. I think it worked. Sharon sounded pleased that I'm finally getting some direction in my life again. She said she would work on it and get back to me with more ideas."

"Sharon sounds like quite a girl."

Eddy sighed. "Yes she is. I'm so lucky, and she's had to put up with me and my fucked-up existence. She is really beautiful—big dark eyes and olive skin. Both her mum and dad's family have some gypsy blood. She looks like she's from Spain, not the East End.

"She's smart as a whip too, despite leaving school at sixteen. One of her favorite amusements is going down to the council chambers when they are in session. She argues those Trotskyite idiots to a standstill. They usually have to gang up and shout her down. She can run rings around them in arguments."

Malcolm said, "Don't you feel a bit bad about really cheating on her? I mean, after all, you really did bang Suzie Wong; that wasn't in your imagination."

"I don't think that counts. It was a setup by Cynthia."

Malcolm guffawed. "Mate, you shagged another woman; believe me, it counts."

He was tired and wanted to go to bed.

"Malcolm, I'm shattered, mate. Send me to my room."

"Do you need some pajamas?" asked Malcolm.

"No thanks; I never use them. I always figured you knew you were middle-aged and had one foot in the grave if you wore pajamas."

"Thanks a lot," said Malcolm.

Eddy awoke in the small hours of the early morning, still a little confused with jet lag and excitement about being back in Hollywood. His mind raced with possibilities. It was not an automatic death sentence being a Hollywood crash and burn.

The improbability of the experiences he had just endured— Hong Kong triads, Chinese Intelligence, the Pacific Odyssey, and a beautiful, bewitching Chinese spy— had all the ingredients for success. He yawned and began to fall back to sleep when the cell phone rang.

Cynthia said, "Edward, I hope I didn't wake you. I suspected that you might still be a little jet lagged. You did not sleep too well the last time we were together. Since you seem to be interested in reviving your film career, you had better come and see me the day after tomorrow. Come to the Lucky Lotus at 7:00 p.m.; you know where it is. Good night; sweet dreams."

"Err ... good night, Cynthia," said Eddy,

His sleepiness had evaporated. How was Cynthia monitoring him? The answer lay right in front of him—Cynthia's cell phone. This was more reassuring than sinister. He felt tired again and was on the cusp of sleep when he recalled the end of his conversation with Sharon. She had mentioned that she was thinking of entering local government politics.

CHAPTER 19

PROPOSITION

A Knockney magistrate fined Nigel Owens for cannabis possession. His father had intervened with the understanding that Nigel would do something useful with his life. Something had come up that might be a possibility. Fred Starling, leader of the Labour-controlled Knockney Council, met Nigel as he was leaving the magistrate's court.

"How did you know I was in the nick?" Nigel asked Starling.

"Word soon gets around when a prominent member of the Afro-Caribbean community gets his collar felt," replied Starling.

"Fred, my sister was at university with you, so please drop the fake Cockney. Or should I call you Adrian, Mr. Lymington-Starling?"

"Okay, Nigel, I'll drop the cockney if you give the Rastafarian lingo a rest. Come on, I'll buy you a drink."

Fred took Nigel to a nearby pub and bought him bottles of Red Stripe beer and rum chasers.

"How do you fancy entering politics?" asked Fred.

"What, so I can deliver the colored vote eh?"

"So that the multiethnic community of Knockney can be represented in local government by someone who has a true understanding of the political and cultural milieu."

"Yeah like I said, you want me to bring you in the colored vote."

"Okay, fair enough; yes, so you can deliver the colored vote."

"I suppose I've got to join the Labour Party?"

"Er … yes, otherwise you'd have to stand as an independent, and then we couldn't help you."

"What about a scat; there isn't an election coming up."

Fred said, "One of our older councilors, the member for the West Knockney ward, is going to announce his retirement in a day or so. He just found out he has terminal lung cancer. He is going to call it a day so he can spend more time with his family, you know, before the end."

"That's a bit grim isn't it, stepping into a dead man's shoes?"

"Well, he's not dead yet, and anyway, that's how it works—you're usually taking over from a stiff, dead or not."

Nigel considered this further, sipping alternately at the beer and then a nip of rum.

"So do I have to come to all the Labour Party meetings and be a good party member?"

"I don't think we need trouble you too much with the day-to-day minutiae of the Knockney Labour Party Branch. You might want to show your face at a few meetings and functions, and of course show up to vote with your colleagues at council sessions."

"Suppose I do stand as the Labour candidate. Who is likely to be the opposition?"

"The Tories are not much threat, but we might get a good showing from the Lib Dems. My guess is your main threat might be a popular independent candidate."

"Is that a possibility; is there anyone?"

"There's Sharon Constable. She's the girlfriend of that has-been film actor Eddy Relish. She comes down to the council chambers now and again and asks a lot of bloody awkward questions," said Fred.

"Oh yeah?"

Fred said, "Yeah, and she knows her stuff too; that's the real bugger. She argued me to a standstill one day. She was quoting from philosophers and historians I'd barely heard of. It was the time the council debated commissioning a portrait of Nelson Mandela and sending him congratulations for winning the Nobel Peace Prize.

Constable argued that F.W. de Klerck, the fascist Afrikaaner who shared the prize with Brother Nelson, was more deserving of our praise.

"She had the gall to argue that it was the foresight and political skills of de Klerck that convinced the ruling white minority to surrender power in South Africa. Mandela had been right to protest and rebel against the iniquities of apartheid. But all Comrade Mandela had to do was wait out his imprisonment on Robben Island and work on his charisma until the rest of the world caught up."

Fred paused to take a sip of his beer.

"Next thing she argues is that if anybody deserves a portrait, it was Helen Suzman. You see, she's a clever bastard like that, played the gender card. Anyway, the comrades were not going to tolerate such revisionist nonsense and simply shouted her down. But she's a local Knockney girl, well known and liked and could be a problem on the stump. She has connections with some of the local underworld, which means that she might be able to field a bit of muscle. You know that big scary bloke Bill Blake?"

Nigel shifted in his seat.

"Yes, I certainly do, and it was his ganja that got me into trouble."

Fred looked surprised, "So you do know him?"

"Not really. I was doing a favor for Winston Jackson."

"Ah, another pillar of the local Afro-Caribbean community."

Nigel scoffed. "Come off it, comrade. What have you been smoking? Don't go saying that down Oliver Tambo Drive or Forbes Burnham Mansions; you'll kill everybody with laughter. Winston's a Yardie hard man."

"See, that's what you can deliver for us—real credentials, an Afro-Caribbean guy, who's even got a conviction for drugs. You'll be a hero to the people."

"Don't forget, I'm not originally from Knockney and where I went to university and who my mum and dad are."

"Join the club, mate; I've been down that road too. As far as the folks in West Knockney are concerned, you'll be one of them; you can't fail. Welcome aboard, comrade."

CHAPTER 20

PLOT

Sharon and Eddy had been on the phone for the last two hours, talking about the script; they had different views about the direction in which they wanted to take it.

"You see, we've got the Eddy character being aimlessly transported from one place to another. There seems to be no rationale to it at all," argued Sharon.

"But that's what it was actually like," said Eddy.

"Yes, but truth is supposed to be stranger than fiction, not more boring."

"I don't think it's boring, I think it's exciting. Well it was kind of exciting—one minute in with a bunch of Chinese gangsters, then in some tropical Asian jungle, and the next in Papua New Guinea surrounded by cute native kids."

"I can see that it was, but what is the point? To me, that whole section reads like something that was scripted by two people exchanging emails—writing one episode after another without any serious consideration to the entire narrative."

"Well, so it was, in a way. I mean, I gave you the basic plot; you embellished it, and then I did my edits. That's how it was. That's reality, Sharon. I'm sorry, but either deal with reality or get off the pot."

"Come again?"

"Or however it goes. If you can't take a shit, get out of the kitchen."

Eddy laughed and Sharon joined in, giggling helplessly.

Eddy said, "Hey stop giggling for a second. I was working today. One of Malcolm's contacts put me in touch with an ad agency. They wanted someone who could do a voiceover for a shampoo commercial."

"What did you have to say?"

"I was an archvillian, and everybody hated me. I was dealing with personal demons. I had issues and dandruff. Then, I started using No-Flakes, and that really got to the root cause of my problem. Thank you, No-Flakes."

"God, that's awful; especially when you switch from Essex-man to Leprechaun Irish."

"Over here, they associate London accents with criminal masterminds. The Irish, on the other hand, are regarded as harmless, fluffy, good-time party animals."

"They need to spend a few days in Derry during the marching season."

"Who was Malcolm's contact?"

"Hoped you wouldn't ask; a sound engineer from Yes! Ooh! Yes! Studios. You can guess what kind of films they make. Anyway, the ad agency paid me in cash as requested, and their receptionist even asked me for an autograph. Are you coming over, or are you're serious about this politics thing?"

"Serious is not really the right word. It's hard to be serious about something that is such a joke."

"So why are you doing it?"

"Well the last straw was the council's new recycling policy. Apparently, in addition to separating newspapers from other paper and glass and plastics, they are now demanding that we recycle condoms and syringes."

"You're joking, right?"

"Now you're getting my point. We have to place used condoms in a little green bag. You get one free bag a week. Gay, lesbian, and trans couples get two free weekly condom disposal bags. Then we have to put our used syringes in a dinky little plastic tub that gets returned to you every week, presumably cleaned and ready for reuse."

"But how the fuck can you recycle condoms and syringes?"

"I am terrified to ask. All I know is that it's part of the drive to clean up the neighborhood. It all started when Fred Starling was showing his great-aunt around the area. It seems her high heels impaled a used condom, and she slipped on a discarded syringe. The rest of the family are all staunch Tories, but she is another black sheep.

"She was a renowned Fabian socialist in her day. All this was very embarrassing. Starling convened an emergency council meeting and said something had to be done about this outrage. In typical Far-Left control freak fashion, they drew up a new set of regulations to deal with the problem. It was all too much, so I decided I had to act; I had to stand for election.

"This is always the way with the left. First, they identify a nonproblem. Then they introduce a solution that makes everybody worse off. They're going to finance the recycling initiative by imposing a surcharge on the rates of local businesses employing more than two people, excluding worker co-operatives and grievance creation agencies."

"Grievance creation agency? What's that? Don't tell me Reverend Bill's involved in it."

"No. They call themselves 'victim support groups.' But my term for them is much better. If I am elected, I'd like to require that they register as such or ban them altogether. Actually, that would require another bylaw, so I won't do it. I'm running under a minimalist platform."

"I've never heard of that either."

"It's basically a reduced-government platform, or minimal platform. I'm going to repeal every bylaw and introduce a new, single code, no more than ten pages long, that will address every aspect of local government regulation."

"A do-nothing party?"

"Kind of. I even have a slogan: 'Vote Minimalist. It's the least you can do.'"

"Shazabooboo. I like it."

"Yeah, I think it will resonate with the locals; the way I see it is it's a way of appealing to both the anarchists and the conservatives."

"I miss you."

"Don't start that. You'll get me all weepy, and I'm in rehearsal for the debate, so I need all my wits about me. I miss you too. I'll talk to you tomorrow."

Eddy spent the next day doing additional voice-overs for more radio ads. A production company called his cell phone and asked if he would like to read for a part in a new animation series.

CHAPTER 21

BARBECUE

The guard crouched in the corner of the crumbling watchtower at midnight. It was dark; a freezing wind blew off the steppe with a chill factor of twenty degrees below zero. Apart from the flames of gas-well burn-off in the distance, the only light visible was that from a watchtower window, a pale light from the open stove that provided some warmth.

The guard had not shaved or bathed for a week. His only sustenance was a basket of preserved mutton. He cut a slice, impaled it on a skewer, and held it over the stove, dripping fat onto the bare wooden floor. He brought it to his mouth and gnawed at the burned, grisly meat; his few remaining teeth well enabled him to chew the morsel.

The guard's grease-stained moustaches quivered as he ground at the flesh, and he stared into the distance through the frosted window. His baggy corduroy trousers were wrapped above his shoes with steel wire, to maximize their insulation. The steel wire was torn from the fence that surrounded the demolition site. The wire had snagged the clothes of a would-be thief trying to enter the facility. The thief's corpse still hung on the fence, and his blood was on the wire binding the guard's trousers.

He heard something above the noise of the ever-present wind. This was unusual. Nothing ever happened at this watchtower. Sounds rarely occurred because there was no agent here to effect sound, other than the wind. There were no trees, birds, or animals; just raw, frozen earth and a road. The road once serviced a dismantled nuclear power plant. The plant was cocooned, lifeless but extremely toxic. A truck traveling that road made no sense.

The guard was a little vexed. He had taken this job because nothing ever happened here. The guard had chosen a life of nothingness. He preferred this to the debilitating misery of coping with a worthless life in a remote Siberian oblast.

The old Soviet system subtracted from life, so a life of nothingness was preferable. Recovery from the Soviet-imposed living death would take more years than he had left to live. He stayed on the job, the authorities being unaware that the road no longer needed a guard and watchtower.

A convoy of seven trucks was making its way from the old nuclear plant. The guard watched them go by, counting each one as it passed his window. The participants in the convoy did not appreciate this surveillance. The seventh truck passed the watchtower, and the convoy stopped.

The guard watched as a figure opened the door of the last truck and slowly climbed down. He pulled a sleek piece of weaponry from the open cab. He pointed the weapon at the tower and released a rocket-propelled grenade. The tower and its occupant were blasted into permanent oblivion—a real nothingness.

CHAPTER 22

PORN

Eddy arrived home in the late afternoon when Malcolm was busy in front of his computer.

"What are you working on?" asked Eddy

"This site is called Man's Best Friend; it's for gay men who like dogs."

"Wow, they really like dogs. What if some kids came across that; it wouldn't it scar them for life?"

Malcom shrugged.

"Parent should have their porn filter on their server turned on; it's what it's there for. Anyway, kids can run rings around their parents with computers and phones. Here take a look at this; it's called Bad Habits and Postulants Progress. We put webcams in the dorm rooms of convent novitiates. As a penance, they expose themselves in their cells and pray for the souls of the voyeurs."

"Christ, no way. What convent would allow that?"

"One that is struggling to remain open; the novitiates usually just sit naked for an hour or so. A red light comes on when the webcam is active.

"Sounds like something Madame Sin would cook up. I can't believe it's a real convent."

Malcolm shrugged again and said, "This is *Natural Geographic*; it's full of pictures of naked tribal women. It is for those older geezers who could not get their hands on porn but knew there were naked women in *National Geographic*. Hey, it's getting on a bit, mate, aren't you going to see the Dragon Lady this evening?"

"Yeah, but I think I'll go over there in an hour or so. I'll get a shower and changed first."

"Yeah, right," said Malcolm. "Getting all nice and cleaned up for Suzy Wong? Well, Suzy Wong's mum"

"Oh, fuck off," said Eddy.

"Well here's something that should cheer you up," said Malcolm, printing out a page from the internet. "Here, read about Eddy Relish and his mysterious companion."

The piece was an article from the *Hollywood Reporter Online*:

> **Burned-out Brit still smoldering?** Apparently, '90s Brit heartthrob Eddy Relish has been spotted in various watering holes and other locales in Hollywood over the past week. He breezed into town virtually unnoticed, on the arm of some mysterious oriental beauty. Relish, you may recall burned brightly in the Hollywood firmament for a few years in the '90s until his engines stalled and his acting career nose-dived so fast that "doing a Relish" became a Hollywood byword for a total career meltdown. Relish kept body and soul together by walking on the wrong side of the tracks. He claimed this was research for a gritty crime drama.
>
> Relish left Hollywood to return to his native England, but failed to reignite his career on that side of the pond, and continued to be associated with the sleazier side of life. The *Reporter* contacted all the major film producers in Hollywood, but Relish has not made contact with any of them. However, industry sources say that Relish may be easing back into the business doing voice-overs for radio ads. Hopefully, he will not have the aura of desperation that surrounded him in his decline. Who can forget

seeing Relish touting himself fruitlessly around
the production companies during his later years in
Hollywood?

According to the barman of Jack's Bar and Grill,
he spotted Relish dining with a compatriot, also
believed to be connected to the film industry. Relish
looked tanned, fit, and relaxed, and even paid the
bill. So what is he doing here, just visiting, or is he
planning a messianic second coming?'

"Not a bad bit of press," said Malcolm. "Methinks I spot the hand
of your benefactress."

"What, Cynthia, you think she planted the story?"

"It wouldn't be the first time, mate! You remember when Tibet
was the cause célèbre in Hollywood when you were last here. Well,
one or two actors got on the wrong side of Madam Sin over that. I
have spent less time with her than you have, mate, but I guessed she
has some connection with the Chinese government. All those stories
about gerbils in socks being stuffed up an actor's arse probably
originated from the Lucky Lotus."

"Jesus Christ," said Eddy.

An hour later, Eddy climbed out of a taxi at the Whiskey A-Go-Go
and walked a block down Sunset Boulevard to the Lucky Lotus. He
could have ridden all the way there, but he wanted to soak up the
febrile atmosphere of Hollywood at night and feel part of it again.
This was a town where every night felt like Friday night just before
going to a good party. The sidewalks heaved with all manner of
people walking between bars and nightclubs.

Rock star wannabes and tourists gawked at the free show. Japanese
salarymen lurched between bars as they conducted business. The
occasional minor celebrity emerged from a bar, wearing sunglasses.
They would stand with apparent unconcern, waiting for the valets to
bring their cars and hoping for recognition.

As Eddy approached the Lotus, he heard the music blaring out.
He noted the huge doormen. These two Samoans had beaten him up

and chased him out of Hollywood. They spotted him at about the same time, and a tremor of panic ran through Eddy. They seized Eddy with hands like bear paws. Confusion and relief replaced Eddy's fears.

"Hey, Mister Eddy, good to see you," said one of the Samoans. "Miss Cynthia said you'd be coming tonight, and we were to look after you real good."

"Yeah, and Mister Eddy, we've got you to thank for us getting this great job," said the other Samoan.

"Eh? How's that?" asked Eddy.

"That time we slapped you about. Ms. Cynthia told us if we must, only hurt you a little bit, not break any bones like our bosses wanted. She promised us good jobs at the Lotus in return."

Eddy's mind reeled a little, realizing that Cynthia had been looking out for him in the bad old days before his flight from Hollywood.

"Well, um … nice to see you again."

"I'm Gilbert; this is George," said Gilbert, who placed a huge hand on Eddy's shoulder.

George leaned in and said, "Mr. Eddy, if anyone gives you any problems, anywhere, you let us know, okay?"

"Wow, yes, sure, and thanks!" said Eddy.

He passed through into the club noting little had changed in the interior since he was here last. The original *Blade Runner* movie had inspired the décor. A semicircular bar dominated the club. Behind this was a stage on which naked and semiclad girls danced. Patrons could not touch or paw the girls. They had to hand banknotes to the barmen, who tucked these into the girls' G-strings or stockings. Fully naked girls would seduce customers by rolling a bill into a cylinder and then teasingly sliding it into their pussy. More bills would then fly across the bar.

Huge video screens were at both sides of the stage and hung from the ceiling. These showed rock videos and bizarre Japanese TV. There were booths where customers sat with girls and secluded curtained nooks where customers could pay for a private lap dance. Behind the Lotus was an anonymous-looking double-story motel.

This was owned by the same company and shared a connecting wall with the nightclub. A convenient door allowed girls and their clientele to pass discreetly from one building to the other.

Eddy surveyed the crowded room; a few tourists had come in to soak up the ambience and were gagging over the prices of the drinks. There was a two-tier pricing system designed to keep out the innocent. Asian executives and Japanese salarymen were clustered in booths and along the bar. The dancing girls and hostesses were a mix of Asians and Europeans. Looking at the European girls, Eddy guessed they were predominantly Russian or Ukrainian, with high cheekbones and platinum hair.

Eddy continued to gaze around the room when he looked up to the gallery that ran around the periphery of the club. He saw a familiar figure silhouetted in shadows gazing in his direction. There was a gentle tap on his shoulder. He turned to find a spandex-clad six-foot-tall blonde woman with intense blue eyes.

She spoke one word: "Come."

The woman led him to the stairs that climbed to the gallery. The crowd parted in front of her as she guided Eddy across the floor. At one point, a group of rowdy rich boys on a night out blocked their path. They began making lewd comments to the blonde woman, but these faded under her icy stare. Gilbert and George moved swiftly through the crowd and created a space to the stairs. Eddy guessed that the rich-boy posse would soon be out on the street.

They mounted the stairs to the gallery, but the figure was no longer there. The tall woman led Eddy through into an office that he well remembered and had come to fear. Cynthia sat behind her desk, wearing her full Madam Sin wig, makeup, and outfit. She gazed impassively at Eddy.

"Thank you, Nadia. You may go."

Nadia closed the door, and Cynthia said, "Well, Edward, how are you?"

"I'm fine, actually more than fine and—"

"You have a few questions, no doubt. Did you like Nadia?"

"Pretty incredible. Where is she from? Russia, I'm guessing?"

"Close, from Finland's arctic north, close to the Russian border. Did you notice the effect she has on people with those blue eyes? Nadia is a Sami or Laplander, descended from a line of shamen. Not too long ago, would have been regarded as a sorceress. Now I use her to bewitch men's souls."

"Lucky men," said Eddy.

By rights, I should be punishing you for disobeying my orders."

"Oh … sorry about that."

"Don't do it again. This time it did not matter. I half-expected you to take a chance when we arrived in Los Angeles. In future, if I give you such an instruction, do not take it lightly. It's for your protection and that of your girlfriend, Sharon."

The mention of Sharon made him blush and feel guilty about being with Cynthia.

"So how is Sharon? Is your script coming along?" asked Cynthia.

"I suspect you know how well it's coming along," Eddy responded with a smile.

"Quite, I must see the final draft before you hawk it around the studios. I do not want you giving away secrets that could get both of us into trouble. Speaking of studios, here, this will help you smooth away problems you may have with any producer in Hollywood."

Cynthia motioned toward the laptop computer on her desk. The screen showed a photograph of a famous Hollywood producer dressed as a baby. He was being spanked by a couple of leather-clad girls; one of them was Nadia. Cynthia closed the image and extracted a memory stick from the computer, handing it to Eddy.

"All the Hollywood hierarchy are on there in some form or other—compromising pictures, embarrassing documents, bank records, secret visits to rehab clinic. Their guilty secrets are all there and all collected by my girls. It's indexed by name."

"I don't suppose I'm getting all this help for nothing. I mean the last time I was in town you seemed to delight in making me look like a complete loser. But, thanks for Gilbert and George; I mean, thanks for getting them to go easy on me all those years ago."

"You're welcome. You were too immature to be of any use to

me before. A decade or so in the wilderness has roughened those smooth edges and put some lines on your boyish face. I will help you reestablish yourself as a film star, but I will ask you to help me from time to time."

"How?" responded Eddy.

"By doing what you do best, acting. I may need to send you into situations where you will have to pretend and dissemble. Actors have prodigious memories, a useful asset for gathering intelligence. Film stars have access to people and places denied to ordinary mortals. Look for example at the parade of film actors and other entertainers that pass through the White House … that reminds me."

Cynthia picked up her office phone, pressed a button, and spoke in Mandarin. Within seconds, there was a knock at the door, and a sallow, slender Chinese man entered carrying a briefcase.

Cynthia motioned him to her desk, and he passed her an envelope from his briefcase.

"This is Ah Chu. It really is his name; please do not snigger. He will get you a Social Security card and work visa. You can stop being paid in cash and avoid problems with the immigration authorities. Sign those forms and give him your passport. I assume you do have it with you?"

"Yes, here it is. I carry it with me everywhere since this country has got so anal about having picture ID."

"He'll have your documents by tomorrow morning and will drop them off to Mr. Bolsum's apartment.

Cynthia took something out of the envelope, which Ah Chu retrieved with the signed documents and left the office.

"I took the liberty of obtaining you a California driver's license."

Eddy whistled and took the laminated card.

"Is it legal?"

"Of course it's legal. I do not want you arrested for possessing false documentation."

"What about the photo … oh, never mind, thanks."

You're welcome; now your first task is very simple. Go and get yourself reestablished in Hollywood; become a big-name star again."

"And this is because?"

"We need you to become a target. No doubt, Sharon has explained to you about the dreadful Mr. Madbul."

Eddy nodded. Sharon had explained all about the renegade Albanian who was intent on rewarding Eddy's friendliness by murdering him. He was even more pleased to be well out of England and under Cynthia's protection.

Cynthia continued. "Well, he's still out there, and he and his ghastly organization, Fa'aht—"

Eddy sniggered helplessly. "I'm sorry, I'm sorry, just couldn't help it. I mean, come on, with a name like that."

"Yes, I agree, it's hard to keep a straight face. However, do not forget this is a serious terrorist organization. Madbul is a creature of our creation; China helped train him, and he represents a threat to our stability. We have large numbers of Muslims on our western provinces. He could stir up problems for us there, as he was planning to do in Europe.

"He has gone to Kazakhstan; he could easily get from there into China. He is very proficient at disguise, which is why we are uncertain about his appearance now. Our western lands contain people of all ethnic backgrounds, including Caucasians. Since he went rogue, we've been concerned about the threat he represents."

"So how does my making a comeback in Hollywood fit into all of this?" asked Eddy.

"As you reestablish yourself, you'll give interviews to the press and other media. In those interviews, you will talk about your hiatus, and how you've spent a great deal of time researching backgrounds for new films. One of these is an espionage thriller about the hunt for a rogue intelligence agent. Tell the Madbul story; tell how you were a target. I will ensure that these stories will be syndicated globally.

"We do not have a decent photograph of Madbul—a consequence of Albanian paranoia about keeping their man totally incognito. You can work with Ah Chu. Apart from his espionage skills, he's also a competent artist. He can render a likeness of Madbul, based on your recollections. These will accompany any articles about you.

We know one of two things will happen. Either we will catch him because someone spots him, or more likely, he will get angry and try to kill you."

"Will I ever stop being bait for this guy?"

"Not until we catch him or kill him. Don't worry, I've grown very fond of you; I will not let you be harmed."

She stood up, walked around her desk, and kissed him on the cheek.

"Oh … okay then, um thanks."

"Now go enjoy yourself. The bar staff knows who you are, so they will not charge you. Call your friend Mr. Bolsum; tell him you are both my guests tonight. Come to the Lotus tomorrow afternoon and ask for Ah Chu, and you and he can work on a sketch of Madbul. Oh, and you'd better hang on to my cell phone for the time being."

CHAPTER 23

SAMOVAR

The flight from London itself was uneventful, but the incessant murmuring of the passenger next to him was beginning to irritate Bill. He had to take some more medication to calm his frazzled nerves.

After the tablets took effect, he felt relaxed enough to listen to the Christian music channel. He enjoyed identifying the Bible quotes scattered through the songs. *Not a bad trip overall*, he thought; a couple of hours in Moscow while they change planes for Astana, and he would be in Kazakhstan by nightfall.

After the plane landed in Moscow, the pilot requested that everybody remain seated, even after the plane had come to a complete halt. Bill's happy mood changed. The medication was still working, but he knew something was wrong. The passenger next to him had also stopped his praying and stiffened with apprehension.

The plane door was opened by the cabin staff, and five fat-necked Kevlar-clad police burst through it and headed for Bill's seat. Bill found himself staring up the barrels of five assault rifles. He made an effort to consider his options but could not think of any.

One of the troops yelled at him in Russian. He could not understand the words, although it seemed to involve a mad bull. He understood he had to accompany the officers. They marched him down the stairs and then bundled him into a waiting black Russian SUV. He was bundled out of the SUV thirty minutes later after arriving somewhere in Moscow. The troops manhandled Bill into room with a desk, two chairs, and a bucket in the corner.

Bill sat motionless trying to fathom what was happening. The well-regimented anarchy that comprised his world had begun to unravel. He pursued this line of thought to what was a logical conclusion—Eddy Relish. Here was the key. Since that little toe rag had blipped on his radar screen, things had gone pear-shaped.

Relish had borrowed a measly five hundred quid on the promise of some acting work with the Knockney Repertory Theatre. Bill had ensured that the work never materialized. He had a quiet word with the theater director about his boyfriend's fondness for tattoos and body piercings. Bill suggested that several six-inch nails driven through the scrotum could enhance this body art.

As planned, Eddy Relish became an unwilling heroin mule. Soon after, Bill's world came unglued. A protective cloak draped around Eddy Relish from the moment he arrived in Hong Kong. For whatever reason, the Chinese government had taken the little sod under its wing. Even worse, the bastards had told him to avoid Eddy Relish. The notion of obedience to an instruction did not register to a psychopath. Bill would bide his time and strike. There was a reckoning to come: "The Lord will take vengeance on his adversaries, and he reserveth wrath for his enemies."[10]

Bill sat and seethed, grinding his teeth and imagining how he would play stick the tail on the donkey with Eddy. A plywood tail would be fixed through the application of industrial staples to Eddy's coccyx. The pressure of Bill's teeth grinding produced an eerie squeaking sound.

Special Investigator Vladimir Romanov entered the room carrying a folder.

"Mister Blake, how nice to meet you; please, stay seated. My name is Vladimir Romanov. You are familiar with Russian history, yes. Romanov is the family of the last tsar. It is believed that my family is distantly related. My grandmother says I have resemblance

---

[10] Nahum 1:1–3.

to Tsar Nicholas, but I think this just old woman's talk. You would like tea, yes?"

A muscle in Bill's eyebrow began to twitch. He could barely restrain his urge to throttle the talkative Mr. Romanov. He had spotted two huge well-armed guards standing just outside the room as Romanov entered. They were armed with a variety of devices such as electric stun guns, mace sprays, and old-fashioned wooden batons. Romanov was a short, stocky, middle-aged man, with receding slicked-back dark hair and a bluish five-o'clock shadow. Bill was not fooled by the man's friendly demeanor. He knew enough about the police to know that this was a serious hard man.

"Tea would be acceptable," Bill said in a monotone.

"Good, good!"

Romanov simply spoke out aloud.

"Please bring tea for myself and Mr. Blake."

A few moments later, a tray with a steaming samovar and glass teacups in metal holders was placed on the table between them. As he fussed with the makings of the tea, Romanov kept up with his incessant chatter.

"Do you know where you are, Mr. Blake? No? You are in part of a Russian historic building, called the Lubyanka; it was famous jail. Many of Stalin's victims begin last journey. It is perhaps a little melodramatic to bring you here, yes? But our offices next door are being redecorated. I mean offices of Russian FSB, the Federal Security Service. You have heard of this perhaps, no? You understand KGB, yes?"

"What's the bloody KGB want with me?" asked Bill.

"FSB, KGB, MVB, OGPU, Cheka, all same really. We are guardians of Mother Russia, and have been since time of tsars. You are surprised, yes? Here, take tea, is sugar and milk if you like. Personally, I not like, but you are English, so please …"

He gestured to the tray and continued.

"Governments come and go, but we have sacred duty to protect our country, particularly now we change from Communism to free market. You know, is funny. I am working now with Russian historian on history of KGB. This man I arrest him many times, and many time he go to prison; he is big dissident in Russia. Now we are friends, and he is helping us to tell our story of fight with Americans in Cold War. Strange times, yes?"

"And what has this to do with me?" asked Bill.

"Nothing, my good friend. I am just talking to put you at ease. Please, not to worry about way you were brought here tonight; was just good ruse to put terrorist off guard."

"What bloody terrorist?"

"Ah, yes, sorry; man beside you, you notice him?"

"The little mumbling twat with the prayer beads?"

"Ah, yes. We think he is very bad man, from Albania, and now on his way to Kazakhstan. We think he is going to make trouble so we want to follow him. So we arrest you, make big scene, take you off plane as a ruse. You think is too elaborate this plan, but bad man, is called Madbul, he is, as you English say, as slippery as an eel.

"He is a trained spy, an assassin. We watch all passengers come and go, watch crew, watch everything. So we make big noise with SPETSNAZ troops, big arrest, lots of people, make distraction. So now we keep you a few more hours and then put you back on later plane to Kazakhstan, where you can go about your metal-buying business."

"How did you know about that?"

"Oh, Mr. Blake, you are in heart of Russian security services. You think we not know about your business with Jew pirate Silberstein. But Kazakhstan is not our problem anymore, and you look like you can take care of self."

Romanov gestured to the folder on the desk.

"You have colorful business in London, Mr. Blake, but you commit no crime in Russia, so if keeping nose clean, as you English say, no problem."

Bill was beginning to relax just a fraction but did not let his guard down. Police were police, no matter if it was an ordinary London copper or James Bond.

"All of this just to keep tabs on one fucking terrorist. Why not simply grab him and shoot him? I would."

"Ah, Mr. Blake, is too crude. How we ever know who bad man know and what mischief he is planning with his friends? So we make our own plan and follow him, let him lead us to his friends, and they lead us to their friends and so on. When we ready, we pounce like cat."

Romanov clapped his hands together sharply. He sat back in his chair, sipped his tea, and smiled at Bill. Bill kept quiet. His contacts with the Russian mafia in London were not extensive but sufficient to impress him that they were devious bastards. Romanov's explanation could be true, but, on the other hand, why pick on him and not another passenger? Was it simply because he had the misfortune to sit next to the bloody wog from Albania?

"So I can go now?"

"If you like; next plane to Kazakhstan leave Sheremetyevo airport in four hours. We can take you back to airport if you want to go now."

Bill grunted, and Romanov got up to take his leave; as he made for the door, a thought struck him, and he turned back to address Bill.

"Before you go, I just have small favor to ask."

"And why would I want to do you any favors?"

"Surely man of your background value good relations with law enforcement agency, no?"

"The less I have to do with your kind, the better," said Bill. "But if I scratch your back, you fucking owe me; that needs to be understood."

"Of course, of course. I have friend in Astana; well, she more than friend; she my lover. Her name is Fayina. My job keep me in Moscow, so it hard to see her as often as I like. I want to show depth of my love. So I ask you do me favor. You please deliver some flowers to her—a bunch of pink carnations. Fayina love carnations; she say they have aroma of heaven. She say angels dance on their petals."

Romanov closed his eyes, lost in reverie.

"What? You must be fucking joking. I haven't got time to be your delivery boy; I've got business to attend to. Call Interflora; now get me to that airport before I—"

"You heartless man, Mr. Blake, heartless man."

"Yes, I am a heartless bastard, at heart."

Romanov said nothing more; his expression had become very glum, and he beckoned Bill to follow him out of the door. At the reception counter, Romanov said something to the staff sergeant at the desk and strode out of the room. The staff sergeant stared at Bill, picked up a phone, and gave what sounded like a command.

Bill looked around and noticed Romanov in an office adjacent to the main desk talking on the phone. The staff sergeant said something to Bill and pointed to a chair, but before he could take a seat, another uniformed agent turned up.

"You Mister Blake?"

Bill nodded.

"You come with me; airport."

CHAPTER 24

CLUBBING

M alcolm joined Eddy at the Lucky Lotus to take advantage of Cynthia's generosity. Soon they were sitting in a booth watching the most beautiful girls in Los Angeles take their clothes off. Malcolm knew many of the girls, some of whom moonlighted in porn videos shot by Malcolm. They would come and sit with them between lap dances or performing on the stages. The patrons of the Lotus noticed this. They had to wave high denomination bills to gain interest from the girls.

Eddy and Malcolm were on their third drink.

"Remind me again how you got here. Why are we even friends? Sorry that came out rather badly," said Eddy.

"No worries. You always were a two-pot screamer," said Malcolm.

"What? Oh, right. One sniff of the barmaid's knickers, and I'm all over the place."

"I think you mean apron."

"You sniff what you want; I'll sniff what I want."

They fell back laughing, whipping tears from their eyes.

"Okay, so you remember I was in this band before you were even born."

"Jeff Sodgewick and the Logic Sound."

"Yup, we had a couple of hits in England and in the United States in the midsixties. Funnily enough, we had a number one and number two on the Australian and New Zealand charts."

"No accounting for taste, I suppose."

"It was about the worst thing that could have happened to us. In the late sixties and early seventies, we spent our time touring Australia and New Zealand. In the midseventies we did a huge US coast-to-coast tour with other British Invasion acts. We plowed through the Midwest playing in an endless succession of clubs and hotel lounges. It was winter. Have you been to the Midwest in winter?"

"No, and I don't plan to. So, what, you ended up in LA and figured that was it?"

"More or less; I couldn't stomach touring anymore. Long story short, I met a girl in LA. I was an illegal immigrant for a while, living off what skills I had in electronics, music, photography, whatever. I was lucky; I got a green card in an amnesty and got a reputation in Hollywood as a camera technician. Its sounds glamorous, but it's not. The studios pay zilch because there is a line out of the door for jobs. I was talking to an extra on a film; she told me she moonlighted in porn videos."

"Would I know her?"

"No, this was still before your time, and these days she looks quite different."

"Well, yeah, older."

"Women don't age gracefully in Hollywood. They just transform into the bride of Frankenstein with Botox and plastic surgery."

"Oh ..."

"Anyway, she gave me a contact number, and I just went from there; first film, then videotape, then internet and DVDs. I met you on set when you first came to Hollywood. I told you I was from Knockney."

"Yeah, I remember; I was trying to look cool and confident but was crapping myself with nerves."

"You didn't do too badly."

The room darkened like an eclipse. Eddy and Malcom looked up and saw that Gilbert and George joined them.

"Hey Mister Eddy, Madam Sin give us the night off to take you out to some nightspots; she want you to get seen around town," said Gilbert.

Eddy and Malcolm smiled at each other, downed their drinks, and followed the two huge Samoans out of the building and into a waiting stretch limo; George drove the car, while Gilbert joined Eddy and Malcolm in the rear.

They drove a couple of blocks, pulling up to the Cobra Club, a Hollywood nightspot, with a throng of hopefuls waiting to get in. The four of them got out while a valet took the car.

"Hell, we'll never get in here," said Malcolm.

George turned to them and said, "No worries, Mr. Malcolm; we can get you in anywhere in Hollywood. Madam Sin make sure of that."

The two Samoans gently shouldered their way through the crowd at the club entrance. Gilbert nodded to one of the doormen scanning the crowd. The doorman returned the nod, spoke into his headset microphone, and went back to scanning the crowd. The hopefuls gazed at the little party, wondering who these celebrities were. They must be stars. Who else could show up in a limo with minders and swan right into the hottest place in town. Eddy noticed several of the crowd began making frantic calls on their cell phones.

Inside the club, the rich, famous, and D-listers checked each other out as they circuited the dance floor. On the periphery, in the relative darkness of the booths, groups of people huddled over drinks. Malcolm motioned to Eddy to head upstairs. Eddy looked down from the stairs on the writhing mass of humanity. He saw many faces that had been staring down at him from billboards in LA.

Several people did a double take when they glanced in his direction. Eddy thought he spotted movie producer Cy Sly checking him out from a booth opposite the staircase. Eddy had seen the furtive ducking of the heads of people in the booths, turned toward the wall in a quick twitch, as they snorted cocaine. Once inside the relative sanity of the chill-out lounge, the foursome balanced themselves on some high stools at the bar and ordered drinks.

The two Samoans smothered their seats. They looked like a pair of giant garden gnomes, impaled on their bar stools. They ordered mineral waters and several family-sized bags of Cheetos. The bar rang a local Korean grocery store to deliver the Cheetos. The Samoans confirmed that Cynthia was picking up the tab for the night. Eddy and Malcolm ordered complicated cocktails with elaborate names.

Malcolm said, "Mate, sorry about dragging you up here, but the noise and lights were too much downstairs; I couldn't hear myself think."

They could feel the steady "whump, whump" of the bass notes vibrating through the floor. The cocktails arrived; Eddy took a sip of his, declared it undrinkable, and ordered a large Rosebank, his favorite single malt. After three of these, he was feeling woozy.

"Mell, Walcolm, I think ... I'll start again ... I've got the hiccups. Well, Malcolm, I think we accomplished what Cyn wanted; start for real on the comeback trail."

"Well, you certainly got yourself noticed tonight," responded Malcolm. "Hey, Gilbert, George, are we going anywhere else tonight?"

"Whatever you and Mr. Eddy want to do, no problem," said George.

Eddy said, "Well, we're both a bit pissed, so I figure a few more drinks here until we're a lot pissed. Where's a good place to get a burger in Hollywood?"

"Hollywood Burger," said Malcom.

"Okay, figures; lets head there. I assume we'll get a table," said Eddy. "Hey, did you see all the snorting going on down there?"

"Couldn't miss it," said Malcolm.

Eddy laughed. "Did I ever tell you about the time I went to one of the Oscars, when I was still on top? The cocaine was like talcum powder. The bathrooms at the award ceremony were full of people snorting coke. Men and women in each other's bathrooms, all crowded into stalls sniffing away. You could get high just breathing in all the dust in the air.

"There was one poor old bloke up for some lifetime achievement award. He was shuffling about looking for a place where he could take a dump. He was in tears because his turn was coming up. He was desperate but could not find a vacant stall.

"Poor old bugger, in desperation he barged into the first unlocked stall in the men's room, pushed his way in, dropped his pants and let fly. All these men and women burst out of the loo. One English actress shouted out, "That disgusting little man; how dare he take a shit in the toilet.""

Malcolm guffawed and shook his gray head. They finished their drinks and decided it was definitely time to go to Hollywood Burger. George called and made reservations using Cynthia's name to secure their table.

The party of four made their way out of the club. They were met with a volley of flashbulbs as they stepped out onto the street. A small knot of reporters had assembled and some began snapping photos, while their colleagues were asking questions.

"Hey, Eddy Relish, is it true you're here in Hollywood to make a comeback?"

"Have you been offered any roles yet?"

"Is it true that you turned to a life of crime when your film career failed?"

"Who is this mysterious oriental beauty we've heard about that brought you to LA?"

"Have you heard? Your name has once again become a byword for spectacular career flameout."

Eddy put up his hands in mock surrender.

"Hey, guys, give me a break. I'm just in town visiting friends. Yes, I would be interested in getting back in the business, and I am working on a script that might provide a good vehicle to do just that.

"Who was the mysterious lady? Just an old family friend.

"I'm taking life one day at a time; I'm doing a bit of voice-over work.

"I think turning to a life of crime is a bit strong, I had to do whatever it takes to keep body and soul together. I was even being stalked by an Islamic terrorist at one point, a bloke called Abdul Madbul. I'd even done the guy a good turn, would you believe?

"Am I wiser as well as older? I got a valuable life lesson, and I would like to think so. I was just a kid when I was here last time, so what did I know?"

Gilbert and George flanked him as he spoke, their two large frames keeping the reporters at arm's length. Malcolm, valuing his privacy, stood to one side. After about twenty minutes the reporters had what they wanted and let him go. The four of them got into the stretch limo and glided off to Hollywood Burger.

"Well, mission very definitely accomplished I would say, wouldn't you, old mate?" said Malcolm.

"Shit, I've just realized I didn't tell them where I was staying," said Eddy, a hint of panic in his voice.

"Don't worry about that; I don't think you'll have any problems getting calls and offers.

Malcolm paused. "Er … I don't want to be inhospitable, but you might want to think about getting yourself a, like, place of your own."

"Oh, yeah, you're right mate. I don't want to impose."

"No worries; anyway, let's go eat."

Next morning Eddy stirred in bed and began the slow process of getting up. Malcolm heard him, knocked on the door, and came in.

"Hey, check this out."

He flung a bunch of printouts from various tabloids and trade paper websites. They all told pretty much the same story about Eddy's return to Hollywood. They recounted his spectacular decline and fall, but sounded upbeat about his chances of success.

"You've got messages on the answering machine. I told you they'd figure out where you were staying."

"Who are they?" asked Eddy.

"Cheeky bugger, listen yourself; I'm not your bloody secretary!" Malcolm laughed. "Okay, one of them, though, is from your old mate Cy Sly."

"Now there's a name to conjure with. Did you know the material Cynthia gave me is very interesting? Cy has a taste for underage girls; he goes to places like Mexico, India, and the Philippines to indulge his sweet tooth. When he is in town, he slakes his passion with the youngest-looking girls at the Lotus. But did you know that he was behind my career burnout? He boasted about it to one of Cyn's girls when he was pissed one night."

"There was a rumor to that effect; let me guess, he was pissed off about you going out with Lynn Skynn?"

"Yeah, that's right; gave Lynn her first break in mainstream after being a porn star. After she met me, she would not give him the time of day. Instead of getting pissed with her, he took out his rage on me. So I've had nearly ten years of fucking misery just because that old bastard didn't like me bonking Lynn Skynn."

"Yeah, well, welcome to Hollywood. Didn't I warn you about not messing about with Lynn when you first started sniffing around her?"

"Er … yes I think you did. What did I say?"

"Fuck off, as I remember."

"Ah, fair enough, but come on; Sly was totally out of order."

"Whatever. Are you going to see him?"

"Well, I'd better go and see how he's planning to screw up my life this time. Anyway, thanks to Cyn I think I can exercise a little retribution of my own. And I don't have to take whatever he's got on offer."

Eddy got up, scratched his backside and was about to go into the lounge and replay the phone message. He suddenly noticed his passport was on the bedside cupboard, with a laminated Social Security card taped to the front. Eddy flicked through the pages and saw he had a brand new work visa.

"Hey, Malcolm, look at this; seems like I'm all legal for work. When did Ah Chu come by with my passport?"

"No idea, mate; that guy Cynthia's little ninja. He and I have a running battle with my security system. He's always been able to get through my alarm systems when he drops off payments for work. I don't know why, but he never just drops off the bloody check at the front door. I always find it mysteriously propped up on the table. He may have delivered your passport while we were out last night or even when we were sleeping."

"Wow; well it's nice to be legal. So let's have a listen to what wicked old Uncle Sly has got to say."

CHAPTER 25

FAITH

Romanov sat brooding in his office. The uncouth gangster Blake had refused to do him a simple favor, which Romanov would have greatly appreciated. He opened the bottom drawer of his desk and took out a bottle of vodka and two shot glasses. He picked up the phone and pressed a button.

"Epstein, come into my office; I hate drinking alone."

Emmanuel Epstein appeared within a few moments and accepted the vodka. Romanov liked Epstein, who had no desire to emigrate to Israel. Epstein also had good connections with Israel's intelligence community.

Epstein downed his vodka in one swallow, causing Romanov to arch an eyebrow and refill his shot glass.

"You saw the little pantomime this evening," said Romanov darkly.

"Yes; this is good vodka. Is it Georgian?"

"Yes, they make a lot of good things, but they're troublesome, annoying bastards. Look at Stalin."

"I'd rather not, Vladi."

"No, well, he wasn't too kind to the Yids, was he?"

"He wasn't too kind to anyone as I recall, except maybe his daughter Svetlana."

Romanov poured himself a second drink.

"The UK security forces are pathetic; how we lost the Cold War is a mystery to me. As soon as I saw what the SPETSNAZ troops brought in, I knew it couldn't be Madbul. What have you found out?"

"I called the airport security and told them to make me a copy of their CCTV videos of the incoming London flight, and of the departure lounges for the connecting flights of all passengers on that flight."

"Did they actually do it?" said Romanov.

"They sent a memory stick over with a courier. I know the deputy out there; she's my wife's second cousin."

"Ah, so it's true, all you Jews stick together."

"We're God's chosen race, Vladi; unfortunately that's been a mixed blessing. We look after each other; nobody else will, not even God. I had to promise to pay for the music at her sister's wedding next month."

Romanov laughed. "Ah, such a mercenary race you Yids. So what's on the stick?"

"There's a man in one of the transit lounges who we know was traveling on a Pakistani passport. He took an onward flight to Astana. It seems that he and the London gangster had simply switched seats, so the English did actually send us the correct information."

"They're still pathetic," said Romanov. "I asked the uncultured English gangster to take some flowers to Fayina; the pig refused."

"Foolish."

"Very foolish; he failed my good faith test. Here, send this to the Kazakh police in Astana and copy to the CIA post at the US Embassy there."

Romanov took a sheaf of papers out of the folder on his desk.

Epstein looked through the sheets of paper. Bill had been routinely photographed and fingerprinted. Along with the picture and fingerprints was the message: "Madbul photo & prints. Suspect due in at 08:00 on Aeroflot flight 555 tomorrow. Please detain, Fa'aht operative."

Epstein asked, "And the other man, who really might be Madbul?"

Romanov scowled. "Fuck it; it's Kazakhstan's problem. I hope he keeps going east to China and gives those bastards a surprise."

There was a pregnant pause.

Epstein said, "Baykonur is Russian territory."

Romanov downed his vodka.

"Stop being my fucking conscience; all right, send the details about the other man to our FSB post, and ask them to keep him under surveillance."

Epstein nodded, finished his drink and left. While the FSB monitored the real Madbul, the local Kazakh security services and their American allies would no doubt give Mr. Blake a hospitable welcome. Romanov slapped his hands together, as if dusting them off. *A productive day's labor; splendid work*, he thought to himself.

CHAPTER 26

SCRIPT

Cy Sly gazed sourly at Eddy's smiling face leering at him from the *LA Times*. He felt his neck muscles tense and a headache begin when he thought of the little limey shit. Relish had run off with that hot little fox Lynn Skynn. Even with Viagra available, she had run off with a younger man. Despite all he had done for her, giving her a shot in mainstream movies.

He remembered the ridicule; Cy Sly, the boss of MegaTool Productions, the megatool of MegaTool. He had obtained his revenge on the ludicrous Relish—leading him on and denying him a plum role in his own film project. He used his influence to ensure the little shit did not get another break. He remembered Relish haunting the movie production companies in Hollywood, as his career went into a tailspin.

The last he had heard about him he was running tricks and dealing in drugs for that miserable old Chinese dragon lady that ran the Lucky Lotus. He wondered about the identity of the mysterious Asian beauty with Relish, when he arrived in Santa Monica. How was she helping him revive his career? Sly had ordered some of the MegaTool staff to do some digging.

He recalled the phone conversation with one of his production troubleshooters, Vera Britanni.

"Cy, we confirmed that Relish flew into Santa Monica. He arrived on a private Learjet, hired by a Hong Kong trading company. The only person we can confirm on the manifest was Relish.

Cy said, "What about his companion? The Chinese woman?"

"Total dead end; it's like she doesn't exist, no name shows on the manifest other than the two pilots."

"Did you manage to get a look at the security camera footage?"

"Yeah, I flashed some cleavage and a couple of C-notes. There is a woman on the video, but she's wearing a hat with a net veil. The camera image strobes like crazy. She's walking head up, but we couldn't see her face."

"Anything else?"

"We tracked them to Ocean Suites on Venice Beach. The staff remembered Mr. Relish and his friend, a mature Asian woman. The bellhop remembered them; he described Eddy as a skinny guy with a Brit accent. They said that the Asian woman also sounded English and that she looked like a movie star, dressed in silk."

"Did you check the Ocean Suites registration?"

"Yes, the bellhops were very helpful. There was a registration card made out in Relish's name. The bill was paid in cash."

Cy wondered if the mature Asian woman was connected to the Lucky Lotus. From the description given by Vera, it didn't sound like the old hag in the Kabuki mask makeup and wig. He had seen her humiliating Relish in public at the Lotus bar. It warmed his heart to see the little creep getting a tongue-lashing from Madam Sin. He felt much less comfortable later when the old bag had brought over a girl.

She announced in a loud voice, "Hey, Mr. Sly, one young girl like you ask. She all clean down below, like little schoolgirl."

Sly plotted the next instalment of his revenge. It had not been hard to track Relish to Malcolm Bolsum's apartment. He had his assistant, Victoria, leave a message there for him to contact Mr. Cy Sly. He would lure Relish into making a film with MegaTool Productions. He would hand pick a script so bad it would kill Relish's career forever. Not even God himself would be able to revive the corpse.

He mulled over the scripts on the table in front of him, plucked by his staff from the endless stream of hopeful submissions sent to MegaTool.

The first script was entitled *Malcom's X-Men*. The plot summary stated that Malcolm X's death was all pretense. It give him the opportunity to adopt a secret identity as black Professor X. He clones a band of African-American superheroes from the DNA of Martin Luther King Jr., Marcus Garvey, and the Honorable Elijah Mohammed, Louis Farrakhan, Mohammed Ali, and O. J. Simpson.

Together they would fight the menace of the dread Mastermind, leader of the shadowy secret organization White Might. It turned out that Mastermind was none other than President John Kennedy. His assassination was also a sham. It allowed him to forgo his masquerade as a caring liberal and devote his time to waging war on blacks and gays. White Might was the source of AIDS, which cut a swathe through the gay and black communities in the United States.

That should succeed in offending just about everyone, thought Sly. But sometimes oddball movies struck a curious resonance. There were enough conspiracy theories about Kennedy and AIDS to make this plot seem halfway believable.

He flicked through the next script: *Gandhi: The Musical*. This looked like it might have real potential. Cy read on; it was 1946, and strains were showing in the Indian Congress Party. The Mahatma bows to the inevitable—the partition of India—and bursts into song:

Oh, Mr. Jinna,

Won't you come to dinner,

So we can carve up India as best we can?

The Hindus will get the best;

The Muslims can have the rest.

We'll even let you call it Pakistan!

In an earlier part of the script, Gandhi and the Congress Party were fomenting dissent in India. All eyes were on New Delhi and the reaction of the viceroy, Lord Curzon, who expresses his frustration thus:

If I had my shotgun handy,

I'd bag that blighter Gandhi,

Or I'd hunt him with my pack of dogs.

India's British, don't you know,

And it will always be so, and

We'll never give it back to the bloody wogs!

Even Relish would probably spot the doubtful potential of this one.

He moved on through the stack. The next script, *Carry on Jihad*, came from MegaTool's London office.

Cy read the plot synopsis: rich spoiled brat Arab, Osram Bin Liner, doesn't want to follow his father to run the biggest used car dealership in Arabia. Instead, he wants to be a rock star. His CD, *Rocking with the Prophet*, fails ignominiously in England. This drives him into the arms of terrorism. He declares war on England, determined to see the green flag of Islam flying over Big Ben and Buckingham Palace. Bin Liner's archenemy, British secret agent James Blade, is sent to Arabia to foil him.

He turned a few pages in the script, and the scene cut to one of his father's TV commercials for his Jedda used car dealership.

"The blessings of the Prophet are upon you; come this week to Taliban Motors in downtown Jedda and test drive a new Fatwa. Is it not written that you will love this car, inshallah? If not, you'll be defying the will of God, so we'll cut off your head."

"Uh … no, I don't think so," said Sly out aloud.

He had to find something that looked promising but was in fact a genuine disaster. Not a sleeper hit like *Boogie Nights*. On the surface, this had disaster screaming off every page but won a Golden Globe and a ton of other awards and nominations.

Eventually Sly found it, a formulaic hack piece, and the work of a hack TV scriptwriter. Only a hack would reason that if outer space, westerns, and hospital dramas were currently popular, all three combined would be a guaranteed success.

This line of reasoning had produced *Shoot-out at the Andromeda Clinic*. It could be sold as *Star Wars* meets *Tombstone* meets *E.R.*

He read over the plot outline: Hieronymus Bosch and Michelangelo are two of the best intergalactic bounty hunters. They have been hired to track down and capture the mysterious John Frum, chief of the mysterious Cargo Cult, which preys on vessels journeying through the Andromeda Galaxy. Their leads take them to the Andromeda Clinic, run by the brave and dashing Dr. André Trojan, who is bringing medicine to the new frontier. All the nurses at Andromeda Clinic are in love with Dr Trojan, as is the enigmatic female bounty hunter Diamante, who is competing with Bosch and Michelangelo to catch John Frum.

He would shoot it on a shoestring but make it seem that the budget was much inflated. When it failed, it would go straight to video to recoup some production costs. It would stall any Eddy Relish comeback. He would put the word around that Relish was still a byword for failure. With any luck, the little punk would be unable even to get a job in Hollywood busing tables or washing dishes, let alone acting.

CHAPTER 27

RECEPTION

Bill was tired as he walked down the Astana terminal jetway. He had been amazed at the sight of Eddy Relish before his connecting flight left Moscow. He was walking past a couple of youths who were web surfing on a tablet. The picture of Eddy Relish had flashed on the screen, bringing Bill to a skidding halt.

He loomed over the two youths. The picture was on an English language webpage of the Entertainment Network. The two youths said something in Russian to Bill, which Bill interpreted as "fuck off," so he banged their heads together, rendering them unconscious.

Bill read the page at his leisure while the two youths slumped and lolled in their chairs. Some passersby saw the slumped figures with Bill standing over them like a block of granite. Bill saw them staring.

He said, "Even the youths shall faint and be weary, and the young men shall utterly fall."[11]

The webpage gave Bill a surge of malicious energy. He knew where to find the pathetic Relish. What kind of idiot chooses to take refuge in Hollywood, a place whose primary industry is publicity? *The boy deserves what is coming to him*, thought Bill, as did all the arseholes he had encountered in the last few weeks.

He mused to himself: "You snakes! You brood of vipers! How will you escape being condemned to hell?"[12], and he smiled.

---

[11] Isaiah 40:29–31.

[12] Matthew 23:33.

Bill entered the Astana airport terminal building, a prefabricated metal and glass construction. He expected to encounter the usual cluster of airline personnel at the gate, along with airport officials. The last thing Bill expected to see were more bulky men with crew cuts, this time in tight-fitting suits. Five of them were walking toward him.

This time Bill decided he was going to resist. He grabbed a walkie-talkie from the hand of one of the young, bemused airline staff standing by the gate. Bill hurled it at the spook who was leading the charge. The projectile spun and the antennae scored a direct hit on the agent's Adam's apple; he went down, choking.

"Not bad," said Bill.

He looked around for another weapon. There was nothing in sight, so he ran. He saw a food counter in the corner; he would grab a knife and take a hostage. That might be the beginnings of a plan. A bullet in the buttock gave him cause to rethink his strategy. Warm blood began to soak his underpants. Something else hit him, and Bill decided he would just lie down for a minute, maybe assess the situation and ... the world faded.

Far off, Bill heard someone yell, "Target down."

Radio noise and then silence followed this.

It seemed all that happened a long time ago when Bill blinked open his eyes. His hand was chained to a railing. He thought he was in a bed, in a hospital, except the hospital was shaking, and there was a dull hum in the air. He realized that he was on board an airplane. A boy in a uniform was sitting a few yards from him, with an assault rifle in his hand.

The boy called out, "He's awake, sir."

An older man in medical scrubs approached. *Who are these people?* thought Bill.

The doctor loomed larger as he approached and started talking to him in some strange language; it sounded like Arabic, but Bill was unsure. Bill wanted to say what the fuck is this? It would not come out; his tongue seemed to be stuck to the top of his mouth. He could not move, and his head ached. He wanted his mind to go back to wherever it was before he woke up; he had not felt this weak and helpless in years.

"He is totally zonked," said the doctor. "He'll be like that for a while. Bastard's had a cocktail of sedatives the size of Lake Michigan. But he'll pull through. That bullet in the butt was a close thing; he was a hair's breadth from having his spine severed."

"He's lucky to be alive," said the boy soldier.

"Well, that remains to be seen," said the doctor.

They both broke into laughter.

"Oh, I don't know," replied the boy, "Guantanamo's nice this time of year."

They both laughed again.

Bill heard that and twitched an angry, evil, hate-laden twitch.

The people were unaware of it, and the doctor walked away.

"Yup, it sure is nice this time of year," said the doctor. "And we'll be there early; apparently there was a tailwind. We touch down in two hours."

CHAPTER 28
DEBATE

Sharon sat at a table on a stage overlooking the crowded hall. On either side were two loudspeakers, out of which a voice was saying,

"Okay, it's the top of the hour, and this is Roger Joseph saying welcome to *Firing Line*. It's your chance to participate in the radio debate between the candidates for the upcoming by-election for the Knockney borough council seat for West Knockney. This was recently vacated by the retirement of the sitting member, Sydney Ramsbottom. BBC Knockney Radio has invited all the candidates to the Hailie Mengistu Community Centre for this debate. We only received responses from the official Labour Party candidate, Nigel Owen, and one independent, Sharon Constable, running under her own Minimalist Party ticket."

Nigel's name elicited a few cheers and handclaps from the Labour supporters in the crowd, including Fred Starling. Sharon's name provoked a great roar from the audience, which startled the Labour Party faithful. Sharon saw the color drain from Starling's face as he nodded to his deputy, Ellen Mumford, a stocky woman with a brutally masculine dress sense and haircut.

As Sharon watched, Starling and Mumford conferred in a huddle at the side of the auditorium, after which Mumford began using her cell phone, making call after call. Sharon guessed Mumford was summoning more of the party faithful to the community center.

Roger Joseph continued;

> "A lot of your supporters out there, Sharon. Maybe you'll give Nigel here a run for his money. Nigel was until recently a leading light in Knockney's Afro-Caribbean community, where he is more popularly known as "Rasta-Blasta." He has been a familiar sight "pumping up the jam" at many of our best clubs and discos. Sharon is a single girl, who works for the Knockney Health Clinic as a receptionist. Sharon's current partner is none other than Knockney's own Johnny Depp, Eddy Relish, who after a few lean years is apparently making a successful comeback in Hollywood as we speak."
>
> Okay, the rules are very simple. I'll ask each candidate to state his or her manifesto, in five minutes, and then we'll take questions from the audience, both here in the Centre and by phone, fax, and email, to which we'll ask the candidates to respond. Our contacts numbers are on the Radio Knockney website. We tossed a coin before we came on air and Nigel won the toss, so I am going to ask him to kick off the proceedings."

Nigel stepped up to the microphone.

"Thanks Roger. May I thank Radio Knockney for allowing us this chance to deliberate on our respective positions; and to my opponent this evening, who was the only one gutsy enough prepared to go toe to toe in this debate. I'd like to think of myself as a gentleman and offer the 'pole position,' so to speak, to Sharon if she'd care to open the proceedings."

"That's very gallant of you, Nigel," said Sharon. "But I realize the Labour Party only pays lip service to women's issues, despite all the noise it makes otherwise, so thanks but no thanks."

Nigel looked crestfallen that his ploy failed. Sharon guessed he had wanted her to open first and so give him a chance to respond to her comments in his opening statement. He bent to the task and laid out the Labour Party line.

"People of Knockney, your Labour Council has an unbroken record of successful local government in this borough since 1945. During that time, the Labour administration, which I would be proud to join, has constantly striven to deliver the best services to the community. The Labour Party has put people first and money second, whether it is education, health care, policing, social services, care for the elderly, race relations, and the list goes on."

My opponent will no doubt point to the collapse of socialism in Eastern Europe and the triumph of free markets versus command economies. But I would say to her, this ignores the human dimension, and something that continues to be an integral part of the Labour administration in Knockney. At the local level, this council has been proud to keep out the freebooting capitalist exploiters from the borough by developing a series of creative incentives to foster small businesses in Knockney (i.e., businesses no greater than two individuals and creating more employment opportunities for a range of competing businesses, rather than allowing one huge conglomerate to monopolize the retail economy."

"Our record on education is unparalleled. We were one of the first London boroughs to tackle elitism in schools by abolishing the Knockney grammar schools in favor of mixed-ability comprehensive education. I believe that the education opportunities offered in our schools are the best and are free of the appalling class-based elitism that permeates state-supported grammar schools."

Knockney Council also was one of the first to tackle racism, gender equality, and gay and transgender rights in its schools, demanding that these issues be included on the curricula for all schools. Our efforts have received praise from progressive governments in Cuba, Venezuela, North Korea, and Uttar Pradesh."

"I am proud to belong to a borough like Knockney, which has seen its role in a broader perspective than simply the provision of local services. It has included days of action and support for our Venezuelan comrades in their fight against US imperialism, the declaration of Knockney as a nuclear-free zone, the outlawing of homophobic language in public, support for gay and transgender ministers of religion … the list of good works goes on, and these are but a few examples.

Is it any wonder that Knockney is a mecca for so many immigrants? It cannot be chance alone that draws recent arrivals to our part of London more than any other borough. I am proud of this council for putting out the welcome mat by providing free accommodation and stipends for recent immigrants."

"Use your vote wisely; a vote for Labour is to vote for a steady hand on the tiller, for a continuation of the government that knows what is best for Knockney and its people. A vote for my opponent is the first step on the road to anarchy and oppression. Thank you."

Nigel sat down, a shy smile on his face acknowledging the polite applause.

Roger Joseph was reading his monitor.

"Thank you, Nigel. That was Nigel Owen, Labour candidate in the Knockney by-election, and this is Roger Joseph speaking to you live from the Hailie Mengistu Community Centre here in East Knockney where we are hosting a candidates' debate. Anyway, I would just like to remind you that the speakers will be taking questions from the live audience and also from you, our listeners. Again, the number to call can be found on the BBC Radio Knockney website, where you can also send emails."

"Sharon Constable will now speak on behalf of the Minimalist party," said Joseph.

Sharon walked confidently to the microphone and tapped it twice. "Hello? Hello?" she said loudly.

> "Hello Knockney? Wake up. Labour's been here since 1945. Some of you remember what it was like in 1945. You and your families had been through hard times, almost unbearably hard times, but you pulled through. You did it, not the local borough council. You took on the totalitarian monster and defeated it.
>
> However, look what has happened. We are meeting in a room named after another totalitarian monster because he was an African Marxist. What kind of perverse organization is this council? Thankfully, the rest of the world has long known that Knockney Council is a joke. But it's an old joke, and I don't want to hear it anymore. I suspect you don't either."
>
> "I'm not here to catalog the history of bungled incompetence that constitutes this local government's period in office these past forty-odd years. You don't need me to remind you of the litany of initiatives, spawned in the humanities departments of our tertiary education institutions. These idle tenured academics generated a series of positions whose sole common thread was the denigration of our noble civilization.

Councils like Knockney went and put those ideas into practice. The result is what you see today: an impoverished, sad, dirty, and unhappy place.

It does not need to be that way, and the beginning of the solution is rather simple. What Mr. Owen has failed to recognize is Britain's less-than-impressive record of devolving government from Whitehall. Local authorities have very little power. His list of so-called achievements have absolutely nothing to do with actions taken by the local authority, except they supported the wanton degradation of our civil society. Local authorities do not control their own budgets, and they are limited in the scope of legislation they can make. What remains is the ability to mess around and strike thespian poses, acting as if there really were some power vested in these pathetic little bureaucracies."

"As a result, local authorities, and Knockney is the guiltiest of the guilty in this, have used what little discretionary spending they have to sponsor pet causes and to demonstrate the caring, sharing nature of their political souls. They use their position as a platform for moralistic bombast, a pompous display of narcissism posing as morality. When put into practice these always result, via the law of unintended consequences, in worsening the lot of those they purport to represent.

Well, I say leave morality to the philosophers. Politics is not about deciding on behalf of your constituents what is morally correct. It is about creating a legal and political infrastructure that reflects the concerns and desires of those you represent, without inflicting unwarranted harm on anybody."

"My promise to you, beloved and benighted citizens of Knockney, is this: Nothing. Or not much, anyway. I recognize that beyond keeping the streets clean and our citizens safe, I, as a local councilor, have very little control over making meaningful improvements to our local infrastructure. However, I promise to fight for the rights of proper local representation."

My promise is to take Knockney back from the grip of the political buffoons and return it to its inhabitants. This includes everybody; it specifically includes all those immigrants who have come here to participate in that wondrous process of improving their lot by their own talent and hard work. You do not need the condescending pity of the likes of Mr. Owen."

Mr. Owen and his colleagues are probably sincere in their views. But, sincerity is a very overrated virtue. Their sincere incompetence has temporarily severed our links with a great culture. Ours is a historic citizenry that created a corner of civilization in England, a civilization that was forged over centuries through a proud tradition of common goodness and adherence to principles; principles that operate at the individual level, not through a deluge of moral impositions posing as laws."

"I will strive to have all those insanely named buildings return to their original names, or we'll name them after pop stars or something. Next, I will terminate all the victim-creation grievance programs and spend the money on putting in some street lighting. When all that is done, we will review where we stand, and let's see if there is something constructive we can do. But for now, this is the Minimalist platform.

It's a long journey to true democracy, and I have decided to start here in Knockney. I've known many of you for years, and some of you have known me even longer. I do not remember my mum pushing me around the Metro Shopping Centre in a pram, when they first built it, before they renamed it the Zapatista Urban Market. But, many of you do. I trust you, and you trust me. Let's end this charade. Vote Minimalist. It's the least you can do."

Sharon waved and blew funny, phony kisses as if she was some kind of rock star making her final exit. The crowd erupted in loud cheers and whistles with even the elderly people standing up and applauding. Red Fred leaned over to Ellen Mumford and whispered something.

"Well, that was a spirited rejoinder from young Sharon Constable; she's certainly seems to be popular tonight with the Knockney crowd in the hall here. It seems like Labour has its work cut out tonight. Now who wants to ask the first question?" asked Roger Joseph.

One of the Labour Party faithful leaped to her feet, the light glinting off her spectacles.

"I'd like to know how the two candidates intend to deal with eliminating institutionalized racism within our public services and the private sector."

This was clearly a planted question, and Nigel had a stock response at the ready.

"If I may, Mr. Chairman, as a black man, I see racism in action every day. My opponent would no doubt refer to any initiative to redress this problem as, what did she call it? A victim-creation scheme? Shame on her. To be nonwhite in this country is to be a second-class citizen. Doing nothing is not an answer. Ours is a multicultural society, Knockney has a high proportion of immigrants from all over the globe. The first waves came primarily from the Caribbean; indeed I can see some folks tonight who look like they may have stepped off the Empire Windrush."

There were a few chuckles from some retired bus drivers, originally from Jamaica.

"Later we absorbed newer migrants from India and Pakistan who came to work in the clothing, engineering, and catering trades. More recently we have taken in people from Africa and the Middle East as they have had to leave their homes through wars, created for the most part as a legacy of this country's imperial colonial past."

At this point a gnarled old man with a tatty raincoat, trilby hat, and splendid nose got up from the crowd.

He shouted out, "What about the Jews? We came first to Knockney, from Poland and Ukraine in the last century and the one before; you are forgetting us, I think."

This put Nigel off his stride, but the old man was right, and he had no readymade reply. The Knockney Council was pro-Palestinian and had increasingly voiced sentiments hostile to the State of Israel. Nigel recovered his wits, and recognized the man as Rabbi Abromowitz, recently retired from the Knockney Orthodox Synagogue.

"My apologies, Rabbi." He continued. "You're absolutely right, and it only goes to illustrate my point that Knockney has been a safe haven for many years."

The old man sat down.

Nigel revved up again. "And we in the Labour Party have continued to make this a safe haven for people of different colors and creeds by tackling the inherent biases in our intuitions, be they housing, health, education, social services, or policing. I do not believe that doing nothing is the right answer. If we are going to root out racism from our institutions, we have to educate people and transform our society, while at the same time making sure that opportunities are open to all people.

"Some may say that we are biased in favor of the immigrant community, and I would say yes, this is true. The average man and woman on the street is more than adequately represented at Westminster, with its overwhelming white majority. This council offers some redress for this by trying to improve the lot of the marginalized in our society, including the migrant community, who are at the mercy of unscrupulous landlords and businesses. The Knockney Council can and does make a difference to the lives of our migrant community, and we will continue to do so when I am elected to this borough seat."

"Miss Constable? Would you care to respond?" said Roger Joseph.

Sharon smiled and said, "Mr. Owen a black man? That's the best news I've heard in a long time. I've got gypsy ancestors, so if Mr. Owen is black, then so am I, and so is everybody in Knockney. And that means we have solved our minorities problem at a single stroke."

The audience laughed and Nigel grimaced while the rest of his Labour contingent adopted condescending expressions such as shaking their heads and rolling their eyes.

"But the question is an interesting one. Clearly, it presupposes that there is institutionalized racism in our public services and the private sector. Well, the private sector, that plant that has been dying in Knockney for the past forty years, could not survive with institutionalized racism. To ostracize an entire section of the workforce and customer base by reference to their ethnicity would be bad business. As such, nobody in the private sector does it. Public services may tend toward this kind of thing, and if they do, I suggest the Labour Party explain it since its biggest source of funds is the unionized civil service. If the questioner were correct about there being racism in the public sector, then the alleged perpetrators would be the very people who fund the Labour Party."

Let me say this: I think the question is impertinent. Of course it suits the socialists' agenda to talk of institutionalized racism. There are many votes to be garnered from labeling people as victims and then promising to release them from their victimhood. Of course this never happens because the people who operate the agencies would be out of a job if there were no victims to defend. The last thing they want is to see are minorities fulfilling themselves as proud and successful individuals. Therefore, you have a neat little vicious circle: victims need help; they elect the government that will deliver it, and the government creates jobs to operate the agencies, which are then staffed by more voters who will reelect that government to keep themselves in a job. Where is the incentive to get off that merry-go-round?"

"A new generation of people of color has grown up in this country, immersed in British culture. Rightly or wrongly, the children of most of our immigrant population have abandoned much of the culture of their ethnic origins and adopted a new one. Actually, adopted is entirely the wrong word. They have created a new British culture, one that is lively, colorful, and exciting. They have done this spontaneously and organically, most certainly not via any kind of government program.

Where immigrant communities have failed, and sometimes they have failed, I admit, has been primarily due to government policy. Those arrogant, middle-class, highly educated policy-makers assuage their inherited guilt and indulge a minority of immigrants who import their cultures of barbarism and antidemocratic values. They have promoted the erection of barriers between them and the rest of us, all in the name of multiculturalism. They have imposed misery on those poor communities that have had to bear the brunt of this indulgence while visiting hatred on the innocent children of our immigrant families."

Fred Starling leaped up from his seat, his face contorted and his lips snarling.

"Racist claptrap. Apologize immediately. Never in twenty years of public service have I encountered someone with such odious views. I am outraged, and I insist the candidate withdraw her offensive remarks immediately."

Muttering from all sections of the audience quickly grew into a cacophony of shouting and yelling.

"Leave her alone, you big bully."

"Go back to St. Albans, you self-righteous bastard."

Joseph tried to impose a little order, but his attempts could not be heard above the noise; the mayhem was apparently uncontrollable.

Fred's face turned a shade of crimson, and he shouted back.

"You're nothing but a bunch of fascists."

One elderly gentleman stood and shouted back, "I fought the fascists, and let me tell you if there are any fascists in this room, they're sitting on Knockney Council."

Fred had crossed a boundary; he had insulted his constituents live on local radio. Just when it seemed the chaos would terminate the meeting, a chant was heard from the back of the hall.

"People before profit," and then, "One, two, three, four: eat the rich to feed the poor; five, six, seven, eight: organize to smash the state."

As the placard wielding mob moved forward, Sharon grabbed a microphone and shouted into it.

"Wrong slogan, people. We haven't got onto the evils of capitalism yet; we're still on racism, you bozos."

As if controlled by a single nerve system, the mob immediately switched slogans.

"Shut the racist meeting down; right-wing scum get out of town. Shut the racist meeting down; fascist scum get out of town."

"That's more like it!" shouted Sharon

She began conducting the mob, an imaginary baton in her hand as she joined in the chant.

After some minutes of this, the various members of the mob eventually found themselves seats and rolled up their placards, and slowly the noise dissipated. Roger Joseph was able to speak.

"Well, er, yes. Quite a lively debate we are having here. If I could please ask the members of each candidate's teams to leave the candidates to speak for themselves, that would be much appreciated."

Joseph covered his microphone.

"Steven, where's security? Who let those bloody protestors in?"

A young man with a fuzzy beard said, "I'll look into it, Mr. Joseph."

He ran off, trailed by wires and the electronic gadgetry strapped to his waist.

Joseph said, "Yes, lively indeed. I think we should move onto the next question. We have an email here from a listener named Elsie. She writes, 'I own the haberdashery on the Knockney High Street. I've just had to lay off one of the younger assistants because I can't afford her wages after I've paid the rate increase on my shop. And it seems no matter how much I pay in council tax, it's never enough to fix the leaking drain that's right outside my front door and puts off customers. What would the candidates do about this?'"

Joseph continued. "Well, indeed, what would you do about this? I think, as a representative from the incumbent party, you, Nigel, might also like to take this one first?"

Sharon saw Nigel looking long and hard at Fred Starling. Everyone recognized that Knockney Council had a poor reputation for taking care of local infrastructure, while putting its energies into fighting for the most current political causes.

"Elsie, my dear, I'll be honest with you and say right off, I don't know a damn thing about drains, but I do know how miserable they can be if blocked, or leaking as in your case. If elected, the first thing I will do is make some inquiries into why this problem has been allowed to persist for so long. You all heard me make this promise, so you can make sure I honor it if I am elected to the council."

Nice body swerve, thought Sharon.

Nigel continued; "As for the rates increase, I don't think it's any secret that the Labour Party aims to redistribute wealth from those who are fortunate to have wealth, like yourself Elsie, to those that have little or none."

This drew murmurs of approbation from the claque of Labour supporters but a steely silence from the crowd. Joseph turned to Sharon and asked her if she would like to respond to Elsie or the comments made by Mr. Owen.

Sharon stepped up and said, "Elsie, they will never repair the drains in front of your shop because they don't care about the drains in front of your shop. They don't care about anything apart from their pathetic ideology; anything that exists in the real world is an irrelevance, a distraction from the quest for communitarian perfection. Don't believe the lies of the liars. If you vote for me, I really will fix that drain, and I really will try to stop robbing you through the rates. Mr. Joseph, I've had enough of this; it's getting boring and the presence of all these stupid people bearing placards is giving me a headache."

Roger Joseph explained that the debate was scheduled to run the full forty-five minutes, and there were still ten minutes on the clock. So he took one more call from a listener, a man with a question about crop circles, which neither Nigel nor Sharon could make any sense of, after which Joseph asked them to make their final statements and bid everybody goodbye.

An audience member said, "Sharon I have no idea what you're talking about half the time, but you annoy those rascals so much, you must be doing something right, so I'm going to vote for you."

Sharon thanked the woman and switched on her cell phone. There was a voice mail message. It was from a man with an American accent.

"Sharon Constable? Hi. Cy Sly, an agent, asked me to eyeball your script. It needs work, but I think it might have wheels. We need to talk. Call me. Ciao, honey."

CHAPTER 29

SCREENPLAY

Cy had been leafing through some more scripts while under the masseuse on a Thursday afternoon. He had decided to go with *Shoot-out at the Andromeda Clinic* and had told his people to start project outlining. Just before he left the office for his club, another script had landed on his desk. It was called *The Friends of Red Shidley.*

He had brought it to the masseuse to have something to read; as he leafed through it, it began to dawn on him that this was exactly what he had been looking for. This was the most abominably written story he had ever come across.

It was the ideal vehicle for launching Eddy permanently into oblivion and could be shot much more cheaply than *Andromeda* which, even with the cheap and cheesy special effects he had planned, was going to be more expensive than a story set on present-day Earth.

He grabbed his cell and speed dialed his assistant, Victoria Moralité.

"Vickie. *Andromeda*'s toast. I've got something way more suitable. Call me. Ciao, honey."

It was important to convince the unknown writer that the script was barely usable, but it may have promise. Given the high risk, the writer had to take a minimal up-front and hope for the best at the box office. His call to Sharon was to convey his view that the script was not very good.

The problem was that his words of doubt about the script quality would be sincere. Cy was anxious about his ability to make statements in which he believed. It was a relief when he had to leave a message on Sharon's voice mail; this would give him more time to prepare himself.

CHAPTER 30

COMPREHENSION

Bill Blake stirred out of the drug-induced delirium. He found himself fettered hand and foot with chains. He was lying on a small camp bed in a large cage with a tin roof. He ran his tongue around his mouth and then regretted doing this. Apart from the ghastly taste, it set off dull pain in the back of his eyes. He struggled to his feet. There was a dull ache in his left buttock, and he remembered being hit there by a bullet before being stung again with a hypodermic dart.

Looking about him, Bill saw that he was clad in single one-piece orange overalls. He had manacles on his wrists and ankles, connected to a waist belt with chains. Pulling on the chains made him feel like a puppet. Beyond his cage, he could see other similar structures, some with inmates. Behind the cages was a single-story building festooned with aerials.

On the other side was a flat expanse of runway and then the ocean. The sun was dipping down to the sea, and fingers of light played across the open side of the cage. Guards were posted at regular intervals along the perimeter, dressed in green uniforms. One noticed him stirring awake and came over to the cage to speak to him.

"Good afternoon, sir; welcome to the United States Marine Base at Guantanamo Bay. Do you speak English, sir, or would you prefer if I arranged for an interpreter?"

The vein along Bill's left temple throbbed. He opened his dry mouth and spoke a little hoarsely to the young soldier.

"All right, sonny; I speak English. Now what the fuck am I doing here?"

The young marine gestured to a senior colleague.

"Sir, Mr. Madbul is awake, but I think he needs a translator, sir; he sure doesn't speak English."

He turned back to Bill, and mimed eating and drinking, while speaking slowly.

"Food, good, yes?"

Bill's temple vein beat a relentless tattoo, and he gestured for the young man to step closer.

"Listen, sonny. I am English, you little prick, and I am not called Madbul; now let me out of here before I really lose my rag."

Saying this, he beat his hands on the cage mesh.

"Nope, didn't understand that either, except for 'Madbul.' Was that what you wanted to tell me?"

Bill pounded on the cage in impotent fury. Another marine joined them. He began speaking to Bill in Arabic, but was interrupted by a roar of rage. A marine chaplain joined the confused knot of people around the cage. The chaplain had served at a military base in the southeast of England and recognized the glottlestops and strangled vowel sounds of Estuary English.

"Hey, guys, this isn't an Arab; he's speaking English, albeit a little exotic to your ears. What gives?"

"Sir, he's an Albanian Islamist terrorist, with a terror group called Fa'aht," replied the young marine.

The interpreter listened carefully to Bill's raging and screaming, and concluded this was indeed English. Several men dressed in civilian outfits arrived to join the small crowd in front of Bill's cage.

One of them carried Bill's British passport. He scrutinized this, while checking out the now red-faced bellowing creature in the cage. He stood to one side of the group of men, took out a cell phone, and glanced at his watch. He spoke on the phone for about five minutes before rejoining the group at the cage. He stood right in front of the cage and spoke in a low, firm voice.

"Mr. Blake? Mr. Bill Blake?"

Bill stopped pounding on the cage and looked at the man. Finally he spoke.

"Yeah?"

"Mr. Blake, I apologize for you being here like this. Apparently one of our Russian security colleagues has a sly sense of humor, which has resulted in your wrongful incarceration."

Bill's eyes rolled back in his head as incandescent rage flooded through him.

"That little Russian bastard in Moscow; it had to be him. Just because I wouldn't play Interflora for him and his girlfriend, the little prick had me fingered as Madbul. So what now?"

Bill tried to keep his voice level and sane.

"Now, well let me see, I guess a shower, shave, and a steak dinner would probably sound good, eh? Well, this isn't the Hilton, but we'll give you a feed, let you clean up, and then ship you back to Kazakhstan. We have a military base there, and we can get you back on a military transport. This base and that in Kazakhstan are top security facilities, so we will keep you under guard, if you don't mind. I'll see you are moved to a better room than this dog kennel. By the way, Mr. Blake, we know that you have something of a reputation. Your guards will have orders to shoot to kill if you have any fits of bad temper, okay?"

Bill reined in his desire to rip somebody apart with his bare hands.

Two large military policemen appeared. Bill was taken in their custody to guest quarters. As Bill walked away he heard the civilian making a call on a cell phone.

"Cynthia Tsin, please. Ms. Tsin? Hi, I thought you might like to know that Bill Blake showed up here in Gitmo."

Bill wanted to hear more, but he and his escort had turned a corner between buildings, and the man's conversation died away.

CHAPTER 31
STEPPE

A bdul Madbul stared out of the window of the Peace and Friendship Hotel on the dusty outskirts of Karaganda's Old Town. Madbul was certain he had been under surveillance when he arrived in Kazakhstan. This meant that the authorities were hoping he would lead them to other enemies of the state. After spending a few days in Astana, he took an early-morning bus to Karaganda in the hope that he might shake off any surveillance or even identify covert watchers.

Karaganda was the exile capital in a country of exiles. Thousands of prisoners freed from the gulags in the 1950s, unable to go home, settled with their jailers. On the surface, Madbul sensed that there were abundant possibilities to create mayhem in this huge, sparsely populated country.

Oilfields in the east and west of Kazakhstan needed extensive pipelines to export the petroleum out of the country. These would always be vulnerable to sabotage. A greater number of tourists were coming to Kazakhstan, along with foreign workers, as the economy expanded. They too presented targets of opportunity to Madbul and Fa'aht.

There was even the possibility of a strike at the Baykonur Space Center, where the Russians continued to maintain their space launch facility. This was a tempting target since the survival of the International Space Station was dependent on this launch facility. Madbul balanced the potential of this target with the knowledge that any attempts against Baykanour would result in merciless pursuit by the Russians.

He hoped to find more disillusioned youths to recruit to the Fa'aht cause. Native Kazakhs were a minority in their country and were deracinated from their culture. Only a privileged few were reaping the benefits of the money that was pouring into Kazakhstan. Madbul believed the widespread poverty and high unemployment would be fertile soil in which to plant the Fa'aht seed.

Elsewhere, Islam was resurgent in Kazakhstan but was grounded more in Kazakh nationalism and not hatred of the West. Madbul spoke to a group of young Kazakh men and women at a mosque in Astana. The boldness of the women and their disavowal of the veil shocked him. One of the women explained that Kazakh women had been warriors and even fought against men in wrestling competitions. One of the men had suggested that Madbul could benefit from wrestling with a Kazakh woman. This met with a peal of laughter. Madbul had turned on his heel quivering with loathing, wishing he could have slaughtered these heretics.

He walked outside to escape the depressing confines of his room. Beyond a few other crumbling rundown buildings, there was nothing but endless steppe. His gaze alighted on a poster for Karagandinskoe beer, brewed by a Turkish-owned brewery in Karaganda. This soured his bleak mood even further. A fellow Muslim country owned the brewery producing demon drink. Only members of Fa'aht were the true believers. The world would be a better place cleansed of all infidels and heretics.

He hated to admit it, but he was at a loss about what to do next. Wandering the scrubby grasslands, he hoped God would show him the way. Some wind-blown pages of a Russian entertainment magazine wrapped themselves around his leg. Madbul's eye was caught by a picture of Eddy Relish, stepping into a limousine in Hollywood. Madbul read the page, disturbed that Relish mentioned his name. He was horrified there was a sketch of his likeness accompanying the article.

His path was clear; he would go to America and eliminate this irritant. Getting into the United States presented few problems. He would make his way overland to the Pakistani tribal lands in the Hindu Kush. From there he could secure passage to the coast and work his passage on a vessel bound to Canada. Once in Canada, it would be easy to cross the lightly patrolled northern border and then make his way to Hollywood.

CHAPTER 32

METAL

Bill finally arrived in Kazakhstan. He had to be present at the transfer of the scrap metal from the seller in Astana. Mr. Zhang had arranged a subsequent buyer but had stipulated that the transfer needed witnessing in person by Bill.

The army transport plane finally touched down at a military airfield just outside Astana. He stood on the tarmac as his eyes surveyed the area, but there was not much to see. The light was glaring, but the sky was overcast from the ever-present smog. He had no idea what time it was. He was still feeling dazed from jetlag. His medications were in his luggage in the aircraft hold. The events of the past week and the absence of medication had Bill teetering on a near-psychotic meltdown.

He took a deep breath. *Someone is going to die*, he thought. *I don't know who or how but they are going to die, the bastard. Or maybe bastards, I don't know, I'll see how it goes.*

One of the Kazakh airport guards interrupted Bill's violent reverie. He told Bill in broken English that CRC had arranged transport for him after he had retrieved his luggage. Bill looked at him with disdain but followed him. As they walked, Bill pulled out the business card that Zhang had given him—the meeting place for the exchange of documents.

Bill said to himself, "All right, let's get this fucking process in process."

In a storage area, Bill collected his bags. Bill's driver was waiting outside in a Toyota taxicab, its engine idling in wait. Bill got in the cab and almost immediately jumped back out again. He had no way of communicating with the driver. The address on the card given to him by Zhang was in Russian and English. Bill found one of the American airmen, who summoned the same Kazakh airport guard. The guard looked at Zhang's business card and told the driver where to go.

The journey was long enough for Bill to take his medication and resume a certain degree of calm He arrived at the ministry in a reasonably buoyant mood. At last, he was joining the community of traders in legitimate commodities. This gave him a sense of well-being, the first step away from that dark and grubby universe he had always inhabited.

There remained the business of mutilating the Relish bastard. He wished he could get his hands on the Russian ratbag Romanov. Bill could deliver a few well-targeted perforations that would make the Ruski reconsider his sense of humor. For now, however, those issues could be dealt with on another day.

Bill took his bags from the trunk and ran up the stone stairs leading to the front door of the mausoleum-like ministry building. He strode over to the reception desk. He was about to announce the purpose of his visit when a voice spoke from behind him.

"Mr. Blake. How are you?"

Sitting on a bench was Zhang himself. He folded the newspaper he had been reading.

"I was so sorry to hear of the interruptions to your schedule. Quite unacceptable. The perpetrator of that practical joke should be admonished. It is one thing to play a prank, but it is quite another to abuse the channels of law enforcement, especially those dealing with the universal threat of international terrorism."

"Yeah, well it was a fucking … sorry, water under the bridge now. I must say, you are looking well, Mr. Zhang, and what a pleasant surprise to meet you. I had been led to understand that I would be meeting your rep, Mr. Zhu."

"Well if there is a silver lining to your cloud of misfortune, it is that I was planning to be here at this time. Therefore, I was able to meet you personally. Come, come, we will go somewhere more salubrious. Have you taken lunch yet?"

Lunch, thought Bill, *is it lunchtime*. He had no idea what time of day it was but had the presence of mind not to show his alarm.

"No, as a matter of fact, I haven't."

"Well, you must join me. I will take you to one of my favorite Kazakh restaurants. President Nazarbayev recommended it to me personally. We can discuss the details there."

At lunch, Zhang apologized for the burdensome requirements of the transaction. When Bill had taken possession of the metal, he would complete the deal by an email to his Cayman Islands bank, using a password prearranged with CRC, which was acting for the Kazakh government.

After lunch, they returned to the ministry, where Zhu was waiting for them in the lobby. Bill and Zhu exchanged greetings, and Zhang bade his farewell.

"I must leave now, Mr. Blake. It was so nice to see you again."

"Same here, Mr. Zhang; please send my best wishes to Ms. Liu."

Zhang smiled and left.

Bill and Zhu walked up two flights of stairs to a dark corridor and entered an elaborately decorated office where Bill met the official with whom he would sign the papers.

Zhu said, "Would you care to see your purchase? It's not far away."

"Yes, thanks. I'd like to see what I'm buying."

Despite the fatigue, this was the first of what Bill saw as his transformation from local thug to international executive. Seven container trucks stood in a weed-filled clearing. The air was hot, dusty, and unpleasant, but to Bill it was a stunning sight.

"Beautiful. It brings a lump to my throat. God, I love capitalism. Who would have thought that an orphan boy from London would be standing here completing a transaction with you, a poor orphan boy from Ning Du?"

Bill and Zhu had got on rather well during the earlier negotiations and had exchanged details of their respective upbringings. They chatted for a little while and then returned to the ministry to complete the transaction. Everything went according to plan, and by nightfall, Bill was the legal owner of 350 tons of buzz berry and armature wire.

It was early evening, still daylight, and Bill had retired to his room on the seventh floor of the Intercontinental Hotel. He lay on the bed, retrieved his Bible, and leafed through it. He must have dozed off because it was dark outside when he awoke. Someone was banging on his door.

He shouted, "Fuck off."

The banging persisted outside and inside in his throbbing, exhausted head. He rolled off the bed and walked to the door.

"Yeah?"

"Security," said a voice. "Please open the door, sir."

Bill did as requested, just to get rid of the irritant. Standing there were three men: a tall, intimidating Kazakh with a thick moustache; a smaller, younger man dressed casually in a golf shirt and light brown brogues; and a thick-set, thick-necked individual who was planted underneath a baseball cap.

Before Bill could speak, the three men were in his room. The man in the baseball cap started talking.

"Mr. Blake, we understand that you bought some scrap metal today. Am I correct?"

"Er … yes … no … I mean, if I did, what's that to you, fuck-head?"

"We have reason to believe that the shipment of scrap metal that you acquired today is illegal."

The man in brogues butted in.

"It is in contravention of the International Atomic Energy Authority's UN-mandated rules on the transfer of nuclear waste and was supplied by operatives of Fa'aht, the terrorist organization to whom any payment of funds is a breach of the UN Nuclear Antiterrorism Accord."

He looked at the tall Kazakh.

"These same individuals are implicated in the murder of one Soliev Khan, security guard at the former Alia Nuclear power plant."

Bill stopped listening and contemplated escape. Previous experience with the police suggested that the best thing was to remove himself from the situation. The doorway was blocked. Bill ran to the open balcony door and stepped outside.

Bill saw that the balcony of the room next door was within reach and decided to aim for that. Climbing onto the railings, he launched himself outward and upward. He heard two muffled thuds and felt two hammer blows to his back. Bill grasped the railing of the neighboring balcony, but all the strength in his arms vanished. He lost his grip and fell backward into space.

CHAPTER 33

ANXIETY

E ddy Relish stood in the offices of the Lucky Lotus in front of Cynthia Tzin.

"I listened to her debate on one of Malcom's laptops. Soon after she called me, about midnight her time."

"What did she say?" asked Cynthia.

"We talked about the debate; I congratulated her on her performance, and then she said she'd got a message from someone calling about our movie script. He said his name was Cy Sly.

What should I do, and how the hell did he get his hands on the script?"

He was hopping from foot to foot and only just resisted the urge to tug at Cynthia's sleeve.

Cynthia leaned back in her chair.

"The answer to your second question is that I obtained a copy of the script and saw that it ended up in Mr. Sly's office. As to what you do, well, let's think about that."

Eddy gasped with amazement and outrage "You did what … I mean, why … how could you?"

"How, was very simple. I am sure you've already worked it out. I dislike operating in a vacuum; even Ah Chu has grown weary of monitoring your communications with Miss Constable. I thought I would speed things up a little. I read the script through to ensure you were not giving away any of my secrets. Afterward, I passed it to one of Mr. Sly's staff, who was in here a few nights ago. I asked him to ensure that his boss saw the script. I knew he would not let me down. He is a married man with a liking for Asian women. I asked him to do this little favor for me. One of my girls, so far unattainable, became disposed toward him.

The reason why was to give you even more advantage over Sly. If he goes ahead and uses your script without the agreement of both you and your partner, then he will be legally vulnerable. Sly is no fool, however, which is why he is trying to contact Sharon. But he does not know that you are the coauthor of the script. Of course, the script still requires a serious amount of editing."

They were interrupted by Cynthia's office phone.

"Yes? Oh, hello, Nancy."

Cynthia frowned and turned away from Eddy while she talked.

"Are you sure? More to the point, how certain are they that he is dead? Hmm, do you believe it? No postmortem photographs; that is rather telling, don't you think?"

Cynthia suddenly switched to Mandarin and continued an intense discussion with her colleague. She put down the phone and spoke to Eddy, who was sulking in an armchair.

"That was Nancy Liu at the London Embassy. She reviewed a report that indicated security officials in Kazakhstan killed your nemesis, Bill Blake. However, despite him being shot in the back and falling at least one hundred feet, there are discrepancies in the story and, more tellingly, no photographs of Blake's corpse."

"Bill Blake dead; doesn't seem possible," said Eddy.

"Well, it may indeed be impossible," replied Cynthia. "Nancy was sure that there was a great deal of fudging and obfuscation going on by the Kazakh security forces and from our friends in the Central Intelligence Agency."

Eddy shook his head. "How was the CIA involved?"

"I believe Mr. Blake conducted the purchase of some radioactively contaminated scrap metal. This could be sold for many times its purchase value, as long as the radioactive contamination was not disclosed. Central Asian states have been peddling scrap metal for many years from derelict nuclear facilities built by their previous Soviet masters. They neglect to inform buyers that the metal is highly contaminated."

"This international intrigue lark seems a bit much for the Reverend Bill. I mean, he's more your neighborhood thug, like the Krays. Oh, sorry; they were London villains, but …

"I'm well aware of the London gangster fraternity, Edward."

"Well, it still seems out of character for our Bill. Anyway, what do you think I should do, keep an eye open just in case he survived the shoot-out in Kazakhstan?"

"Precisely. Now, what's your next move with respect to Mr. Sly? I was led to understand that he will approach you to be the star of the movie *The Friends of Red Shidley*. Will you accept? He almost certainly wants to ensure that your nascent comeback stalls in its tracks. The script is awful, despite a promising story line. I understand your partner, Sharon, may be a highly intelligent young woman, but she is not a talented writer. The script needs a major overhaul by an expert Hollywood scriptwriter.

"My advice at this stage is to let Sly pitch the film, look at the script and enthuse over it, and then suggest having it rewritten to improve it. Call Sly's bluff. If he is intent on dealing you another death blow, he'll argue the script is in good shape as it is. I will use my influence to have Sharon invited to Hollywood. I will let you know when the invitation has been sent. As the author of the script, she can negotiate with Sly. At some point, however, she should introduce you as her coauthor, which will wrong foot him further. How you play it from there is up to you."

Eddy nodded taking in Cynthia's instructions. It all seemed so complex, though. There were many steps to remember, so having Sharon on hand to help would be a good idea.

Cynthia leaned back in her chair.

"I do look forward to meeting this young lady friend of yours. I hope she won't hold it against me for making use of you for a night."

CHAPTER 34

NEWS

Sol Silberstein laughed. "Dead? That two-bit crook is dead, and you have his money. Oh, please, that is so funny. Oh, Maestro, I prostate myself before you in humble awe."

Thomas whispered, "I think the word is *prostrate*, Mr. Silberstein."

"Excuse me, Thomas. You think the word is what? Let us ask the maestro."

Sol was in a good mood.

Zhang said, "Yes, I think maybe the word is prostrate, but I am less than fluent myself in the language of Shakespeare. If that is a trait we both share, then, to the extent that it groups us together, I am proud to be less than fluent. Without your kind introduction, SS, none of this would have been possible. And to show you my gratitude, I would like to share my good fortune with you."

The three men were sitting in the conservatory of Sol's suite at the Inn on the Park, just off London's Piccadilly. The sunshine was filtered through the huge ferns and crawling plants that decorated the glass walls. Zhang had asked for the meeting, suggesting that they meet for lunch. Sol agreed and invited him to his suite, an accommodation that he maintained throughout the year.

Zhang said, "I have decided to charter a plane to fly to Las Vegas next Tuesday. I invite you, Marigold, Thomas, and any other guests to join my wife, Ms. Liu, and me. It is a little celebration of my fiftieth anniversary in the metals business.

Sol laughed again, and said, "Please, Maestro, tell us again about your rise from humble beginnings; I don't think Thomas here quite appreciates the true honorific of your nickname Magnesio, and how well earned it is. Pay attention, boy, and stop daydreaming about Miss Woo. What? You think your old uncle is too senile to see you become like a mooncalf every time she's around? Maestro, please."

Thomas blushed, indicating to Sol that he had indeed been thinking of another chance to meet Boddy Woo. Sol had suspected that Thomas, who had met her on a number of occasions, was harboring thoughts of exchanging more than just contracts with her.

Magnesio smiled indulgently.

"It was fifty years ago this year that I joined the Victory Through Strife Metals Recycling Co-operative in Ning Du. As you know, like many others, I had, shall we say, had a difficult time during the Cultural Revolution. I spent most of the time entirely outdoors on a vegetable farm. After my denunciation by the Red Guards, I kept my head down, digging up cabbages. The move to the Ning Du plant was quite a step up."

"My first job there had been to separate the copper and the steel from the cable wire that arrived by truck from all over Hunan Province. My duties at the plant were to tear at the strips of wire with a pair of pliers. Pliers as blunt as a pig's arse, if you'll forgive my vulgarity. It was not hard work because the co-operative's expectations in terms of productivity were low. In those days, it was far more important to maintain a 100 percent attendance record at the party's three-hour rhetoric sessions. They were held every afternoon just after the lunch. With lunch running from noon until 1:00 p.m., it meant that I really only worked from nine in the morning until noon.

"Thanks to the endless barracking of the Red Guards, I had the outward appearance of being a loyal party student. I easily mastered all the intricacies of that year's directive from the Central Committee:

Adhering to the three irrefutables: the integrity of the party, the wisdom of the leadership, and the resourcefulness of the proletariat.

My participation in the discussions in these sessions was born out of having survived the onslaught of the Cultural Revolution. I recognized that the only way up and out of this tedious existence was to actively cultivate an interest in the party and to turn this tolerance into a weapon."

Zhang paused to sip some tea.

"Thankfully, Chinese Communism was on its way to unshackling the economy, and the money to be made off the back of the state's monumental trading apparatus became irresistible. By the end of the decade, I was running China's scrap metal trade, and, well, the rest, as they say, is history. So there is much to celebrate."

"Thank you, Maestro. Of course I will be there, and I know Marigold will too. It must be all of three weeks since my wife was last in Vegas; she is already suffering withdrawal symptoms. I tell you, that wife of mine will bankrupt me before long. I only wish my dear brother, Ephraim, could join us. I call him the Prisoner of Zug. At the last count, he is wanted in fourteen states in the United States for alleged breaches of the Federal Reserve antifraud laws."

"I was thinking about that," said Zhang. "I will set up a video link so that we can party online, so to speak. It will be a day to remember—a celebration of global capitalism."

"Splendid idea," replied Sol. "The Grand would be ideal, fitting indeed. Since that pansy lion tamer was mauled, they have been looking for a new act. Maybe we could be that new act. Magnesio and his Friends. Anyway, thank you so much. I assume your beautiful assistant is making the arrangements?"

Zhang nodded.

"Good. I'll have Thomas … Where the fuck are you?"

There came the sound of a toilet flushing, and Thomas emerged from the bathroom shaking his hands dry.

"Always not there when you fucking need him," snarled Sol. "Call Boddy and get the plans."

"The plans, Mr. Silberstein?" asked Thomas, flinching.

"If you didn't spend so much time in the toilet … What do you fucking do in that toilet anyway? It's not normal. If you were doing your job properly, you would know 'what plans.' The arrangements for the Vegas high jinks to celebrate Magnesio's fifty glorious years in the metal business. The business that we all love and for which we toil; the business for which we make heartbreaking sacrifices— sacrifices like having to deal with birdbrained assistants when I could be strolling down the sixteenth fairway at Augusta."

CHAPTER 35

SORROW

Sharon was walking to work to start her afternoon shift at the Health Clinic. Her mobile phone rang. The caller ID said it was Clore.

"Do I want to talk to him? Not really, but what the hell ..."

"Sharon, I have some news."

"Well spit it out!" said Sharon.

"Bill Blake's dead."

"Bill's dead? How? What happened?"

Clore repeated the Kazakhstan story as told to him by Interpol. He described the background to Bill's role in the scrap metal contract.

Sharon was intrigued and thrilled. This meant the removal of one of the threats to Eddy. She was also delighted that Eric's plan had succeeded. Eric had wanted revenge for Bill's barbaric behavior toward his family; but even he could not have anticipated such absolute vengeance.

Sharon wanted to ask if Bill's dying words were some Bible quote. As Clore spoke, she had noted a tremor in his voice.

"Are you all right, Inspector?" she asked.

"Well, no, since you ask, I'm not all right."

"Why? I would have thought this is good news for you and your colleagues at the Metropolitan Police, not to mention the people of Knockney. One does not want to talk ill of the dead or gloat over the death of another human being; actually, yes I do. I might organize a little party—"

Clore cut in: "Okay, okay, enough."

"Well, I'm sorry. But I can't see why this can be anything but good news."

"That's not the way I see it."

"Inspector, is there something you want to tell me?"

"Can you meet me at the Plume?"

Oh, God, here we go again, thought Sharon.

"No, I'm sorry; I can't do that, Inspector. I'm on duty in ten minutes."

Sharon was making a determined effort of late to demonstrate her sense of responsibility given her political stance for the election. She was by far the keenest staff member of the clinic.

She continued, "Can't you just tell me now? Of course, if it's none of my business ..."

"All right. I don't know why I'm sharing this with you. I mean you're not my confidante, and you don't come over as a particularly caring or sensitive person."

"Thank you, Inspector, I appreciate the compliment."

"But I know you deal with things the way they really are, not the way you think they should be. The fact is ... the fact was ... Bill Blake was my brother."

Sharon was stunned and, for once, speechless.

She found her voice and said, "Inspector, I'm sorry to hear that. I mean I really am. That's so ... why didn't you say before? Was this common knowledge?"

"No, nobody knows. I found out by accident. I am an orphan myself, and I was always interested in who my parents were. When I became a copper, I had access to records denied to the public, and I found out that my parents had two sons, Bill and me. Bill was still a nursing baby when my mum and dad were killed, drowned on a trip to the seaside. So we were separated, and that was it, until I found out years later we were brothers, and now he's gone."

Sharon began to feel sorry for the inspector. His life was

descending into a spiral of pathos. She said she would call him when she was free, and they could meet. After she hung up, she continued on her way to work, still surprised at the news she had received.

She thought about how the Reverend Bill never seemed to be arrested or convicted. Everybody knew him to be guilty of the most heinous crimes. Could the inspector's revelation and Bill's evasion of justice be connected?

CHAPTER 36

KARMA

Tiger Tokugawa, the oyabun of the Yamaguchi-gumi crime syndicate, sat back in his leather executive chair and pensively sipped at his whiskey. His eye ranged along the shelves of the bar across the room idly noting the various whiskies—both single malts and blended whiskies, many brands rare and difficult to acquire.

The room in which Tokugawa sat was the "den" in his apartment, which served as both his office and his sanctuary when he needed to be alone. A discreet knock at the door interrupted Tokugawa's solitude. He knew this must be one of his most trusted lieutenants; only they would dare to disturb the oyabun's sanctuary.

Tokugawa sighed and said, "Come."

His number two bodyguard, Hara, entered the room. He looked apologetic at disturbing the boss; he bowed and advanced toward Tokugawa. In his hand was a piece of paper.

"It's an email from Miki, Boss," said Hara.

"Oh? She never sends emails. She normally calls me."

Tokugawa straightened up in his chair.

"What does it say?"

Hara looked abashed and uncomfortable. "It's personal, Boss; maybe you should read it, and I should go."

"Oh?"

There was a silence at the end of which Hara stumblingly summarized the gist of the message.

"She, that's Miki-san, has found some strange Englishman, close to death and had taken him under her wing. She is bringing him back to Kobe, through Vladivostok, using our smuggling route where we ship cars to Russia, in return for—"

"I'm well acquainted with our Vladivostok operation," said Tokugawa.

"Oh, so sorry," said Hara with his eyes downcast.

Tokugawa said, "Read me what she's written."

Hara writhed with embarrassment. He began reading in a quavering and hesitant voice. He did not want to lose any more finger joints on his left hand.

"'Oh, Tora-chan, the spirit of life is strong in this man, and in his own country he is an English boss like you. The stupid Kazakhs and Americans hunted a man they cannot kill; he was shot and fell over a hundred feet. He escaped from the Astana morgue, and now I keep him safe. I want to bring him to Japan so he can recover.'"

Tokugawa's face did not betray any emotion. He took the email and nodded silently to Hara to leave, which he did, looking thankful and relieved.

Tokugawa rolled his eyes, drew on his cigar, took a deep swallow of whiskey, and pondered what to do with this "stray cat" and why Miki was so taken with this Englishman. This did not bode well.

Tokugawa continued to brood. Miki was both Tokugawa's mistress and number one bodyguard. Normally she never left his side. She was sending him an email and not calling by phone. Emails were for underlings. Tokugawa knew this was to preserve face, since he could not immediately countermand her actions.

She was in Kazakhstan, to scout out new Japanese investments in the country, particularly hotels; and to get her out of Japan. The crazy bitch had upset too many people. He was tired of having to bail her out of trouble and placate ruffled feathers. She upset everyone— Yakuza, businessmen, and politicians.

He wished she was more submissive like other Yakuza women, but then she would not be Miki without that wild destructive streak. Japanese businesses were scouting out opportunities in the Central

Asian republics. Tokugawa wanted to ensure that the Yamaguchi-gumi received a cut of the action. Miki was dispatched to Kazakhstan to do his bidding.

He did not want to continue drinking or brooding alone. He shouted out, "Hara!"

The door opened, and Hara scuttled in looking apprehensive.

Tokugawa was silent a moment, contemplating the submissive Hara, knowing him to be a ruthless Yakusa soldier, never flinching from his duty. Hara's hands were intact apart from two joints missing from his left hand little finger.

"Pour me a drink from the bottle on the bar; get one for yourself—a large one if you wish."

Hara's eyes widened with surprise, but he did as commanded.

Tokugawa beckoned to the still-standing Hara to sit in a seat opposite the desk.

"Hara-san, what do you know about Miki?"

Hara's eyes blinked at the unexpected honorific and Tokugawa's conversational tone.

"Just rumors, Boss. Nobody would dare ask her ... or you about Miki. The men, well we all, call her Crazy Miki ... sorry, Boss."

"I know; it's okay. Just make sure that you and the men keep that nickname to yourselves. It is appropriate though. How's your drink?

Hara gulped a generous mouthful, and Tokugawa could see Hara's immediate appreciation.

"It's not Johnny Walker Red Label is it?"

"No, Boss, it's not."

Tokugawa took a drink himself.

"Miki is the product of a Japanese girl and a Japanese American soldier stationed at a US military base on Okinawa. His wife came from the Japanese mainland, and they had met and married, setting up house on the military base, despite opposition from the girl's family; you know how we Japanese are."

"Yes, Boss."

"It was a rotten marriage; the animosity from his in-laws eventually drove Miki's father to seek a divorce. Her mother could not cope with the grief resulting from the breakup of her marriage; she committed suicide when Mike was seven. Miki's relatives took her in but treated her like a slave. After a day at school, enduring the jibes and teasing that she was only 'half Japanese' and with a mountain of homework to do, she had to minister to her grandparents and her aunts and uncles.

"Harsh, Boss; even for a Japanese that's tough. I hate to admit it, but she would have been better off being Korean; they really make life tough for kids."

"Hai, I don't think our Japanese kids know how lucky they are. Maybe there is a streak of Korean in Miki; she just became fiercer as she grew older. She told me the first to feel it was one of her cousins. He used to grope her when they were alone. He tried this once too often and suddenly had a sharpened pencil buried deeply in his arm. Of course, the family fell on her, and she was beaten and confined to her room for a week after this. The grandparents and the rest of the family would try to make her behave like a good girl. Here, pour us a refill."

Hara did as ordered and sat down again.

"Miki ran away when she was fourteen, stealing money from her relatives. In Tokyo, she learned to fend for herself on the streets and later as a bargirl. There were rumors about men being slashed and stabbed for being too careless where they put their hands. Do you remember when we met her?"

"Yes, I drove Takamine to the hospital to get stitched up.

"He was lucky not to spill his guts on the floor. I didn't even see the cut; she was so fast when Takamine grabbed her ass—just a blur, and then Takamine staggering and looking at the red stain.

"He told me afterward that it didn't even hurt; mind you, he'd drunk enough, but still …

"She just stood there, absolutely no fear. None. You and the others were ready to cut her down, but she faced you down. Not like a cornered rat … but like … a lioness. I pride myself on being able to judge people's characters; it's part of the job. I could see a divine madness in Miki's eyes.

"Me and the men couldn't figure her out, still can't. She's thin as bamboo, with skin like a Geisha's face, but deadly with any blade, even a paperclip! I wonder where she learned the skill? Sorry, Boss, not my place to ask."

Tokugawa nodded, and then said, "I don't know myself; we've never really talked about it. I never asked her to get tattooed but she did anyway; a dragon on her back with its tail wrapped around her waist with its tip ... you can guess where."

Hara said nothing but grunted a laugh.

"I wouldn't mind except she has no respect for decorum and keep it covered up. You remember that politician's wife that looked down her nose at Miki. She might have had her jugular slashed if I had not steered Miki to the bar."

"Was that why you sent her and the men to Kazakhstan?"

"Yes, I needed her out of the country to cool off and to let ruffled feathers be smoothed. Our hotel chain expansion in Central Asia offered an opportunity."

"Forgive my impertinence, but how did she react?"

"I think sulky contrition is the best description. Still, she's a good girl when she wants to be. Miki's been spying out opportunities and greasing palms when needed. I talked with Matsuoka; I gather that Miki's been working hard and playing hard. Our men are trying to keep up."

"What do you want to do, Boss?"

"Now? We'll drink a lot more whiskey. Then you'll go and tell all our men and contacts to make sure Miki can bring her stray dog home."

CHAPTER 37

EXCREMENT

F red Starling was chairing one of Knockney Council's Public Works Committee meetings. Starling had called the committee meeting after the accusation at the recent political debate that the council did not care about the borough's drains and hygiene.

Starling and the other council members were only vaguely familiar with the Public Works Committee. Their main concern was creating numerous other bodies to swell the ranks of the dispossessed. This ensured a seamless maintenance of municipal power in the Knockney Town Hall. The proliferation of new advisers, team leaders, and coordinators ensured that council clerical staff was overburdened with work other than their original designated tasks.

Starling had asked the clerk of works to report to the committee. The clerk's report on Knockney's ancient and crumbling sewer system was grim news indeed. He laid out the extent of the work required to repair the disintegrating sewers.

The assembled councilors went on the attack, asking the clerk of works, a Mr. Dorian, why he had allowed the drains and sewers to fall into a state of disrepair. Dorian was cloaked in an air of fatalism. This resulted from his endless struggle to meet the basic services necessary for Knockney. He had to battle daily with council disinterest and a budget that was drained to finance council activities such as an Exposition of Anti-globalization Poetry and the Campaign to Combat Climate Change Denial.

Dorian explained in a calm voice that forty years of neglect and a shrinking budget meant that only basic maintenance work had been possible. The population of Knockney had risen as more immigrants settled in the borough. This placed additional strain on the overburdened sewage system.

"The sewers should have been upgraded and modernized in the 1980s," reported Dorian, "but the council at that time chose not to do so, even though there were government grants for that purpose."

Councilor Ellen Mumford removed her wire-rimmed spectacles and, running her hands through her closely cropped hair, asked in a strident aggrieved tone, "So what happened? What did the council do?"

"Well, I can't remember that far back without consulting the records, but I do know that through the 1980s and '90s, the council annually hosted the Knockney Arts and Music Festival, a free pop music festival that was staged in Grey Park—"

"Where?" snapped Mumford angrily.

"My mistake, in Aristide Park. The Knockney free pop festivals were deemed to be a great success. However, council assumed most of the costs of these events. Major sewage work assumed a low priority. That was also a time of the major influxes of immigrants—Asians expelled from Africa and many others from wars in Africa and the Middle East."

"Well, what about from the 1990s to the present?" asked Starling.

"As I've outlined in my report, conflict, unrest, or economic problems in the Commonwealth or neighboring countries would result in refugees flooding into the borough. It was council policy of welcoming and housing refugees. Dealing with these unfortunates drained the municipal purse. In the 1980s and '90s, the council was preoccupied with opposition to the Conservative government. Initiatives such as declaring Knockney a nuclear-free zone, building monuments to leaders of the developing world, celebrating LGBT awareness, and, of course, the later campaigns against Labour Prime Minister Blair all superseded the sewage system as a council priority."

The assembled councilors stirred uncomfortably and continued to glare at Dorian.

"Then in the 2000s the council voted to freeze the rents for council houses and apartments, rather than sell them to the occupiers. Property values also declined as a succession of local businesses failed, which attracted more immigrants who could only afford to live in places like Knockney. Maintenance costs on council properties rose while rent income actually declined in real terms.

"Then there were the condemnations and days of action to protest the US invasions of Panama and Grenada, and opposition to the second Gulf War, all of which were orchestrated campaigns that drew on council funds. The council chose to mount many major protests and campaigns. These included protesting the persecution of South American agricultural leaders such as Pablo Escobar, and more recently Joaquin Guzmán, Rafael Quintero, and Ismael Zambada.

"Lucille Whyte-Lothar, chair of the Knockney LGBT Group snapped, "It seems to me that you, Mr. Dorian, are trying to shift the blame for your incompetence."

Dorian replied, "Madam, if you consult the council records you will note that I and my staff have continued to communicate our concerns and anxieties—not only about the sewage system but also other municipal engineering responsibilities."

Starling stirred uneasily, aware that he had read some of these memos with deep disinterest. He simply signed the circulation slip and passed them back to his clerical staff for filing.

Whyte-Lothar was not dissuaded.

"I resent the implication that this council's progressive approach to recognizing the needs of persons of color, LGBT community, and the oppressed peoples of the third world has somehow contributed to the decline of our sewers."

Dorian inclined his head slightly.

"Madam, it makes no difference on what the money was spent, be it on pop festivals, poetry readings, days of action, or declaration of a nuclear-free Knockney. The facts remain that there is only so much money available for the council to provide services to the community, and if the council deems fit to spend it elsewhere and not on the sewage system, then the system will inevitably fall into disrepair. If you'll forgive me, Ms Whyte-Lothar, everybody in Knockney needs to 'spend a penny' regardless of color, creed, gender identification, or sexual orientation, and it all goes down the same drains—drains which are now falling apart."

Whyte-Lothar bellowed with rage.

"Brother chair, I must protest this blatant racist and homophobic attitude being displayed by the clerk of works. I demand that the council make a vote of no-confidence and look for a replacement for Mr. Dorian."

Starling tried to placate Whyte-Lothar.

"Now, now, Lucille, I know that Mr. Dorian's comments might seem a little insensitive, but I don't think we want to dismiss what he is saying out of hand. We clearly have a problem here, and Mr. Dorian has highlighted this for us."

Starling's mollifying tones belied his anxiety that a vote of no confidence in the clerk of works would be a meaningless gesture. He was a professional employee of the council, and sacking Dorian would bring down the wrath of the public-sector unions on the Knockney Council.

Starling quickly proposed that the council form the Sewage and Hygiene Initiative Taskforce to study the problem. He asked Lucille Whyte-Lothar if she would chair the SHIT, and asked Dorian to be the vice chair and to assist Whyte-Lothar.

Whyte-Lothar acquiesced with reluctance, stating that the first agenda item would be to deliberate on the composition of the SHIT to ensure that it contained a balanced participation of all stakeholders in Knockney. Mr. Dorian adopted a supine expression. Starling breathed an inward sigh of relief.

CHAPTER 38

REMEMBRANCE

"**S**haron, guess what. Sly's people are going to invite you to Vegas," Eddy yelled down the phone.

"Okay, I'll think about it."

"Don't think about it. You are always thinking about things. Just do it. It's your big chance."

In a way, the idea was attractive to Sharon. Next week was Celebrate Diversity Week in Knockney. This was the council's annual drab-fest, created to counter the obnoxious capitalist agenda of rewarding success and punishing failure. It was one of Fred Starling's prouder innovations, though he was careful not to take all the credit. Sharon could avoid the event by going to Las Vegas.

The election was looming, and it might not look good if she won and then disappeared. On the other hand, it might not matter so much. If she won the seat, what could anybody do about it? She had promised to be a "do-nothing" candidate. What could be more appropriate than to leave for America the week after winning?

Sharon replied, "Okay, I've thought about it. I'll come."

"That's my girl. You will be hearing from Sly's assistant, about your travel arrangements. Don't let on that you know me, okay, and then we can spring that little surprise on Sly when we meet him. Man, do you know what time it is? It is 2:30 a.m., and I am awake and sober. How did that happen? I have to go. Talk to you soon."

Sharon decided to go for a walk. When she got to Grey Park, she heard the sound of planes overhead and looked up to see the RAF World War II formation team passing by. She turned a corner and came upon the park's war memorial.

It was Remembrance Sunday, and a small group of old men in duffle coats, pullovers, and blazers were standing to attention, having laid a couple of modest wreaths at the foot of the small memorial.

A few of them were wearing old army berets or forage caps. All of them had medals pinned to their chests. There were no bands and no official council presence, just a small group of pensioners in the cold gray light of a November noon.

Knockney Council had abandoned commemorating this occasion for many years because of the lack of diversity among the old soldiers.

"Every one of them is an old, straight, white guy celebrating war. It's an affront to youth, LGBT communities, persons of color, and peace advocates," said Lucille Whyte-Lothar, who had proposed the new council policy.

Sharon stood alongside the old soldiers. As the planes disappeared over the rooftops, she continued on her way.

CHAPTER 39

EDUCATION

Eddy knocked on Cynthia's office door and walked through. Tonight she was not wearing her fearsome dragon-lady outfit. Instead, she was clad in elegant silks while she studied documents on her desk. She gazed at Eddy, coolly assessing him and making him feel as always like a schoolboy.

Cynthia spoke at last. "You are going to Las Vegas to meet with Cy Sly and discuss your film?"

"Yes, he wants to discuss making *The Friends of Red Shidley.* I'm meeting Sharon there. Cy wants me to meet the author of the screenplay. Well, that should be fun."

"What about other offers? I believe other producers are beating a path to your door?"

"Well, my voice-over work is coming along well. Disney wants me to voice a major character in their next PIXAR animation. Disney, Paramount, and Sony are all asking to see me, and I have made my first TV commercial; it's for British Airways."

Eddy broke into the patter for the commercial.

"F. Scott Fitzgerald said there are no second acts in American life. Well, it's not true. I'm back, and I got here on British Airways, another great success story."

Cynthia laughed. "You got back to Hollywood courtesy of Heroin Airlines, as I recall."

Eddy laughed with her.

She continued in a business-like manner.

"Good, your success is important if you are to be of any use to me and China."

This made Eddy stiffen with apprehension.

"I've been thinking about that, you know … will I have to, you know, like, err … betray England, be a traitor?"

He shuffled his feet nervously.

Cynthia smiled and said, "I can't promise anything, but I think I can say that I don't expect you to go off and steal plans for British secret weapons or to rifle the drawers of the consular office in Los Angeles. If it will put your mind at rest, China's basic aims and ambitions do not conflict with those of Britain."

She paused. "How much do you know about China?"

Eddy sighed. "Bugger all, apart from, you know, the Great Wall, pandas, Chinese takeaways, and when I was a school kid we thought, you know, Chinese girls had horizontal … you know, to go with the slanted eyes."

Cynthia raised an eyebrow and clucked disapprovingly.

"Did you know how many 'modern' inventions originated in China? Paper money, moveable-type printing, the magnetic compass, gunpowder and artillery, porcelain, the seismograph, astronomical clocks, and even the wheelbarrow?" Cynthia raised an eyebrow and then walked over to an adjacent table and drinks cabinet.

"Really, even the wheelbarrow?" asked Eddy.

"Even the humble wheelbarrow," repeated Cynthia.

She handed Eddy a whiskey and soda.

Cynthia continued. "Did you know that by the sixteenth century, China was the world's economic superpower, and the world beat a path to China's door for its products? By the early eighteen hundreds, China accounted for about a third of the globe's trade and production. Alas, my poor country was plunged into a period of almost 150 years of war and unrest—the Opium Wars, the Taiping Rebellion, the Boxer Rebellion, the Japanese annexation of Manchuria, the Rape of Nanking, and then the civil war. The list goes on, and some of it can be squarely laid at the door of Britain."

This made Eddy squirm.

"It's been a long slow climb back to take our place in the world and its economy. China dominates global business, which is no bad thing, given the way it has been run to date."

Eddy was unsure why Cynthia was lecturing him about this. He knew better than to interrupt when she was in headmistress mode. He kept quiet, absorbing what she told him, and wondering what Sharon would make of it.

"Have you ever seen the Chinese handle money, Edward? We treat it with a mystical reverence you will not see in any other race, except perhaps the Jews. We Chinese truly understand the connection between wealth and power. Those idiots, the Gang of Four, reduced the country to penury, until Deng Xiao Ping returned to power and unfettered the mercantile genius of our country. He said; to be rich is glorious."

Eddy shifted uneasily on his chair. He thought there was an irony that the two most important women in his life, after his mother, were Sharon and Cynthia, and it struck him for the first time how similar they were. Brilliant, mercurial, and self-confident, he just wished he understood half of what they said.

"Do you know what the real triumph of communism was in the twentieth century Edward?"

Oh, Christ, Eddy thought, *here we go again.*

"It was to inflict the cult of egalitarianism on the world and dupe people into the belief that all men are created equal."

"Aren't they?" Eddy asked naively.

"You see what I mean? You have been duped along with the rest. I imagine you remember the Cold War and the so-called triumphs of Soviet-era Russia with the spies it placed in the West."

"I thought they really had done a huge amount of damage," replied Eddy.

"Oh, granted they may have created some problems for Western European countries. After all, it doesn't help if senior men in the security services are working for the enemy. But think, did it lead to the collapse of the West? Far from it.

The East German STAASI thoroughly penetrated West Germany. Even German Chancellor Willy Brandt's best friend and confidant was a communist spy. Look at East Germany, where the STAASI chief Markus Wolfe had half the population spying on the other half. My goodness, the STAASI was virtually a job creation scheme. In the end, Soviet communism collapsed under its own contradictions. But the Russians did have some spectacular victories you probably are unaware of."

Cynthia took a sip of whiskey.

"Not all spies or agents are James Bond. Some can be simply agents of influence, who work to achieve positions where they peddle ideas and nudge government policies. Usually, they remain hidden, unless exposed as was a *Guardian* journalist revealed to have been on the receiving end of Moscow gold.

"I believe there was also a novel called *The Spike*, which in fictional terms described how stories unfavorable to the Soviet Union and its allies were 'spiked.' Persons in the media paid by the Russians deliberately withheld stories from publication. One must appreciate the accomplishments of those Russian Marxists: they created such squalor, oppression, and misery and yet fostered a belief that they had created paradise on Earth."

Eddy perked up; this was more interesting than a lecture on Chinese economics.

"You said they had triumphed. How?"

"You have to look at each country in turn to see the insidious effects of their work. In Britain, the best examples are the National Health Service, which has been elevated to a religious icon in England, and the demonization of the education system. The NHS has become a greedy monster that absorbs more cash and resources without ever improving. You cannot save someone from dying in their youth and not expect to incur a greater cost in the future. It is basic economics.

"Even the postwar Labour Government that implemented the NHS recognized this but hoped with typical English optimism that they would muddle through. Then, the abandonment of coherent immigration controls means that the NHS has to treat people with illnesses long eradicated or never encountered in Britain. I suppose there may be some educational value in exposing young medical students to cases of dengue fever and Guinea-worm."

"And the education system?"

"Britain's grammar schools system was the envy of the world. It provided a first-class education to anyone with even modest means. Imagine the destruction of that system by the very people who had been beneficiaries. One of our great political leaders, Cho-en Lai, was incredulous; some visiting Labour Party politicians boasted to him that England was going to close its grammar schools.

"The foundation of national success is the way a country educates its people. Sabotage that foundation and the country will go into decline as its technical and artistic base shrinks."

"Well, that's not happened in Britain, has it?"

"Not entirely, no. The Soviet Marxists underestimated the Darwinian tenacity of the British in educating their children privately, at any cost. Look at all the hypocritical socialists in Britain, politicians included, who promote state education and then educate their children privately."

"What about elsewhere in the world?" asked Eddy.

"Let me see. France, well that's easy, just encouraging the French natural passion for leisure and reducing the working week to thirty-five hours; you can't get a lot done in that amount of time. Holland was one of the Soviets' more amusing efforts, through encouraging the liberalization of controlled drugs such as marijuana and of pornography.

"I think the Soviets miscalculated, believing the country would descend into a dystopian mire of self-indulgence and narcosis. That it did not was an example of the Soviets capacity to misunderstand human nature. Even a child knows that you cannot subsist on an endless diet of sugar.

"Where else? Germany? Apart from reunification, which is another story altogether, there was the rise of the green or environmental groups. This means that the cost of doing business increases as industry must continue to try to conform to stringent environmental laws.

"Of course, the USA is another example of this. Indeed environmentalism has been elevated to a religious movement. The greens have come full circle, returning from Judeo-Christian beliefs to a form of animism that their primitive ancestors would recognize."

Cynthia saw Eddy's confusion over the term *animism*.

"You can look it up on Google. Where was I? The American green movement is much worse in many ways than its European counterpart. The US environmental groups are seeking fundamental social change and are financed by charitable foundations, established by the very industries these groups seek to see destroyed.

"Lenin said, 'capitalists will sell us the ropes with which we will hang them.' How can a country compete economically? By the way, Edward, most of Hollywood is in thrall to environmentalism and the current meme, climate change."

"What about the whole debacle with British Rail, you know, nationalization, privatization, and now renationalization. Was that a Soviet trick also? I mean, if it was, they've got a lot to bloody answer for."

Cynthia laughed. "No, we did not invent trains, and you can't lay the British Rail debacle entirely at the feet of the Soviet Marxists, although they were influential in getting so much of British industry into the inept hands of government. No, I'm afraid that sometimes politicians are quite capable of make a frightful mess of things without agents of influence nudging things along."

Eddy pondered for a few moments on the enormity of all Cynthia had told him.

"It's like the *X-Files* crossed with Adam Curtis documentaries. Might make an interesting film or, better yet, series of films."

Cynthia smiled and said, "Indeed."

CHAPTER 40

TRIP

Sharon was still elated from her election win as she checked in at Heathrow for her United Airlines flight to Las Vegas, via Washington, DC. The only dark cloud on the horizon was her increasing concern about Eddy. She wondered whether he was telling her the whole truth as she read more stories about his surfacing in Hollywood.

Eddy continued to be very vague about the Chinese official from the security services who had taken him island-hopping across the Pacific. Eddy had described her as a "high-up Chinese government official" and "an elderly lady who mostly ignored me."

Phrases such as "mysterious oriental beauty" had not cropped up in their conversations but were mentioned in the pieces she read in newspaper and Internet articles. Sharon scrolled through her memory. She realized that when she tried to get information on this "mysterious oriental beauty," Eddy changed the subject. Sharon reviewed this behavior against Eddy's past transgressions and came to the inevitable conclusion that their movie script may not be quite the work of fiction Eddy had been suggesting.

Sharon put this thought to one side, to be resurrected at the appropriate moment. It was going to be a long flight, and Sharon planned to review the script of the film. The prospect of her being able to do this in peace suffered a severe setback when she took her seat on the flight, only to find that her neighbor was Lucille

Whyte-Lothar, chair of the Knockney LGBT Action Group. Whyte-Lothar glowered at Sharon as she sat down.

"Morning, Lucille. Where are you going?" asked Sharon.

She chose not to acknowledge Sharon at all and instead buried her face in her paperwork. Sharon managed to catch a glimpse of the document title that Lucille was reading: "Affirmative Action: Strategies in a Multicultural Century," and underneath, the words: "The Annual National Diversity Institute Conference: Promoting Leadership in an Evolving Multicultural Landscape, Hyatt Regency, Bethesda, MD."

"Can I read that when you've finished?" asked Sharon.

Lucille just carried on reading and ignoring Sharon. Sharon retrieved the script and started to review it. The more she read, the more she realized the story had no structure. The characters were shallow and behaved in ways that bore no resemblance to real life. Sharon wondered what qualities the producer saw in the script.

Whyte-Lothar had left the plane at Washington, DC.

Sharon shouted after her, "Who's paying your expenses, Miss Equality?"

Sharon continued to Las Vegas, sleeping most of the way. On arrival, she maneuvered her way through the slot machines in the baggage hall and picked up her bags. She walked into the public reception area.

"Baby!" shouted a very familiar voice.

Eddy picked up Sharon and carried her, singing, "You are my sunshine, my only sunshine; you make me happy when skies are gray. You'll never know, dear, how much I love you; please don't take my sunshine away."

He had not been happy like this in years.

"Eddy, get a grip," said Sharon.

This was not a time to ask a born-again loser to control his emotions. She gave him a big kiss and let him guide her through the slots to the taxi stand, and they took a cab to Paris, Las Vegas.

Sharon read in the hotel promotional literature: "the hotel was a reconstruction of a Hollywood executive's idea of a cinematic realization of the City of Light in the Jazz Age; a Gershwin's Les-Six inspired tableau of a young, single, spirited Gene Kelly dazzling and being bedazzled by the exquisite sophistication of Europe."

Eddy and Sharon retired to their room and enjoyed an evening and night of seemingly endless sex, to a degree that surprised both of them.

Sharon said, "When you haven't shagged the one you love for a while, it brings out the best in you, don't you think?"

"Why do you always have to intellectualize everything?"

They both burst out laughing.

CHAPTER 41

VEGAS

Sol Silberstein was idly reading the Venetian hotel's promotional literature. It described the hotel as: "a reconstruction of a Hollywood executive's idea of a cinematic realization of Venice in the fifties; a Stanley Donen stylized tableau of a young Audrey Hepburn dazzling and being bedazzled by the exquisite sophistication of Europe."

Zhang's entourage had arrived and checked into their rooms. Zhang, Nancy Liu, and Sol Silberstein and his wife, Marigold, strolled through St. Mark's Square. Troubadours were engaged in carousing around the central plaza while gondoliers punted tourists through the canal that winds its way around the vast main floor of the hotel. All of this under a fake Mediterranean sky that cast a blue light on the people below.

Sol's cell phone rang.

"Yeh?"

His face contorted into a look that combined puzzlement with annoyance.

"Meet me at the lobby in ten minutes."

He put the phone back in his pocket.

"I'm sorry. Problem with one of our metals books; some fucker ... er, sorry Nancy, some unscrupulous trader is playing games again. I've got to sort it out. I'll meet you at Zefferino in ... oh ... fifteen minutes?"

Sol bounded up the stairs and found Thomas deep in conversation with Boddy Woo, Zhang's assistant. Sol grabbed his arm and whisked him away, Thomas turning his head back toward Boddy as he was dragged toward the exit.

"I'll call you later."

A Russian trader, Sergei Reuben, was squeezing Sol's December nickel delivery. Sol had a large short position that he knew he could fill but only if a shipment he owned from Canada arrived in Rotterdam on time. However, a lock operators' strike on the St. Lawrence Seaway was threatening to delay the shipment. Reuben was funding strike payments to the lock operators and simultaneously buying huge amounts of out-of-the-money call options on December nickel, driving prices upward.

Reuben's intent was clearly to sell his nickel position to Sol at the point of maximum pain. Boddy Woo passed all this on to Thomas. Her cousin worked for Reuben; business was business, she had said to Thomas, but family connections were more important.

When they got outside, Sol said, "Tell this bastard that if he does not close out our whole December position at evens, then it is payback time. Tell him our Katangese friends are itching for a chance to work in Switzerland."

Sol had managed to secure a pardon for Reuben, after he fell out with President Joseph Kabila, who threw him into the hell of Kinshasa's Makala Prison. In return, Reuben had promised never to squeeze any market in which Sol had a position.

Sol had huge investments in the Democratic Republic of Congo. He was on excellent terms with Kabila and with various mercenary armies and militias, especially the Katangese. His Katangese associates were renowned for their efficiency and brutality. They had no fear of operating in Europe even in the leafy suburbs of Switzerland where Reuben lived. Buying Sol's position would be painful for Reuben but not as painful as what the Katangese would do to him.

Sol had wandered outside, where it was over one hundred

degrees Fahrenheit. Sol was hot and was agitated, which raised his temperature more.

"Let's get inside. I feel like a tandoori chicken."

"I can recommend a good Indian restaurant, over on—," said Thomas.

"You fucking dopey twat. I don't mean I want to eat a fucking tandoori chicken; I mean feel like a chicken in a fucking Tandoor in this heat. Now get in there and sort this thing out while I go back to my friends, wherever they are. My God, what did I do to deserve this?"

Sol went back inside and found the group assembled at the bar in Zefferino. They enjoyed a pleasant meal and talked about the plans for the main party at the MGM Grand the following day. After consuming several espressos laced with Sambuca, they took a limo ride down the strip and enjoyed the various sites of tasteless grandeur.

CHAPTER 42

ACHE

Bill Blake's consciousness returned through a fog. The throbbing in his back reminded him he had been shot, and he remembered falling, hitting the awning over the foyer of the hotel, bouncing off, and landing on a car. He woke up on a mortuary slab. There was a thick, dull pulsation in his head. He tried to sit up but was too weak, and he nearly blacked out from the agony.

He ran his hands over his body and realized he was still in the clothes. Gritting his teeth, he rolled onto his side and lowered his legs onto the floor. His feet touched the ground, and he realized that this was a bad idea. His legs hurt badly and had no strength in them. He was not sure if they were broken or just badly bruised. His arms appeared to be in reasonable shape, capable of bearing his weight as he lowered himself to the floor.

Just as he was doing this, a young Asian boy in a white lab coat entered the room and gasped as he saw the reanimated corpse struggling to get off the slab. The mortuary assistant ran forward to help Bill. He was surprised when Bill deliberately swept the assistant off his feet. He fell, cracking his head on the floor and rendering him unconscious. Bill pulled himself forward on his elbows. He rifled the young man's pockets, finding a wallet with little in it except a few Kazakh Tenge notes and a packet of condoms.

Bill grunted to himself, "So the young lad was going to get his leg-over eh? Either that or he was hopeful. 'But every man is tempted, when he is drawn away of his own lust, and enticed'[13]."

Bill pocketed the Tenge notes and kept going, dragging himself out of the mortuary. He reached the doorway and tried to stand. His legs would not bear his weight. He could move them a little, and he could feel a remote sensation if he pinched the skin. There was a lot of pain coming from deep within the limbs. Bill was in a quandary—how to get out of here and how to avoid the bastards that had shot him.

Edging out of the mortuary room, he looked up and down a dimly lit corridor. He had no idea what the time was; his Rolex watch had disappeared, probably stolen. He noticed a clock on the corridor wall, above a notice board, reading 1:15. Given the quiet and lack of people about, Bill figured it must be the early morning. Bill crawled out into the corridor making slow, painful progress. His legs twitched and pulsed with pain. Bill came to a T-junction and looked right and left.

To the right the corridor merged into another T-junction. To the left was a glass door beyond which was dark. There was a reception area with an office counter. Bill realized that a guard or receptionist was probably on duty. He dragged himself slowly along the corridor trying to make no sound, until he reached the reception area. He listened and heard the noise of a TV set but had no sense of how many people may be inside.

Taking a chance, he shouted, "Oiiii."

The TV sound was muted, and a head peered across the counter. The broad counter shelf almost obscured Bill, pressed against the wall beneath. *Only one person*, thought Bill. He bellowed again, and the person looked down beneath the reception counter. The figure gave a feminine gasp, followed by a jingling of keys.

The reception door flew open, and a uniformed figure emerged. She stepped around Bill and spoke to Bill in Russian, then Kazakh.

Bill whimpered "Please, please help me."

He realized the woman guard thought he might be a drunk who

---

[13] James 1:13–15.

had wandered unseen in from the street. She had not realized he had crawled from the mortuary. The guard moved in closer, thinking Bill was harmless. As soon as she came within range, his arms shot out and seized her ankles, repeating the same trick used on the mortuary assistant.

She fell backward, cracking her head on the concrete floor. She was unconscious but made little groans and sighs. Bill rifled her pockets, finding some more Tenge bills, a pocketknife, and a set of keys. She wore a gun belt with an automatic pistol, spare ammunition clips, and a flashlight. Bill pocketed these and set off on his painful progress out of the main door of the building.

The foyer of the building was deserted and led out onto a dimly lit car park. Edging onward in the night, he crawled through the door and down the steps into the car park. Only a few vehicles were there. Around the car park was a strip of garden, bordered by a straggly hedge.

Bill crawled behind the hedge and lay on the grass between it and the building. He lay panting and gathering his wits, waiting for the terrible pains in his body to subside. A car pulled in, and two burly uniformed figures emerged. Bill watched as they sauntered over to the building but entered by another door.

Bill wondered if this was a police station or the secure wing of a hospital. Regardless, he had to get away. He began to crawl again, staying within the narrow space that hid him from view. He circumnavigated the car park, reaching one of the two gates in the walls surrounding the building.

A sentry box was at the gate, but no one was inside. Beyond was what looked like a main road, with the occasional vehicle passing. Bill crawled out into the gateway, staying close to the gatepost. Vehicles drove past, but no one spotted the figure lying prone in the shadows.

Looking out of the gates and up the street, he noticed a large well-lit building to the left of where he lay. Looking back to the building he had left, he could see Cyrillic text bracketed by two large green crosses.

Bill realized it was a hospital not a police station. The uniformed men entering the building were ambulance drivers or other security guards. The armed guard at reception was to ensure people were not stealing drugs or alcohol.

Someone in the hospital would find two unconscious people and raise the alarm. His trail would be easy to follow; he was still leaking blood from his wounds. His next problem was to get out of this place and recuperate in safety. Looking at the large well-lit building about one hundred yards down the road, he made out the sign that read in Cyrillic and English, "Hotel Yamaguchi." The buildings to his right looked like apartments. Directly across the road was a patch of empty ground between two buildings.

Bill had been staying at the Intercontinental Hotel but had noticed the new gaudy Japanese hotel on his way to and from his meeting with Khan. He glanced at his watch, but remembered it was not on his wrist. He remembered the time from the morgue clock and figured it must now be getting on toward 2:00 a.m.

He could make out the glowing embers of a fire. Bill realized that vagrants were camped out on the empty ground, probably bingeing on vodka. He had seen scores of ragged people thronging the streets, drunk on cheap alcohol.

Zhang had made a joke about it with Bill, saying Astana was the new "party capital" of Central Asia, where even the peasants could afford happy oblivion.

"Is it not like your own London many years ago, Mr. Blake, when gin was so cheap the inns could advertise 'drunk for a penny, dead drunk for tuppence.'"

Bill had shaken his head and said, "For the drunkard and the glutton shall come to poverty: and drowsiness shall clothe a man with rags."[14]

Zhang had raised an eyebrow.

"Very poetic Mr. Blake."

Bill waited for a car to pass and made a desperate scrabbling

---

[14] Proverbs 23:21.

crawl across the road. His knees and hands were bloody from the effort of dragging his heavy body across the ground. A couple of human forms huddled around the remains of the dying fire to the left. Bill himself huddled against the right-hand wall of the building bordering the empty ground. He stayed in the shadows.

Bill was exhausted, and the pain in his back and legs was now joined by the scrapes and cuts from crawling. Bill took stock; he was still dressed in a suit but it was in tatters. He had a gun, a knife, and some Kazakh Tenge. He had only a sketchy idea of where he was in Astana and no friends apart from his contact, Zhang.

He was badly injured. In his violent life, Bill had dished out a lot of punishment. He knew he was seriously hurt. If his back was not broken, it had sustained a serious injury. Two bullets were lodged somewhere in his thorax There were no exit wounds in his chest. He guessed the bullets were lodged in muscle, since otherwise he would have died by now from internal bleeding. Bill pushed himself up into a sitting position with his back to the wall and legs sticking out in front of him.

A large Toyota land cruiser roared to a stop by the wasteland, startling Bill. A squat, fat Japanese man hastily emerged, staggering over to where Bill lay against the wall. The man proceeded to be sick all over Bill. Bill was too stunned to say anything. He was doused in a torrent of beery vomit.

The Japanese man's two companions staggered over to him. Both relieved themselves in the dark. Bill was the recipient of this new drenching. He roared his outrage. The group of men jumped back and then one burst out laughing.

CHAPTER 43

WEBSITE

Eddy yawned and scratched his head as he emerged from the shower. Sharon lay deep in sleep, exhausted from jet lag and the marathon bout of sex. He kept the curtains drawn, dressed quickly, and crept out of the room to get some breakfast.

In the hotel foyer, he stopped by the sundries shop and picked through the magazine rack. Vegas being an entertainment town, the store stocked all the trade papers. He idly picked through them and was pleased to see a three-quarter page article in the *Hollywood Reporter* entitled, "English Relish is definitely back on the menu again in Hollywood."

Eddy drifted into the hotel restaurant and was shown to a table by a waitress. He ordered eggs, bacon, hash browns, and toast, with coffee.

He was about to read the article when his cell phone rang. It was Malcolm.

"How are you doing Eddy? Shagging your brains out, nursing your bruised willie, making up for a prolonged period of abstinence by making a complete beast of yourself, eh? Oh, I forgot, you haven't gone without entirely, eh? You slipped Aunty Cynthia a length didn't you, dirty bugger!"

"Good morning. To what do I owe the pleasure of this call?

Malcolm said, "Listen, guess what? My best mate, the mysterious

Ah Chu, actually came round and knocked on my front door, the first time in living memory."

"I thought I was your best mate. So what did the guy want?"

"He came to tell me that an apartment in a neighboring condo had just become vacant. I told him you were away in Vegas, which I figured he must know. I went over there with him to look at the place. It is similar to mine, bit bigger though, and fully furnished. The rent is reasonable, rather on the low side I thought, and I figured there must be a catch, and there is."

"Well don't keep me in suspense, what the fuck is wrong with the place? Has it got no toilet, noisy neighbors, rats in the skirting board, what?"

"Ah Chu showed me the lease; the place is owned by Lotus Properties. Is that enough of a clue?"

"Do I detect the fragrant hand of Aunty Cynthia in the convenient arrival of this property on the market?"

"Dead right, I would say."

"Well, better the devil you know, I guess, though I suspect Sharon may throw a spanner into the works at some point. So what did Ah Chu say I should do?"

"Just sign the lease. He's faxing it to you at your hotel, and fax it back to him. He gave me the keys so you can move in when you get back to LA. I checked Lotus Properties in the Yellow Pages; the fax number is the same as the Lucky Lotus, surprise, surprise."

"I'll just tell Shazza that you found me a place; I need to pick my way very carefully through that minefield. So what else you been up to?"

"We just wrapped shooting on a new skin flick, covertly financed by your best pal Cy Sly, the real owner of Eros Productions."

"Yeah, the material Cyn gave me indicated that he generates independent funds for MegaTool films through his lucrative little side venture. Did you know that when he goes on his little 'safaris' to Asia and Latin America, to shag young teenage girls, he's also scouting for prospective talent for Eros films. Anyway, what epic were you working on this time?"

"Ah, a little masterpiece for downloading from the Bad Habits and Postulants Progress website called *The Sisters of Saint Sodom*. It is set in St. Simon's convent, in the imaginary Democratic Socialist Republic of Bendova, before the collapse of communism. The Army of the Revolution appropriates the convent. The place is full of young novices and postulants whom the soldiery constantly grope and rape.

"A skin trade veteran, Muffy Diver, plays the mother superior. She complains to the army colonel, played by another skin flick stalwart, Rock Hard. Did you know his real name is Richard Hardstaff? I never figured out why he bothered to adopt a porn name."

"Yeah, Dick Hardstaff, I mean, it's perfect."

"Anyway, Colonel Hard says what can he do, his men are horny soldiers after all, and the place is full of young women. The revolutionary government hates the church, so they ought to be grateful they are not all taken out and shot. Then his sergeant comes up with a solution to everyone's problems.

"He suggests that the soldiers shag the nuns up the bum. This will allow the nuns to maintain their vows of chastity, while relieving the horny compulsions of the men. Our military theologian also points out that this will be an unpleasant experience for the nuns. It would be both a sacrifice and an act of mortification. The girls would gain grace in heaven for this act of charity; I think you'll agree it's a theologically sophisticated argument."

Eddy guffawed, "You're kidding, right?"

"Absolutely not; mother superior reluctantly agrees, the girls bend over the refectory tables, bite their lips, and recite decades of the rosary, while the young men slake their lusts. Mother superior also joins in, although she gets carried away and, if you'll forgive the pun, in the climax of the film, does a spectacular DVDA."

"A what?" asked Eddy.

"Double vaginal, double anal; Muffy's famous for it; it's her trademark as it were. In the old pre-Viagra days, it was rare to shoot a successful DVDA. Getting four guys into position, all with their equipment at the ready, was a hit-and-miss affair. The final shot of the film is one of the novitiates sheepishly changing the nameplate

on the convent gate from St. Simon to St. Sodom. You won't believe
how many enemas and Preparation-H we went through shooting this
epic!"

"Nice one. I hope it's a good little earner for you. You never
know; you might pick up a porn industry award. That'll look nice on
the mantelpiece."

"Funny you should mention that," said Malcolm. "I was going to
tell you I'll be in Vegas tomorrow for the annual Adult Entertainment
Magazine Venereal Awards. A couple of the films I shot are up for
awards. The award show is going to be held in the MGM Grand's
Convention Center."

"That's the same place where this Chinese guy, Magnesio, is
holding a big soirée. His real name is Zhang. Cynthia told me she is
going to this big celebration of Magnesio's fifty years in the metal
trade. Apparently he earned his nickname after cornering the market
in magnesium and making a shit-pile of loot."

"Are you going too?" asked Malcolm.

"I'm not sure; Cyn told me to come to the function room and call
her on her cell phone, and she'd get us into the bash. Apparently all
kinds of celebrities will be going to the party, and it wouldn't hurt
my rising profile to be seen at an event like this."

"So why the reticence, or do I detect a little reluctance on your
part for Cynthia to meet with your lady, Sharon?"

"Yeah, much as I'd like to go to Magnesio's bash, there's the little
matter of when Sharon meets Cynthia and me getting caught in the
middle."

"Serves you right, you dirty bugger. It was a woman that did you
in last time, remember?"

"Well, it's going to happen; I guess sooner rather than later.
Anyway, we'll look out for you tomorrow at the MGM Grand."

"Yeah, it's worth spending a few minutes watching the triumphal
arrival of the ladies and gentlemen of the adult entertainment world."

They chatted for a few more minutes, and then Eddy rang off
to order breakfast and read his paper. Eddy reflected on the last
few months and how his life had taken a spectacular turnaround.

Nevertheless, he had an uncomfortable feeling that Cynthia and Sharon would mix like sodium and water. He thrust the thought aside and checked out the article in the *Reporter*.

"English Relish is back on the menu again in Hollywood"

The man who has become part of the Hollywood lexicon for failure is definitely making serious ripples if not waves in Tinsel-town. Doing a Relish became as much a part of the Hollywood lexicon for spectacular crash and burn.

Relish slipped into Hollywood a few weeks ago, ostensibly just visiting friends. He has quietly been reinventing himself as the comeback kid. He has not made a great song and dance about his return, but has been building up a steady portfolio of work, primarily in radio commercials and voice-overs for various animation films. When he was Hollywood's glamour boy in the 1990s it was often overlooked that Relish had serious talent as a vocal mimic. His recent TV ad for British Airways has put him firmly back on the Hollywood radar screen.

He is still wiry and good-looking, with cheekbones and a profile to die for, but the years of hardship in the wilderness have toughened those boyish good looks. He has the air of someone who has not only stared long into hell but has spent a long time there. Word on the street is that he has also been working on a screenplay, based on his own experiences after his decline and fall. In a recent interview, Relish recounted some of his adventures including, he claims, an encounter with an Islamic terrorist called Abdul Madbul. Relish claims Madbul was stalking him in England. Being stalked by studio executives is the only danger Relish faces in Hollywood.

Relish is also attracting attention from the TV side of the industry. One studio exec has seriously considered Relish for a new sitcom. Relish is believed to be having discussions with Cy Sly this weekend in Las Vegas. Sly is attending a major party at the MGM Grand, hosted by Chinese metal magnate Zhang Xing Liao.

Eddy nodded approvingly, not caring if Cynthia was behind this or not; he was back in the limelight again. All he had to do now was to start making movies again. The waitress placed his order on the table and refilled his coffee cup. As she did so, she glanced at the paper still opened at the Relish article. The picture accompanying the article was an old one from his glory days, but she recognized that it was the same man sitting at her table.

"Hey, sir, is you, no?"

She continued to look admiringly between the paper and Eddy himself. Eddy grinned self-deprecatingly and put his fingers to his lips in a mock instruction for the woman to be silent and not give the game away. On a whim, he took out his pen and autographed the page, giving the paper to the waitress, whose name he read from her badge was Rosita. She simpered and giggled like a teenage girl and took the unexpected gift.

She told Eddy she would rent a Spanish language video of one of his films. Eddy wolfed down his meal and rose from the table. He dropped a twenty-dollar bill for a seven-dollar meal, floating out of the restaurant feeling ten feet tall. Eddy Relish was definitely on the way back.

CHAPTER 44

HAMPER

"Hey, Hirasuna, you just puked up over the big ugly gaijin," said Igashi.

"No, Hirasuna, puked up a gaijin; he's such a greedy cunt, he must have eaten the waiter at that restaurant. He's such a greedy drunken prick that he must have eaten him, thinking he was just a big sheep," said Matsuoka.

"Eeeeee, Hirasuna-san, what a greedy cunt you are. You were so hungry that you ate the waiter," said Igashi.

Miki Ogamura heard the drunken laughter echoing out of the darkness between the two buildings. She was growing impatient with her henchmen, Idiot Igashi, Fat Hirasuna, and Many Tongues Matsuoka. It had been a successful day wringing concessions out of the Kaszakh government, but she was tired from the negotiations and subsequent drinking endless toasts with their Kazakh hosts.

Miki said, "Hey, what's so funny about Fat Hirasuna throwing up? Or do you three idiots always get such a laugh out of puking? Get back in the car before I cut off your tiny dicks! I'm tired, and I want to go to bed."

Just then Bill lashed out and grabbed one of the Japanese men, knocking the man to the ground and then grabbing him around the neck and putting the gun to his head.

The two other Japanese jumped back and pulled out long knives from under their suit jackets.

Igashi shouted, "Miki-san, the bastard gaijin has taken Hirasuna prisoner. What shall we do?

Miki shouted back, "Igashi, do you wonder why we call you Idiot? Kill him!"

"Miki-san, the bastard's got a gun; he might kill Hirasuna," shouted Many Tongues Matsuoka.

Miki Ogamura snorted, dismounted from the Land Cruiser, and marched over to the little group against the wall. Matsuoka and Igashi moved to one side while fat Hirasuna wriggled in Bill's steely grip, trying all the while to breathe. Miki took in the situation at a glance.

"Hirasuna, you useless pile of monkey shit, you've got us all into this situation by your piggy appetite and too much beer. I should let the big gaijin shoot you. Matsuoka, you speak some Russian. Ask the prick what he wants."

Matsuoka aired his Russian on Bill to no effect.

Bill spoke up. "Can any of you speak English?"

"You Engerish?" responded Matsuoka.

"Yes, English," replied Bill. "Now, you're going to help me, or I'll blow this fat bastard's head off."

"What's he say?" asked Miki impatiently.

"He wants our help," said Matsuoka.

"Funny way of asking for it," grunted Igashi.

Miki sighed and looked at the big man. It was hard to make much out in the dark. It was clear he was not some drunken vagrant, and although in a bad way was still dangerous. She wondered if they should simply leave Hirasuna, but Tiger Tokugawa would be annoyed. It was against the Yakuza code to abandon a soldier.

She squatted on the ground, not hunkering on her heels as Asian women do, but balanced on the balls of her feet, leaning forward and supporting herself on the fingertips of her left hand. She smiled at the man in the dark and spoke to Matsuoka.

Miki said, "I'm going to stab the arm holding Hirasuna; when I do, kick his wrist hard."

"You might end up killing Hirasuna, Miki-san," Igashi said.

Hirasuna gurgled in assent, but it was too late; Miki struck Bill's arm with a stiletto conjured out of nowhere.

Bill howled as the blade stabbed his bicep, not too deep to do any serious damage but enough to distract him. Matsuoka delivered a hard kick to Bill's wrist, numbing it and causing the gun to slip from his hand. Matsuoka quickly kicked it to one side, while Hirasuna wriggled free, gasping for breath.

Idiot Igashi stood open-mouthed at the perfectly choreographed sequence.

Igashi said, "Ha, now we kill the big bastard cunt gaijin."

Miki laughed and said, "Okay, idiot boy, go ahead."

"Err, what, me? You want me to kill him?"

"I thought you were just volunteering. Go on brave boy; cut his throat. Here, take my knife; we'll get out of the way."

Igashi looked from face to face in a quandary, before Miki laughed at him again.

"You dickless wonder Igashi, is it any wonder we call you Idiot. Look at him."

She pointed at Bill.

"Even without the gun, he is fearless and dangerous."

Bill nursed his sore arms but glowered menacingly at the four Japanese. The woman seemed to be the leader. He had expected them to attack him again, but she was keeping them at bay. Despite the pain and injury, he would have enjoyed sparring with them. He knew there was a tiny chance they might offer a way out of this predicament.

"Help me," said Bill.

Matsuoka spoke. "I don't believe it! He still wants us to help him! I'll help the cunt all right; I'll cut his dick off and make him eat it!"

He brandished his knife, but Miki sprung up and slapped him.

"Oh no, you won't."

Hirasuna turned to Miki. "Please, please, Miki-san, let me find the gun. I want to pay this steaming turd back for what he did to me."

"Fuck off; you'll do no such thing, either of you. Now, Igashi, go and fetch a flashlight from the Land Cruiser. Matsuoka, translate for me."

"Errr … okay, what do you want to say?"

"Ask the gaijin his name."

Matsuoka turned to Bill, who was glowering up out of the shadows. "What your name?"

Bill blinked and replied, "Bill Blake."

"Miki-san, his name is Bill Blake."

"Ask him how badly is he hurt," said Miki.

"How bad you hurt?" asked Matsuoka.

Bill made an inventory of the injuries, falling into a similar minimalist language.

"Legs hurt, no good; back in pain, shot; you understand, bang-bang, yeah? Head, pain; hurt bad, okay?"

Matsuoka pressed on. "Where you come from?"

Bill pointed to the building across the road.

Matsuoka said, "I think he's in bad shape. It sounds like he's been shot in the back; his legs are badly hurt, and he has some injuries to the head. When I asked him where he came from, he pointed across the road to the hospital. I'll bet he was taken there by the police; he can't have come from far away in this state."

Igashi returned with a flashlight. He turned it on and shone it at Bill, who was dazzled. Even in ragged clothing, broken and in pain, doused in vomit and urine, he radiated menace. Miki gazed into his eyes and recognized a kindred spirit. Bill gazed in sullen defiance, still waiting to see what their next move would be.

A police siren sounded in the distance. Miki and the crew looked at Bill and toward the alarm blaring in the distance. Hirasuna backed the Land Cruiser onto the wasteland. They all grabbed Bill, who was too surprised and exhausted to resist.

They quickly took off to the Hotel Yamaguchi, before the police cars arrived at the hospital. They bundled a groaning and complaining Bill into a large laundry trolley in the basement. They used a service elevator and pushed Bill to a private suite on the top of the hotel. They gingerly lifted Bill onto a bathroom floor.

Miki had her crew summon a doctor, who stitched up Yakuza and other criminals in Astana. The doctor cut off Bill's clothing and patched Bill up as best he could. The doctor was concerned about further injury to Bill's back.

The doctor took Matsuoka to one side and spoke to him about Bill's condition, which he relayed to Miki.

"Miki-san, Doctor Kevorkian has removed two bullets from the Englishman's back. He says the man is lucky to be alive. He has probably broken several vertebrae in his back, but thinks that his spinal cord is not severed. He says we should get him X-rayed as soon as possible and move him as little as possible. He's also pretty certain that he has fractures in his legs, and possibly a cracked skull. He thinks it is remarkable that the man is alive at all.

"He does not think he has any serious internal bleeding, other than the two bullet wounds. Kervorkian is ex-military and says the bullets are standard 9 millimeter rounds. He reckons they must have been fired from a silenced pistol with reduced muzzle velocity, which is why the bullets did not go right through him.

"Kevorkian thinks the spinal injuries might create some mobility problems for the man, even after healing. He suggests we sedate him heavily and then get him to a hospital as soon as possible. I told him you might want to take him back to Japan; he doesn't advise this, but if we do, he thinks he should be immobilized and kept sedated for the entire trip."

Idiot Igashi burst into the suite, grinning from ear to ear. Miki sent him to ask the hotel manager, a retired Yakuza, to speak to local police contacts.

Miki motioned him to be silent.

Kevorkian finished up and gave Miki an itemized bill in US dollars for his services. Miki scrutinized it thinking the doctor was overcharging them, but it was late. Miki went to a room safe and counted out the doctor's fee.

The doctor left, and Miki said, "Okay, idiot boy, out with it."

"His name is Bill Blake, and he's an English gangster. He is here to do a deal buying scrap metal from the Kazakh government. The deal was put together with a Chinese official called Zhang. Everyone calls him Magnesio. He is based in London but has an office here in Astana. Our man downstairs phoned cops and security agencies, calling in favors. It seems Magnesio was using Blake in a cat-and-mouse game to curry favor with the Americans. He arranged a deal to sell him some radioactive scrap through one of his front companies. Then he snitched on him to the Americans and the Russian FSB.

"The American and Russian security people shot him trying to escape from his hotel, and he fell about one hundred feet but landed on the big awning outside the foyer. He bounced off this onto a parked car. When they picked him up, there was no pulse, so they assumed he was dead. Now they are all in a panic. The dead man came back to life, and that's when we found him."

Igashi stood beaming like a schoolboy making his report. Hirasuna and Matsuoka scratched their heads, while Miki thought about all this. Then Igashi spoke again.

"Oh, I nearly forgot. The local Kazakh cops and security services were in on the deal. Magnesio paid them to ensure Blake was killed."

Miki thought about this and looked up something on her cell phone browser.

"You know what this means, if Magnesio is involved?"

They looked blankly at Miki.

"Errr ... no," said Hirasuna.

"Umm ... Magnesio doesn't like Englishmen?" said Matsuoka.

"Magnesio is a cunt?" said Igashi.

Miki surveyed the criminal brain trust.

"And who does Magnesio answer to?" asked Miki.

"His wife?" ventured Igashi.

The other two Yakuza slapped him on the head, but Miki spoke up.

"Not bad, Igashi, but you don't know why you're right, do you?"

"Err ... no."

"Tokugawa-san mentioned to me when he sent me out here. He said I might meet Zhang in our business dealings out here. He warned me not to let his gentle manner deceive me. I just looked up Zhang on my phone browser. Magnesio's wife, Nancy Liu, is the cultural attaché at the Chinese Embassy in London. Cultural attaché is as good as saying she is a spy. Have any of you figured it out yet?

The three Yakuza stared at Miki, who rolled her eyes with impatience.

"Multibillionaires like Magnesio don't go getting their hands dirty personally arranging hits. Besides, just shopping Blake would have curried favor with the Americans. No, this is different. Why should Magnesio put himself at risk by having Blake killed? I don't know, but only someone very powerful could have convinced him to do this. The obvious choice must be Nancy Liu."

Miki was pleased with the news. It might be enough to convince Tokugawa that the Yakuza should take an interest in the welfare of Bill Blake. After sending her email, she arranged further treatment for Blake at a private hospital to render him ready for the trip to Japan.

Although still suspicious, Bill realized he had no choice but to accept help from the Japanese woman. Matsuoka explained to Bill that he would be taken to Japan. Bill reckoned this could only be an improvement on Kazakhstan. The last thing he recalled was the injection of a tube connected to a drip.

CHAPTER 45

RENDEZVOUS

A bdul Madbul was the Great Satan, arriving in LA, as he had planned from Canada. He worked his way south, picking up odd jobs with the migrant armies of agricultural laborers. His next task was to get money and firepower. All he had was a switchblade taken from a black youth. He and his two friends had mugged him on the outskirts of Compton. They were lying dead in a Dumpster, their throats cut.

Madbul remembered his extensive training at the hands of the Chinese. He was to make his way to a Hollywood club called the Lucky Lotus in LA. He should find the proprietor and identify himself using coded phrases. Each Albanian agent had his own unique set of phrases and passwords to identify himself to the Chinese.

He knew that China and Albania had long drifted apart. No more fraternal banquets of diplomats in Tirana or Beijing, sluicing down rice wine or plum brandy, and swearing eternal friendship. These days, the Chinese were coupled with the Americans, despite the continued tension over Taiwan.

The covert surveillance by the Chinese in Knockney also continued to trouble him. What the hell were the Chinese doing looking for Eddy Relish? Were they looking for him also? He recognized the dangers in revealing himself to a Chinese operative in LA, but at this point, he had no choice. Fa'aht cells were independent units operating with the loosest coordination across the globe. He might track down a cell here in LA, but it would take time, time he could be devoting to killing the hated Relish.

Madbul found a pay phone and looked up the Lotus listing in the phone book. He called, asking if he could speak to the owner. He was put through to an extension.

"Wheyyy?" said a harsh voice.

Madbul said in English, "I will take Tiger Mountain by a stratagem."

"Did third uncle advise you to do this?" said a voice in English.

Madbul completed code. "No, it was told to me in a dream."

There was a brief silence, and the English voice spoke again.

"Please come and be my guest at the Lucky Lotus. I'll see you at four o'clock this afternoon."

CHAPTER 46

SCARS

B ill Blake gazed at the ceiling. He was scrolling through some of his favorite Bible passages in his mind. He flexed and tensed his body to get a sense of how well he was healing. His body was immobilized to prevent damage to his spinal column. Nonetheless, he could feel more sensations in his legs.

A Japanese doctor had given him a detailed inventory of his injuries. The two bullets had lodged in his back muscles, not penetrating to his lungs or passing near his heart or vital arteries. The fall from the hotel balcony had resulted in most of the damage. His fall was broken by the hotel awning. The impact and ricochet onto a parked car had cracked several spinal vertebrae. He had also broken both his legs, created a hairline fracture of the skull, and badly bruised his kidneys.

A heavily built Japanese man walked into the room. He stared down at Bill for a long time. Bill saw the woman he knew as Miki, standing at his side.

The man finally spoke in accented English.

"Mr. Blake, I am Tokugawa. You can call me Boss Tokugawa or Mr. Tokugawa. My friends call me Tiger, but I do not know yet if you are a friend. Miki thinks we should take an interest in you."

Although muzzy and tired, Bill knew within seconds that his fate hung in the balance. Tokugawa radiated power and brute strength. His face was square, crowned with sleek black hair swept back from his forehead, with wings of iron gray at his temples. Tokugawa gazed down at Bill with eyes as black as jet and an expression of grim calm. After a long silence, he spoke again to Bill.

"Miki has told me some of your story. You appear to be a resourceful man, but also a man who is out of his depth in the Far East. I have made some inquiries about you, with some associates in London. What were you doing in Astana, buying toxic metal from Magnesio?"

"Mr. Zhang?"

Tokugawa growled impatiently, "Yes, Magnesio; compared to him, you are like a child in a grown-up world."

Bill stirred uncomfortably under this interrogation. Tokugawa was laying bare his ignorance of the metal markets and the world beyond the confines of Knockney.

Bill said, "I was doing what any businessman would do; I was trying to turn a profit."

Tokugawa said, "An admirable objective, Blake-san, but you were deceived by both Silberstein and Magnesio. Silberstein made the deal for the money, but Zhang—Magnesio—used the opportunity to curry favor with the Americans, by passing on information about the deal. The metals you bought were radioactively contaminated. The Americans are terrified of this dirty metal getting into the hands of terrorists. If ground down into powder and used with conventional explosives, it could contaminate the center of a large city and render it uninhabitable for centuries."

Bill felt the familiar supernova of rage build up behind his eyes. Ever since he had put that shifty little prick Eddy Relish on the plane for Hong Kong, his well-ordered existence had disappeared. His life had transformed into an alien landscape where Bill was like a billiard ball, careening wildly around the table by an unseen hand. He was Bill Blake, the scourge of the East End, a byword for pain. His entry into a pub reduced a merry hubbub to nervous silence.

He thought about the fax he had received from Eric Dwyer, only a few weeks ago in Hong Kong, but it felt like a lifetime. Bill thought he would pay a visit to Mr. Dwyer on his eventual return to

Knockney and familiarize him with the pleasures of driving six inch nails through flesh.

This was as nothing to what he would do to Relish when he caught up with him; despite the warning off he had received from Zhang's bint-wife. Dwyer, Relish, Magnesio, Silberstein, all of them would become acquainted with the joys of an industrial nail gun. He would particularly enjoy introducing Relish to the sublime misery of an anal fistula.

Bill was suddenly aware of a harsh squealing sound in the room. Tokugawa and Miki were looking at him with puzzled expressions. The noise was coming from him, as he ground his teeth together in his fury. He forced himself to relax.

Bill said, "Since you would do a thing like this, I will surely take revenge on you, and after that I will cease."[15]

Tokugawa inclined his head to one side. "So, Mr. Blake, you favor us with one of your biblical quotations. Perhaps you should also read the sutras of the Lord Buddha.

"What shall we do with you? I have indulged Miki's whim to save you, but I don't think you should outstay your welcome. Your body is healing; no doubt you might like to catch up with Silberstein and Magnesio and discuss your recent period of bad luck with them. I believe we can help you to confront them.

"I have received an invitation to a party in Las Vegas hosted by Zhang. We will fly there in my private jet, stopping on the way in Saipan and Guam, to look at some of our hotel properties there."

Tokugawa turned on his heel and left with Miki, who favored Bill with a smile and wave as she left the room. After Miki and Tokugawa had left, Bill continued to mentally scroll through the Bible and flex his slowly mending body. He knew from Miki, through a translation by Matsuoka, that any day now they would leave for Las Vegas. She told Bill that Tokugawa had his underlings arrange for Bill to travel with them to the United States. The Yakuza would provide him with

---

[15] Judges 15:6–8.

false travel documents and ensure that immigration officials who were in the pocket of the Yakuza met them.

As a bonus, he knew from the various English language tabloid magazines that Miki had brought him that the little punk Eddy Relish was likely to be in Vegas too. "I will make mine arrows drunk with blood, and my sword shall devour flesh; and that with the blood of the slain and of the captives, from the beginning of revenges upon the enemy."[16]

---

[16] Deuteronomy 32:41–43.

CHAPTER 47

MEAT

Nigel Owens walked into Pol Pots, Knockney's ceramics and earthenware collective, looking for Fred Starling. Nigel knew that the collective was ostensibly one of the more successful small businesses in Knockney, but this owed more to local government grants from the council rather than business acumen.

It was rare for them to sell any of the pieces of pottery, and the main source of income came from the store's café. Nigel looked around the café guessing Fred would be hiding here from the media storm raging over Kockney.

Nigel blessed his good luck that he had lost the local election contest. He had accepted the electoral opportunity to please his father after the marijuana debacle. He now realized just how fortunate he was not to be associated with a council that funded an enterprise honoring the man responsible for the Cambodian genocide.

Nigel saw Fred at a corner table in the darkest part of the pottery café, away from the window. The breaching of the Knockney Labour fortress had been a significant news item, which Fred could probably have weathered, ridiculing Sharon's immediate departure for Las Vegas as a political lightweight.

Unfortunately for London's "hermit kingdom" it emerged that a woman resident in Knockney, from the Havelock-Ellis Islands in the South Pacific, and her Liberian boyfriend, had been operating a racket whereby children from this impoverished archipelago were supposedly sent to start a better life in the UK.

Nigel had read the investigative reports in the various newspapers and heard the news on Knockney Radio. The children were sent to a woman known as Auntie Agnes and used as slave labor by her and her boyfriend to work in the couple's apartment sweatshop, turning out beautiful embroidered fabrics and clothes for sale in upmarket boutiques in London's fashionable West End. The children would accommodate new arrivals by killing and eating any of the least productive children, or those that fell sick.

The Havelock-Ellis Islanders had no interest in independence despite being a British territory since the mid-nineteenth century. The Havelock-Ellis Islanders were eligible for British passports and could travel feely to Europe. There were few opportunities for people in these islands, other than growing coconuts or catching fish. The scheme established by Auntie Agnes seemed so attractive.

Nigel crept up to Fred and tapped him on the shoulder.

Fred shook his head mournfully. "Hello, Nigel. How did you know I was here?"

"A little bird told me. Don't worry, I haven't let on you're here. Not a good time for you and the comrades, is it. I have to admit, I am not so upset now about losing out to the Constable girl. I mean, I'm all for respecting alternative cultural norms, but cannibalism is a bit extreme."

Fred glared at him. He could not bear more than ever to have his faith mocked. Nigel saw Fred's expression and adopted a more sober demeanor.

"Okay, bad joke."

Fred relaxed and said, "So what you going to do now, continue with the radio and deejay work?"

"Yup, funny you should mention that; I've been booked to deejay a party in Las Vegas. Would you believe to celebrate some Chinese bloke's fiftieth anniversary in the metal trading business. I thought it was just a massive windup at first. I mean how come Knockney's finest, Rasta-Blasta, gets to play Vegas? I got an email through our radio station's website, from a Boudicca Woo, executive assistant to Zhang Xing Liao, of the Chinese Recycling Council.

Fred looked impressed.

"One of our Chinese comrades has hired you to provide the music for his party?"

"Well, it's not as though I'm putting on the vibes for Chairman Mao, Fred; Zhang is as capitalist as they come. I understand that one of the main guests of honor, according to Ms. Woo will be Sol Silberstein."

Fred grimaced. Silberstein was the kind of capitalist that he and the Knockney comrades condemned.

"Don't tell me you're actually going to take the job?"

Nigel laughed at Red Fred's naïve, po-faced note of censure.

"Sure, it's no worse than doing a Yardie gig. Anyway, it's all on the level; I get a first-class ticket to Vegas, a week in a hotel, and $10,000, half of which was wired to my TSB account this morning. Some of us have to work, Fred; we can't all subsist on the local government tit."

Fred was too tired to argue and felt embarrassed at the election debacle, so just shook his head. *Fred looks more than tired*, thought Nigel; *he looks old and ill*. On the table in front of Fred were various British daily papers, mostly tabloids:

"Cannibal Auntie Horror in Darkest Knockney!" said the *Sun*.

"Knockney Cannibal Tragedy Blamed on Incompetent Council," said the *Mirror*.

"Cannibals? Get a Mouthful of Our Dusky Savage, Kimberly!' said the *Daily Sport*.

Nigel asked Fred, "Did the council have any inkling that this was going on?"

Fred sighed. "I've talked with our Social Services Department, and they suspected something was wrong."

"Let me guess, they were terrified into inaction by the fear of being accused of racism?"

Fred was silent, his mouth a grim line as he stared at Nigel, before nodding.

"It's worse; we've a big file of complaints to the police from neighbors of the couple, documenting signs of malnourishment and physical abuse."

Nigel could see that Fred was actually on the verge of tears.

"Some of the neighbors really gave the police and SSD a hard time about these children. Sometimes, they were seen on the street but would not behave like ordinary kids. They would march behind the adults in silence, holding hands, gazing at the ground. Some of the neighbors also noticed that certain children disappeared from time to time. If they asked Agnes or her boyfriend, they were told that the missing kids had gone back to the South Pacific for a holiday."

Fred was silent again. Nigel went to the café counter and paid for two cups of tea. *Even the pottery staff seems submerged in gloom, thought Nigel. This might be because their source of council largesse is about to dry up.*

"Have you read the papers?" said Fred when he thanked Nigel for the tea. Fred seemed to have a compulsive need to unburden himself.

"They started … they started eating the kids to cover up the death of one of the children, who was killed by the boyfriend. They'd still be doing it if they hadn't got greedy and careless. Apparently, they marketed some of the flesh as 'bushmeat,' you know, cooked wild animals. There's a huge demand for bushmeat in the immigrant community. Apparently Agnes and the boyfriend abducted a local Togolese-born twelve-year-old girl to kill and butcher. They figured that an orphan living with a drunken uncle would not be missed."

Nigel gave a grim laugh and said, "They literally bit off more than they could chew."

Fred winced, but Nigel went on. "They were doubly stupid; I mean, that kid was going to school, holding down a night job, and looking after her drunken uncle. She wasn't going to go quietly. It says in the papers that she bit Agnes on the hand when she tried to shove her into their apartment, and she kicked the boyfriend in the balls. Then the stupid bastards went after her. Did they think they were going to outrun a whippet-thin twelve-year-old girl scared out of her wits? And they left their apartment door open, an open invitation in the Milton Obote Mansions to be relieved of your possessions."

"How come you know so much about what happened" asked Fred.

"I had a chat with Aspirin Harry."

"Who?" asked Fred, mystified.

"Look in the papers, there's mention of a Harry Harrison. He's known on the street as Aspirin Harry. He's what the police would call a known confederate of Bill Blake. He works as a bouncer at various Knockney nightspots and moves his ill-gotten swag through Bill's various enterprises."

"How do you know all this?"

Nigel thought, *because I don't live in a fucking ivory tower, you twat.*

He said, "I dunno; I'm a deejay. I meet a lot of people in social situations all the time. Harry's one of them. He's helped me load and unload my gear at different clubs and dances."

Fred asked, "Why's he called Aspirin Harry."

Nigel laughed and said, "Compared to Bill, Harry is a regular well-adjusted villain, looking on his profession as a valid career choice. When he hurts someone, there is nothing personal in it. It's a habit to give someone a dose of painkillers after he's slapped them around. He's even been known on rare occasions to drive his victims to that hospital, what's it called? The one that's named after one of those African dictators."

Even in his depressed state, Fred bridled at Nigel's casual description of Kwame Nkruma.

Nigel noticed Fred about to get on his soapbox so he pressed on.

"Apparently a couple of teenage kids ducked into Agnes's apartment looking for lightweight stuff to pick up like CD and DVD players. One of the bedroom doors was bolted and locked with a large padlock, though the key was in the lock. They unlocked it, and, well, you know what a house of horrors was inside."

"And Harry, how did he get involved?"

"When the kids ran out puking up, a Bosnian Muslim refugee

and his wife passed by. They'd smelled that kind of horror before in Yugoslavia. The guy went in, came out, and started shouting. That brought people out of the other apartments onto the landing, including Harry. He told me he strolled up to the open apartment door just when Agnes and the boyfriend returned. Harry said she tried to shoo everyone away, but Harry decided to have a look for himself, and he's a hard man to say no to. He said the Bosnian was in shock saying 'please call police, you must call police.'"

There was a long silence as Nigel remembered what Harry had said to him as they had joined for a late-night drink on the previous evening, the eyes in his great scarred face staring into infinity.

"I'll never fucking forget what I saw in that room. Little kids, lying in their own filth, and these pathetic bits and pieces of the dead ones hanging from hooks in the ceiling."

Nigel continued. "Harry made someone call the police, while he told Agnes and her boyfriend to sit in the lounge and keep quiet. Harry reckoned the mob outside the apartment would have torn them apart if they had seen that chamber of horrors, so he just stood guard in the doorway. He said he'd never been so relieved to hear a police siren."

Fred was silent again, realizing that his career in politics was over, and that he would be forever known as the local government leader who had let this happen on his watch.

Nigel tried to cheer Fred up.

"Did you know that Agnes's Liberian boyfriend was actually descended from Lebanese and Liberian stock? He was continually asking Agnes not to keep introducing him as being 'part librarian and part lesbian.'"

Fred did not react. Nigel heard the noise of lots of vehicles in the car park and looked out of the window. A convoy of cars and TV vans was pulling into the Pol Pots car park. The media had run Fred to earth.

CHAPTER 48

KIT

Abdul Madbul was driving in a rental car to Las Vegas. He had thought about stealing a vehicle but decided that the possibility of being stopped by the police, though remote, was an unacceptable risk. Creating a fake California driving license had been child's play. Hidden under the front passenger seat was a pistol, silencer, fifty rounds of ammunition, and $5,000 in cash.

He had obtained this from the Chinese woman at the Lucky Lotus. He still felt uneasy about revealing himself, but without any allies to help him in the United States, targeting the hated Eddy Relish would be difficult. Killing Relish had been a necessity to prevent identification in England. In America, the public execution of Relish, in the godless heart of America, would terrify the nation and strike a blow for the cause.

Madbul continued to feel uneasy. Things had gone well with the Chinese woman—too well. He had circled the Lotus several times during the afternoon of the previous day. The nightclub did not open until well after dark, but in the late afternoon the side door was unlocked. Club staff and dancers reported for work. He entered into the quiet and gloomy interior. He knew he was watched on security cameras, so he did not remove his hat and sunglasses.

Madbul stood on the threshold of the main lounge letting his eyes adjust to the low light levels in the room and waited until someone noticed him. A six-foot blonde-haired girl with disturbingly luminous blue eyes approached him.

"Come."

She led him to a semicircular booth where a middle-aged Chinese woman sat to one side of the booth gazing at him. Madbul slid into the booth and positioned himself with his back to the wall and at an angle to the Chinese woman.

"Mr. Tiger, I presume."

Madbul merely nodded and sat in silence.

"I am called Madam Sin. How can I help you, Mr. Tiger?"

"I need a gun, with silencer and ammunition, and some operational money."

"I can provide such things. If you have any problems or are caught by the Americans, I will of course deny any knowledge of you. Will $5,000 be sufficient?"

"Albania will be grateful for your help."

"China does not forget her old friends, Mr. Tiger, despite those with whom we must now do business."

Madam Sin lifted her head slightly, and a small, cadaverous-looking Chinese man emerged out of the shadows, making Madbul's heart skip a beat. All through this exchange, he had been scanning the room, noting the comings and goings of the staff and for any sentinels watching him.

He had not noticed this slender Chinese man, but Madbul knew that he must have been there. Madam Sin spoke to the man in Mandarin, and he disappeared behind the main stage, returning after a few moments carrying a hold-all, which he placed on the table.

Madam Sin said, "Take the bag, Mr. Tiger; it contains your weapon and $5,000 cash in used low denomination bills. Good luck."

She left the booth and walked to a staircase that led to the gallery around the lounge. Madbul watched her leave and then glanced back to the small Chinese man. He had disappeared, returning to the shadows.

Madbul drove through the night to Vegas on Interstate 15, passing through the Mojave Desert. Madbul felt he should be feeling more relaxed and confident, but too many things were nagging at him. The polite acquiescence of the Chinese woman, Madam Sin, was too easy.

Why would a Chinese operative be so obliging? The old days of mutual collaboration were long gone, although not replaced with any hostility. When China took the capitalist road, the two countries had drifted apart, like a married couple whose kids have all left home.

He had expected more reticence from the woman, but she seemed amenable to helping him. She had not inquired at all about his mission, which raised his hackles and increased his anxiety. Madbul kept circling back to the two Chinese watchers in Knockney, when he was stalking Eddy Relish.

There were too many things that nagged at him. Worst of all, since leaving the Lucky Lotus, he felt he was under surveillance. However, he could not spot or expose any watchers, as he had in Kazakhstan. He took some small comfort from this. He knew how good an operative he was. Given time, he should be able to spot and kill anyone tailing him.

Madbul yawned; he did not want to nod off to sleep and crash. He pulled the car over to the hard shoulder of the highway to rest for a couple of hours. Before he slept, he looked at the *Hollywood Reporter* and the mention of the party at the MGM Grand for Zhang Xing Liao. He was certain Relish would attend. He browsed staff vacancies at the MGM Grand, on a cell phone bought in a CVS pharmacy, and the floor plan of the Marquee Ballroom.

CHAPTER 49

DEAL

Eddy Relish was shown into Cy Sly's suite at Paris Las Vegas by his personal assistant, Victoria Moralité.

Sly was in an expansive mood.

"Eddy, kid, good of you to come! Sit down; hey, Feliz, get Eddy whatever he wants to drink."

Eddy just asked for a glass of water and sat opposite Sly on a sofa in the hotel suite lounge.

Sly continued. "Eddy, you look great. Doesn't he look great, Vicky?"

Victoria simply smiled and handed Eddy a glass of ice water.

Sly continued. "I just read through the script of *The Friends of Red Shidley* again, and I gotta say this has got legs; it's got winner written all over it. Listen, I've asked the writer, a Brit girl by the name of Sharon Constable, to join us this morning; she's staying in this hotel. She'll be here in a few minutes; Vicky told me she checked in last night. I was going to send a limo for her, but she told Vicky not to bother, that she was being met by a friend. Vicky, call her, will you? Let her know that Eddy is here, and she should join us."

Eddy leaned back in his chair and flicked through a copy of the script.

"I don't know, Cy, I read this through, and to be honest, it reads like the work of amateurs. Sure, there are some great locations in the script and some interesting characters, but one minute it reads like a Guy Ritchie London gangster flick, and the next second it's like a Golden Harvest kung-fu epic meets a James Bond knockoff. All the strong parts are the characters that Shidley meets on his travels. His part is very flat; he's more like a cipher. Plus it's very bloke-ish."

Sly looked puzzled at the word.

Eddy continued. "All the characters, even the women, are drawn from a man's perspective."

Sly smiled and tried to allay Eddy's fears.

"Sure, the script needs some work; this Constable chick is just an amateur. But all scripts are really a work in progress; you know that, kid. Christ, how many rewrites were made on your last movie?"

"I can't remember, it's such a long time ago," said Eddy.

"What … oh … yeah, okay," said Sly, "but you know what I'm saying, right? Scripts are never just a finished article, right? Christ, I mean we usually have rewrites going on right before the shoot; even during the fucking shoot, am I right?"

He chuckled as he said this. Victoria walked in followed by Sharon.

Sly started to make introductions, "Eddy, this is—"

"Sharon Constable, yeah, I know. I left her sleeping off her jet lag this morning. How are you feeling, darling?" said Eddy.

Sly looked perplexed. "What, did you two meet last night?"

"Yup, last night and many nights besides. Cy, me old mate, Sharon's been my girl for a few years now, and it was her idea to turn my most recent escapades into a movie script."

He turned to Sharon and took the screenplay from her hand.

"Here's the most recent draft, *The Friends of Red Shidley*, by Sharon Constable and Eddy Relish. We both know how crap this little number is, so why don't we talk about other possible projects that I might look at."

He smiled his best smile at Sly.

Cy Sly's look of surprise now hardened into one of rage.

"What the fuck! You little punk, you think this is funny? I'll—"

"You'll do what?" said Sharon. "Ruin Eddy again because he got his leg over with Lynn Skynn? Get over it, move on, and find closure, as you say over here."

"Fuck you, you bitch, I'll—"

Victoria Moralité looked into the room in alarm, hearing the shouting.

"Get the fuck out and shut the door!"

"Do you speak to all your girls like that?" asked Eddy.

Sly was nearly purple with rage; his shock of white hair seemed to fluoresce as his anger intensified.

"Listen, you little punk, I drove you out of Hollywood once, and I can do it again. One word from me, and you'll be a leper. No studio will pick you up; you won't even be able to voice-over a porno flick."

"Ah, interesting you mentioned porno," said Eddy.

"Eh, what, why, what about porno?" asked Sly.

"Oh, just that I think the Hollywood community would be interested to know about Eros Productions."

"What about Eros; I mean, who are they? Are they a porno company?" asked Sly.

"Yes, one of the biggest, actually, very successful, churning out millions in profit every year; you should see their balance sheets," said Eddy.

"Balance sheets, what the fuck are you talking about? No one gets to see Eros's balance sheets, the … I mean, how I would know what they looked like?" said Sly.

"What's even more interesting," added Sharon, walking around the room and pouring herself a glass of water, "is the way new talent is recruited by Eros Productions."

Sweat beaded Cy Sly's brow; his choleric purple was fading. Eddy and Sharon were circling around him like sharks.

Sharon continued, "Yes, the young Filipina and Mexican girls who are promised fame and fortune in the movies; only they are not told what kind of movies. Shall I go on … no? Hang on, Mr. Sly, aren't these some of your favorite holiday destinations?"

Sly's expression became cunning.

"You'll never prove anything."

"Prove what?" asked Eddy.

"Eh … yeah, exactly" said Sly with mock confidence.

Sharon and Eddy stood together holding hands and staring at Sly.

Sly wiped his brow and looked at the two of them, just staring at him. It unnerved him. How much did they know? A few whispers surfaced now and again about Cy Sly's sweet tooth and his liking for teenage girls. No one had ever linked him to Eros. He had been confident that his tracks were covered through his holding companies and offshore accounts. He took another tack.

"Listen, I don't know what kind of scheme you and your bitch have cooked up, but you'd better watch out, buddy. I'm fuckin' connected, eh? My real name is Silvestranni, okay? You know what that means?"

"Is it like pastrami?" asked Sharon.

"Fuck you, bitch! It means I got connections, you dumb broad," said Sly.

"Oh, I think he means the Mafia, Eddy."

"Is that right, Cy? Do you mean the mafia?" asked Eddy.

"You better fucking believe it," said Sly.

"Ah, well, trouble is, we don't, do we, Shazabooboo?"

"Indeed no, Eddy."

Eddy said, "In fact, we think that Cy is connected with a very profitable porno company. We have no problems with this. However, we think the Hollywood community may be a little surprised at how MegaTool's finances continue to stay so robust. Certain ladies in Hollywood may not be so inclined to star in MegaTool films or direct them. Probably a lot of the guys too. But who are we to cast aspersions? Perhaps when it all comes out in the *LA Times* and the *Hollywood Reporter*, folks will just be like us and say, "Each to his own."

But what might really make them raise their eyebrows is the exploitation of young teenage girls. Most of them are under sixteen, brought by devious routes into the United States to keep the Eros production line profitable. They might also be a little disturbed that our Cy is a bit of a 'chicken hawk,' as indeed might the police and FBI."

Eddy paused.

"What do you think, Cy?"

Cy said nothing but had turned pale under his tan.

Sharon poured him a drink, a stiff scotch with a little water, and offered it to him. Absentmindedly he took the glass, swallowing a deep draught. Sly was still trying to figure out how much Eddy and Sharon knew. The hints they dropped had been enough to chill him to the bone.

He said, "You can't prove anything."

"Maybe and maybe not," said Eddy, "but do you want to take that risk? Do you want reporters sniffing about in the Cayman Islands and Bermuda?"

That made Sly look up.

"Oh, and we don't just mean the pussy-cat reporters in the States" added Sharon. "We're talking the real deal, the Fleet Street reptile squad; you remember them, every time there's a Hollywood scandal."

Sly did indeed remember. When British reporters landed en-masse in Hollywood, it was like a school of hungry piranhas turned loose in a goldfish bowl.

Eddy continued. "So, Cy, let bygones be bygones eh? Let's work together to restore the luster to the Eddy Relish star. You are still the best of the best of the Hollywood producers. I could simply walk and put my faith in other production companies. But, I think I'd like to make my comeback in a Cy Sly production—to show the world that the hatchet is buried … in the ground and not in my back eh?"

Sly looked around as if trying to find a way out and then looked resigned and weary.

"I can't guarantee any film will be a success."

Eddy said, "I know that, Cy, but at least we can make a film that will sink or swim on its own merits, without your helping hand to hold its head underwater," said Eddy. "Now what serious projects have you got in the pipeline, and please not *Shoot-Out at the Andromeda Clinic*, okay?"

Cy's eyes narrowed again. Eddy had thrown out another clue that he knew a lot more about the goings-on in MegaTool and Cy Sly's life than he had realized. Cy began to do an inventory of the projects on which the MegaTool staff and writers were currently developing.

"We're thinking about doing *The Brothers Karamazov*, you know by the Russian guy, Christ, what's his name?"

"Dostoyevsky," prompted Sharon.

"Yeah Dotoy … Dostsky, yeah, well, by him, anyway," he snapped.

"That's a bit gloomy isn't it?" asked Sharon.

Eddy looked doubtful; he knew the book but had never read it.

"Is it?" asked Sly. "Well, it could be a good Oscar prospect if we pack it full of plummy voiced Brits; serious literature and good actors always go over well with the Academy. Now let me think; we were also thinking about Thomas Mann's *The Magic Mountain*."

Sharon snorted, and said, "Blimey, Mr. Sly, but you do like highbrow books."

"What?" asked Sly.

"Sharon, like me, was wondering about this selection. What's it about, Shaz?"

"Well, the short answer is that it's a story about how a person's environment affects self-identity."

Both men looked nonplussed, which told her that the short answer was not going to be sufficient.

She said, "It's the tale of Hans Castorp, a shipbuilding engineer from Hamburg. He visits his tubercular cousin in a Swiss sanatorium. Hans spends a great deal of time talking about life and philosophy with an Italian academic, and is later diagnosed with TB himself. He remains at the sanatorium for seven years.

"Hans does not return home until the outbreak of World War I, in which he fights and survives. Hans finally comes to understand that one must go through the deep experience of sickness and death to arrive at a higher sanity and health."

Sharon paused and said, "Not a rib-tickler or an action movie, I would suspect, Mr. Sly."

"Yeah, well if you want to win film awards …"

Sly left the sentence unfinished, as a thought struck him.

"You know what else we got in the works? I was reminded when you mentioned World War I; we're going to start shooting next month in Romania; it's called *The Somme*."

Both Sharon and Eddy chorused, "Eh?"

"I know, I know, it sounds a bit off-the-wall for Hollywood to do a major World War I movie set in 1916, before America entered the war. Why not do a movie about the marines at Belleau Wood in 1918. But the Somme was the single biggest battlefield slaughter of all time; Christ, the Brits lost about sixty thousand men on the first fucking day. After it was all over, there was something like four hundred thousand Brit casualties. The Germans lost something like the same number, and the French about a quarter of a million. You telling me there isn't a great film there? The screenplay is just about the first day, and follows the lives of ordinary soldiers in the trenches on both sides."

Sly became alive again as the prospect of the movie excited him.

"Shit, *The Titanic* looked like a real turkey on paper, but look at the business that did! We got the best writers, cameramen, directors—the works—on this one. We can cast you in one of the colead roles in the British side."

Eddy looked hard at Sly. "This is straight up? No fucking around?"

Sly looked hurt.

"Eddy, come on; hey, Vicky ..."

The door opened immediately.

"Yes, Mr. Sly?"

"Give Eddy the script and shooting schedule for *The Somme*. Let him see who we've cast already and who the crew is going to be on the movie. Hey, that pal of yours Malcolm Balsam, or whatever, I think one of the unit camera crews is picking him up as a technician. Okay, convinced now?"

Eddy and Sharon looked over the folder of documents that Vicky retrieved from a large briefcase in the adjoining room. Sly might be in Vegas to party, but that was no reason not to take care of business.

Sly continued. "Listen, we'll announce it tonight—that you are joining the cast of the movie. We'll nail down the part later. Here, keep the screenplay and tell me who you want to play."

Eddy asked, "Tonight?"

"Yeah, you and your girl will be my guests at the big party at the MGM Grand, the one everyone has come to attend. Some rich Chinese scrap metal trader seems to have invited half the fucking entertainment world, including your truly, and I get to bring two guests. So go on, look at the script. We'll make an announcement at the party. Hey, Vicky, contact Wang? Dang? Tell him to add Eddy and Sharon to the guest list. Ask if it's okay for us to make an announcement tonight."

"Sounds good," said Eddy. "Shazaboo, do you fancy losing some money in the casino first?"

"No, I don't think so; I fancy winning some," said Sharon.

Eddy felt on top of the world. He and Sharon sped groundward in the elevator. Sharon brought Eddy back to Earth a bit sooner than he expected.

"Well that went well. Good job you have this elderly Chinese woman looking out for you. I wonder if she'll be at the party? I can't wait to meet her."

From: bwoo@crc.gov.prc

To: c.clore@metpolice.gov.uk

Attachments: Zhang Party.pdf

Subject: Come to the Grand, A Surprise is at Hand!

Dear Inspector Clore:

Mr. Zhang Xing Liao of the Chinese Recycling Council cordially invites you to a party, which he will be hosting at the Marquee Ballroom, MGM Grand Resort, Las Vegas. The party will celebrate Mr. Zhang's fiftieth year with CRC. Your first-class e-ticket is attached to this email, as is the date and time for the party. Please feel free to change the flights if these do not suit your schedule.

You are booked into a suite at the MGM Grand Resort, and you will be met by a limousine service at Las Vegas airport. Your invitation was recommended by Ms. Nancy Liu, cultural attaché of the PRC Embassy in London, to thank you for your recent assistance with security matters of mutual concern to both the UK and People's Republic of China. Ms. Liu has taken the liberty of contacting the Office of the Metropolitan Police Commissioner to obtain official sanction for your attendance at Mr. Zhang's function.

If you have any questions, you may call me on 1 886 523 6777. Sincerely

Boudicca (Boddy) Woo, Executive Assistant to Mr. Zhang

CHAPTER 51

PLUSH

E ddy and Sharon braved the late afternoon heat and walked to the MGM Grand from Paris Las Vegas. They walked past the Mirage volcano, erupting for the first time in the evening.

At the Grand, Eddy called Malcolm on his cell phone. They navigated between various landmarks and made contact at the Convention Center. Malcolm was effusive in his greeting toward Sharon, who warmed to him. Malcolm introduced his date, Liz, a striking middle-aged woman. Liz was English but spoke with an American inflection in her voice.

Liz mentioned that she had just finished working on a film with Malcolm. Eddy realized who this woman must be.

"Oh, you must be Muffy Diver, the one who does the double errr …"

He pulled up short realizing what he was saying, but not before Sharon had hissed at him and punched him hard on his left arm.

"Oh don't worry, Sharon," said Liz. "I'm quite used to it. After seventeen years in the business, I am not coy and bashful about my career in X-rated movies. It can be a bit trying when men spot you in supermarket queue or at a gas station."

Malcolm said, "Come on, let's go and watch the stars arrive. Liz can give you the benefit of her insider's knowledge."

They lined up behind the velvet rope that cordoned off the plush red carpet. The stars of the adult video world were arriving for the awards show. Wee Willie Winkie was playing the event, and their music floated out above the crowd, relayed by speakers from the auditorium.

As the porn stars arrived, a battery of TV spotlights and camera flashes greeted them. Many of the women were a tribute to the plastic surgeon's art, with gravity defying breasts, full rounded buttocks, and luscious lips.

Liz pointed and said, "That's Misty Mountains."

Eddy said, "Christ Almighty, it looks like she had shoved two motorcycle helmets down the front of her top."

Liz laughed and said, "She told me she's downsizing. She can't keep pace with the medical bills for her back. Misty has to spend most of her off-screen time wearing a back brace."

Next up the red carpet were two men: American porn superstar Dick Long, accompanied by rising Thai male adult actor Long-Long Dik.

"This is as stage-managed as the Oscars," said Liz. "Those two guys didn't just arrived by coincidence. Neither did these two; they're twins; well, you've probably guessed that."

"Are there many identical twins in the porn industry?" asked Sharon.

"Yes, a lot, quite a few triplets and even quads," said Malcolm. "These two are Nasti and Nyce. They scored a big hit with their video *Love Therapist/Love the Rapist.*

Liz said, "Most of the people you see this year will be gone by next year. Not many of us stay in the industry for very long. It used to be so much well-paid fun, but with AIDS it's become a high risk occupation."

"I thought people were tested," said Sharon.

"We must be tested for a range of STDs every month, but people can get faked results. Some of us will only work with men we know. Young people think their relationships can survive, but not in porn. Girlfriends of straight men doing gay for pay think it's okay until they see their man fucking another man. I don't know why, but it really kills the love buzz. You can understand why we have so many drink problems and drug overdoses. The industry is always on the lookout for fresh talent. If you want to stay in the business, you have to go more extreme."

Sharon said "What—"

"I do double-anal-double-vaginal scenes, sometimes other variations, but always me in a cock sandwich. Still, it is not a bad way to make a living."

The arriving actresses played to the crowd and assembled media. They never missed an opportunity to expose and flash their impressive breasts at the cameras, frequently feeling each other to gauge the naturalness of the implants. Several actresses recognized Liz and came over to speak to her.

One of them even hitched up the hem of her very brief skirt, pulled aside her G-string, and showed off her new clitoral and labial piercings. Malcolm looked on, while Eddy simply gawped, and Sharon resisted the urge to burst out laughing. She noticed Eddy was aroused by all the flesh on display and cooled his ardor by punching him again on the arm.

"Come on lover boy, it's time we were going to Mr. Zhang's party. Malcolm, Liz it was nice to meet you."

Liz and Sharon exchanged cell phone numbers, and Sharon said she would give her a call when she visited Eddy in Los Angeles. She also told them to come over to the Zhang function at the Marquee Ballroom later in the evening.

Sharon said, "Eddy has some pull with Chinese these days, so I am sure he can get you in."

Malcolm rolled his eyes suggesting that Eddy might expect a bumpy ride tonight. Eddy followed Sharon to the Zhang party.

CHAPTER 52
PARTY

Zhang and his party, which included his wife, Nancy Liu, and Sol Silberstein and his wife, Marigold, were enjoying a drink in Function Room B, screened off from the Marquee ballroom where the evening's festivities were to take place.

Sol refilled everyone's glasses and said, "Magnesio, Maestro, tonight is your night; please lead us in a toast."

"To the glorious Communist Party." Zhang raised his glass.

Zhang continued. "The party to commemorate the party. A party that would shame Gatsby's most extravagant attempts to lure the lovely Daisy back into his loving arms. You, Marigold, will be my Daisy tonight. Come."

Zhang gaily held out an elbow through which Marigold linked her arm. Marigold's bad taste and vulgarity had found its perfect locale; Las Vegas was her cradle.

Zhang and Marigold led the party out of the room; a most absurd sight as Zhang's head bobbed level with Marigold's-gravity defying cleavage. Sol turned to Nancy Liu, Zhang's wife, who was gazing without expression after her husband.

"Nancy, shall we?" said Sol.

Nancy favored him with a smile, linked arms, and they followed Zhang and Marigold.

Sol took a look around the room to make sure nobody had left anything important behind. Other members of the Zhang and

Silberstein entourages, mainly their overworked personal assistants and other staff, finished their drinks and hurriedly followed the main party, including Thomas and Boddy Woo.

As the party entered the main ballroom, the majority of guests had arrived. The guests comprised a mix of actors, musicians, artists, writers, business tycoons, and current and former heads of government. They arrived along with their entourages and bodyguards.

From the stage, a young black deejay was creating a throbbing dance groove, and many of the partygoers were taking to the dance floor. Sol could mark Zhang's progress around the hall by following the elaborate blonde hairstyle of his wife, which acted like marker buoy. A cluster of people came to pay their respects to the legendary Magnesio.

Nancy Liu had excused herself and gone to meet with another Chinese woman, leaving Sol alone. Marigold's laugh reached Sol, even through the barrage of music coming from the sound system. Marigold had downed several glasses of champagne on Zhang's circuit of the ballroom, and Sol decided it was about time to mount a rescue mission.

CHAPTER 53

TERRAIN

A crowd of onlookers at the ballroom entrance chatted among themselves spotting all the celebrities.

Sharon heard one lady say, "Look, there goes that actor, Eddy Relish; I hear he's about to hit the big time again. Maybe that's why there's a party, and maybe these are all the friends of Eddy Relish."

Sharon saw Inspector Clore, standing away from the crowd with a look of severe disapproval on his face.

"What are you doing here?" shouted Sharon.

Clore turned slowly, and a smile almost cracked his face. "Hello, Miss Constable. I received this mysterious invitation, with a plane ticket and a hotel reservation. I thought, why not; my career has stalled. What do I have to lose?"

Clore sighed then said, "Oh, beg pardon, congratulations on your election win."

"Thanks," said Sharon. "Come on, Inspector, don't be so gloomy. Why not just enjoy yourself?"

Eddy said, "Hello, Inspector, a little out of your jurisdiction aren't you? Are you here to extradite me or something?"

This was the first time he had seen Clore since the inspector caught him handling a load of stolen microwaves.

"Leave him alone, Eddy," said Sharon. "The inspector's been through some hard times. Give him a break."

"Yeah, like he gave me one, I presume."

Sharon saw something catch Eddy's attention. She followed his gaze. A beautiful Chinese woman walked toward them. Eddy would not meet her eye. This must be the Madam Sin character in their script.

When Cynthia reached the couple, she proffered a fine-boned hand around the wrist of which was an emerald-encrusted bracelet and on her fingers, ruby, jade, and diamond rings.

"Edward, so nice to see you; you look splendid, and this must be the lovely Sharon? I've heard so much about you, my dear. You look elegant tonight."

Sharon was wearing a Versace creation she had bought that afternoon in a hotel shop, charging it to Eddy's room. Eddy wanted to buy an extravagant Nudie creation, but Sharon persuaded him into buying a denim dinner suit.

Eddy was speechless faced with both Cynthia and Sharon.

Sharon was undaunted and said, "Hello, there; welcome to Celebrity Central. How nice to see you. And you are?"

Cynthia looked at Eddy. "Edward. Aren't you going to introduce us?"

Sharon intervened, in a stage Cockney accent: "I was only pulling your leg, Miss Sin. Of course, I know who you are. You're an old name 'round our way, isn't she, Eddy? Go on; tell her."

"Okay, Sharon, enough, all right?" Eddy was terse and anxious.

Sharon smiled and then looked at the floor as she waited for Cynthia to respond. She was intrigued by what Cynthia might have to say.

Cynthia was unperturbed. "Interesting event, don't you think? A Chinese government bureaucrat is throwing a party to celebrate his success in the most unadulterated capitalist activity—commodity trading."

"Indeed," replied Sharon. "If I was a smarter person, I would detect the angle that's in there somewhere. Anyway, I want to thank you for taking care of Eddy. He's been through a lot, and I want you to know that I appreciate the support you have given him."

"Oh, that was nothing more than business. Edward is a talent that deserves to thrive, not wither on the vine, and I was glad to assist. Congratulations on your election success, Miss Constable, or do you prefer to be called Sharon?"

"I don't mind either way. As you were saying, it is interesting how Mr … what's his name, Eddy?"

"Who?"

Sharon followed Eddy's gaze, which was fixed on a blond-haired man who had just entered the room, escorting an enormous cat.

"The commodity trader," said Sharon.

"Mr. Zhang," offered Cynthia.

"Yes, Mr. Zhang. It's interesting how he has been able to generate so much wealth while occupying a government position," said Sharon.

"Well, indeed," said Cynthia, "but you need to understand that the rivers of commerce flow through diverse terrain."

"Yes, I think I do need to understand that. Because otherwise I would need to beg forgiveness for suspecting that the stink of corruption pervades the enterprise."

Before Cynthia could respond, Eddy nudged Sharon.

"Did you ever see anything like that?" Cynthia turned her head to where Eddy was pointing and nonchalantly looked away.

"That's Sigurd, of Sigurd and Leroy," said Cynthia.

"Who?" asked Eddy.

"The famous conjuring act that has been playing at this hotel for the last thirty years or so," explained Cynthia. "His partner was mauled by one of their white tigers, and they had to close down the show. Sigurd can't bring himself to leave the place. They say he's planning to have his ghost walk the halls in perpetuity, once he's dead."

"Which he may well be already; he don't half look pale, whiter than his tiger," said Eddy.

"You know, I think I could grow to like Las Vegas. It's an invigorating monument to absurdity. I think the Dadaists would have enjoyed it here," said Sharon.

Eddy said, "Did I ever tell you, I saw a barber's shop in Honolulu called DaDa Hair? I think it was a Korean barber's."

Sharon and Cynthia stared at Eddy, who muttered an apology and continued gazing around the room, checking out the guests.

Sharon said, "As I was saying, before Eddy interrupted our conversation, China—"

"The future is China. We are presently in the early stages of an inevitable process that will see China establish itself as the world's largest economy and also its most advanced political society."

Eddy looked bored and said, "Look, I am sure this is all very interesting, but I think I'll go mingle a bit. Do you mind?"

He was looking at Cynthia.

Sharon spoke through lips drawn as tight as bowstrings, with heavy emphasis on every word: "No, I don't mind; go and mingle."

CHAPTER 54

DEBATE

Eddy sauntered off, and Sharon turned back to Cynthia. "Most advanced political society? I would—"

Cynthia said, "Not only has China solved the problem of maintaining stability in a society drawn toward chaos by the unsupervised meanderings of the masses, it has also established the principle that the proletariat willingly expresses its needs and desires through the subsuming of authority in a strong leadership.

"It is amusing to see how the world has begun to hail China's economic achievements as evidence that it has adopted the capitalist model and acknowledged the supremacy of Western liberal philosophy. In reality all that is happening is that Middle Kingdom has continued down its true road, as laid out in early Maoist thought, just as the dialectic method anticipated."

"Absolutely. Couldn't agree more. In other words, China has finally emerged as a fascist state," said Sharon.

"Oh, come now, Miss Constable, that is not a logical proposition. Cynthia raised an eyebrow and smoothed her sleeve.

"Do I detect signs of jealousy?"

"And why would I have cause to be jealous?" said Sharon.

"Well, perhaps you could tell me," said Cynthia.

"Look, I don't know what's been going on here. I can see from your supercilious expression and patronizing demeanor that you think you occupy some kind of high ground from where you can survey your pawns and your minions. Well, that's not what it looks like from where I'm standing. I look at you, and I see a pathetic knocking-shop madam with a jumped-up sense of her own importance."

"My, how feisty; dare I say vixen-like. No wonder Edward's sense of his own manliness was suppressed. I say *was*, because it became quite evident during our travels that all was not lost. There were in fact methods for liberating his manhood, so to speak."

"Ah, I see. That is what this is all about—a little victory for the aging dowager. She has to go celebrate the temporary attention of a toy boy, by gloating in front of his girlfriend. That is so funny. You know something? Eddy Relish would screw a sneaker when he has gone without for a few weeks. Sorry, but you are past it. Get used to it. Bye, Madam Sin."

Sharon stalked off. She was furious; Eddy had been two-timing her. No surprise in that, but to be confronted with the evidence was, as always, very annoying. She had tried not to give Cynthia the pleasure of seeing how upset she was. Unfortunately, her anger was transparent from the torrent of abuse she had just hurled in Cynthia's direction.

CHAPTER 55

PAYBACK

In the meantime, Eddy had been chatting to Malcolm Bolsum, who'd slipped away from the lubricious atmosphere of the Venereal Awards. Eddy had convinced the security to allow Malcolm access and was updating him on the afternoon's conversation with Sly.

Malcolm guffawed when he heard how they had put the screws on the movie magnate.

"Sly has so many skeletons in his closet that you can hear them rattling from a mile away when he opens the door. He was in a car accident—quite a bad one. They had to cut him out of the car. The cop on the scene was the brother of a girlfriend of mine. So anyway, the in-car CD player was still going as they were trying to get him out. It was a Kenny Gee compilation. Sly was pleading with the cop not to tell anybody that he had been listening to Kenny Gee. Never mind his broken leg, just do not let anybody know he's a Kenny Gee fan. He's so screwed up."

"Yeah, well, it's payback time … uh oh. I rather think shit and fan have made contact."

He could see Sharon coming in his direction. Eddy weaved and ducked behind a group of partygoers, dragging Malcolm with him. The crowd did not provide ample cover, and Sharon spotted him.

Eddy looked back as Sharon approached Malcolm, who was standing with a sickly grin and was shrugging his shoulders.

Sharon ducked around Malcolm shouting, "Eddy Relish, come here, you fucking timeshare dildo. Eddy Relish!"

Eddy took some small comfort that everyone in the room was looking at him. For the first time in years, he was the center of attention again.

CHAPTER 56
GATECRASHER

The music suddenly stopped, the lights were turned up, and a familiar voice boomed out of the PA system.

"All right, everybody, give it up for the Knockney Massive. Mr. Cy Sly, the top man at MegaTool Pictures, wants to say a few words to you."

Sharon and Eddy both stopped running. They turned to face the stage where Rasta-Blasta was presiding over the festivities. He handed a microphone to a figure that mounted to Rasta's vantage point, and another familiar voice boomed out.

"Ladies and gentlemen, I won't delay your partying any longer than I have to. Mr. Zhang, Magnesio, our gracious host, has allowed me to use the occasion of this splendid party to make this announcement. He has also been kind enough to give the ladies and gentlemen of the press access for this brief occasion, so those of you who want to remain incognito should go to the bathroom."

Zhang beamed like a small benign Buddha.

"MegaTool is shooting an epic film, which focuses on the first day of the Battle of the Somme in 1916. I am proud to announce that Eddy Relish will play one of the leading roles in this great film. Where are you Eddy? Let's have a look at you."

Eddy gave his best Hollywood smile and walked through the crowd. He took a wide detour around Sharon, who was still fuming at her cheating boyfriend. Eddy walked over to the stage and climbed up alongside Cy. The reporters were escorted into the ballroom by hotel security. They formed a loose half-moon around the edge of the stage, directing questions to both Eddy and Cy.

Sharon drifted slowly back toward the stage listening to the reporters pitching questions. They gave a good account of themselves, easily fielding questions about their checkered history, Eddy's time in the wilderness, and his successful comeback.

She gradually became aware that Cynthia was standing about an arm's length, which she felt was no accident. She racked her brains for something cutting to say. There were a series of muffled pops from the left side of the stage. She and others looked in that direction. They saw a swarthy-looking waiter gazing intently at Eddie, holding a napkin in two hands.

The waiter looked surprised and made some movements with the napkin, and there was another series of muffled pops. An expression of rage suffused the waiter's face, and he gazed wildly about him, staring in Sharon's direction. He seemed to be looking directly at her, but she realized he was staring past her at Cynthia. He threw the napkin to the ground. A pistol skidded across the parquet flooring of the ballroom, and he lunged through the crowd toward her, pulling a knife from beneath his waistcoat

Sharon backed away a little and at the same time noticed that another waiter, an Asian man, moved from the periphery of the room to intercept the swarthy individual. The Asian man moved through the crowded room like an eel. He would have reached the swarthy waiter but for a former IMF director. The ex-director turned, looking for a waiter to bring him a drink. He blocked the way of the scurrying Asian, proffering his empty glass. Much to the ex-director's chagrin, the Asian waiter body-swerved around him.

The swarthy waiter raced onward, screaming what sounded like "Fart, fart, fart!" His whole attention focused on Cynthia, who tensed and shifted her weight onto her back foot. Sharon stuck out her foot as the man passed her and tripped him. The swarthy man fell, sprawling headlong and losing the knife, which skidded across the floor. Partygoers gasped and spread away from his spread-eagled form.

This was all the respite the slender Asian waiter needed. The swarthy man jumped to his feet, looking around for his weapon. The Asian moved in a blur, striking at him in a flurry of blows. Sharon realized that the swarthy man exchanging blows and parries with the Asian waiter must be Abdul Madbul.

It looked evenly matched. Then the Asian waiter produced a combination of moves that drove his foot into Madbul's groin, doubling him up. This allowed the slender Asian to slam the heel of his palm into Madbul's temple. Madbul collapsed into a groaning heap, while the party guests gasped and talked excitedly about what they had just witnessed.

A group of men in sober gray and black business suits appeared moving through the throng. They surrounded the prone form of Madbul, over whom the Asian man was still standing guard. Sharon saw Eddy shading his eyes to look at the commotion. Sharon glanced at Cynthia, who had relaxed and was running an eye over her silk outfit, as though nothing had happened. Sharon saw Cynthia look at Eddy and smile. She saw the look of comprehension flash across Eddy's face. He had been used to bait this trap for the rogue Albanian.

On the stage, Cy Sly recovered his composure but was unsure what to say, while the press contingent swiveled between the events in front of them and Sly.

Boddy Woo joined Eddy and Sly on stage, asking quietly for a microphone from Rasta-Blasta.

"Ladies and gentlemen, I hope you enjoyed our little entertainment to round off this impromptu press conference. Mr Zhang is celebrating his fortieth year in business by announcing his intention to expand his business interests to include film production. He is using this evening to announce that he will shortly be opening discussions with Hollywood's top production company, MegaTool Productions, about financing a range of new high-quality action movies to be made in Hollywood and Asia!"

Cy looked nonplussed but was too much of a businessman and

a showman to let it show for long. New opportunities had suddenly unfolded before his eyes.

A Cockney-West Indian voice boomed out over the PA, "Let's hear it for Mr Zhang and the MegaTool Massive. Okay, everybody, let's get back to partying."

Wild applause erupted as the lights were turned down, and the dubstep dance rhythms blared out. The men in the suits picked up Madbul and dragged him away. Hotel security escorted the reporters out of the room. They left rather reluctantly, sensing that there was more of a story here.

Cynthia said, "Ms. Constable, it seems I am in your debt for stopping Mr. Madbul. How may I reward you?"

Sharon smiled. "Two things: first, continue to take care of Eddy, and, second, please stop shagging him."

Cynthia laughed and said, "Don't worry; I've spent too much time and resources molding Edward to waste him. As for the ... other, you need have no anxiety on that score; I shall refrain from any further carnality with Edward."

Eddy said, in a disconsolate tone without thinking, "Oh, thank you very much."

This attracted both a freezing glare and a punch in the arm from Sharon. One of the clean-cut men in suits arrived and addressed the threesome.

CHAPTER 57

FEDS

"**M**adam Sin, I mean Ms. Tzin, the US government and Federal Bureau of Investigation thank you for assistance in apprehending this dangerous terrorist."

He turned to Eddy, "And also to you, sir, for volunteering to be the decoy to lure this man out in the open. Ms. Tzin told us that Madbul would make an attempt on your life here in Vegas but that she had given him a weapon with blank ammunition. If I may say so, sir, that was a brave thing to do. We were most concerned in case Madbul checked the ammo closely and realized he had been given blanks. That's why he went crazy when he realized he'd been tricked and tried to kill Cynthia, I mean Ms. Tzin."

Eddy blanched, and the color drained from his face when he realized what the FBI man was saying.

He looked at Cynthia and said, "You could have got me killed."

Cynthia said, "You are being well rewarded Edward."

The FBI man, Agent Kinsey, took Eddy to make a formal identification of Madbul. Sharon went with Eddy. Cynthia mingled with the guests. Eddy saw her join Mr. Zhang and his party, talking quietly and intently. Kinsey's face had looked familiar to Eddy. He remembered him from the little group of officials that greeted Cynthia when she and Eddy had arrived in Honolulu.

CHAPTER 58

FILM

As Eddy, Sharon, and the FBI men left the party, Cy Sly worked the room. He had cornered Zhang about the surprise announcement by Boddy Woo following the capture of Madbul. From his vantage point, he had seen what Eddy had seen.

He was suspicious that the fight between Madbul and Ah Chu was indeed a choreographed event. To his surprise and pleasure, Zhang was positively enthusiastic. He told Boddy to check his diary and work with Sly's assistant, Victoria Moralité, to set up a meeting.

Cy Sly stared very hard at Cynthia. He noticed that she talked very intently to Eddy. He remembered that she had seen Eddy and Sharon with her earlier in the evening. He realized that she was the Madam Sin from the Lucky Lotus, who procured young girls for him. As if she read his mind, she glanced over in his direction, smiling and raising her glass of champagne in salute.

He was aware of the mystery and aura of protection that surrounded the Lotus. A pair of retired FBI and CIA agents consulted on a recent espionage thriller series made by MegaTool's TV production division. During script consultations, the two men had idly mentioned how much they had enjoyed going for a drink in the Lotus and catching up with several old friends and Cold War adversaries.

They also referred affectionately to Madam Sin. They had laughed knowingly about a recent attempt by a politically ambitious city prosecutor to have the Lotus shut down. The man was now fighting to keep his career alive after an investigation for taking bribes from Hollywood drug dealers. Despite protestations of innocence, records showed that he had been receiving regular payments of funds from offshore accounts in the British Virgin Islands.

It was clear to Cy why Relish's star was in the ascendant. This was the source of the leverage to make his comeback. Despite his simmering rage, he recognized that there were times when one should leave well enough alone.

CHAPTER 59

SYNDROME

Two agents were standing over the glowering Madbul in a storage room for tables and chairs. The agents had handcuffed Madbul to a chair and gagged him with a piece of tape. Eddy, Sharon, and Kinsey joined the little group. Eddy looked down at the man who had been stalking him. Madbul, though still groggy, radiated menace.

Kinsey introduced the other two agents. "These are agents Johnson and Masters, and this, of course, is Abdul Madbul, or Stefan Globtic when you knew him, Mr. Relish. Can you confirm this is the same guy?"

He looked at the swarthy face. When Eddy met him he had a ten-day stubble and wore ragged clothes. He tried to fathom the depths of hatred in Madbul's eyes. *What is it*, he thought, *that brings out the worst in people?*

Eddy sighed and said, "Yes, it's him. What will you do with him?"

Kinsey glanced at Masters and Johnson.

"We shouldn't disclose this, but I guess you'd probably find out from your ... uh ... friend Cynthia."

Sharon made a sharp little sniff. Eddy found that looking at Madbul was a safer prospect.

"We'll be shipping him off to a facility we have in Alaska. He'll be interrogated by our agents up there, particularly Special Agent Peter Sagavanirktok, a native Inuit. He's anxious to find out why his relatives have been receiving voluminous hate mail from Abdul and his friends."

"Do you think those reporters will buy the story that all of this was a put-on to announce Zhang's venture into film production?" asked Sharon.

"Yeah, it's a pity; Madbul here could be known as the Farting Assassin, after his performance out there, shouting, 'Fa'aht, fa'aht, fa'aht,'" said Eddy with a laugh.

The three agents just looked at him blankly. Agent Kinsey replied without enthusiasm, "Yes, sir."

Sharon hit him on the arm again while Madbul continued to glare. A door at the back of the room opened and another dark-suited agent walked in.

Agent Johnson sighed. "Oh, shit! I told him to stay in the communications van."

The FBI agent advanced toward them. Eddy noticed his head made small jerky movements, causing an earphone to fall out of his ear. Apart from the head tics, the man was very pale and thin, and looked a little agitated. Halfway to the group, he executed a little skip in his step, causing Eddy and Sharon to exchange looks and the other FBI men to roll their eyes.

When he reached them, he said, "Hello, I'm Agent Cadwalledar. This must be Madbul."

Eddy was about to answer, when Cadwalledar suddenly yelled, "Shit, motherfucker!"

Everyone started, including the seething Madbul.

Eddy was puzzled and looked at the assembled agents.

Cadwalledar spoke up. "Sorry about that, sir, ma'am; I have Tourette's syndrome. Among other symptoms it includes coprolalia, or involuntary cursing, particularly if I'm nervous or excited. Fuck, shit cunt!"

Eddy laughed. "You're joking, right?"

Cadwalledar replied in an earnest voice, "No, sir, I really do have Tourette's syndrome, but, thankfully, the bureau, the FBI, is an equal opportunity employer."

"Which means," continued Johnson, "that Special Agent Cadwalledar is one of the bureau's most accomplished cipher experts. Indeed his ... condition is something of an asset in that regard, since it gives him an elevated ability to see patterns within coded messages and terrorist internet chatter.

Eddy laughed. "Christ, it must be fun being on a stakeout with this guy."

The two other agents rolled their eyes again, and one of them actually said half under his breath, "Don't go there."

Sharon thumped Eddy again on his arm, which was growing numb. Eddy could not resist and turned to Cadwalledar and went, "Boo!"

"Fuck you, motherfucker."

Eddy laughed again and said, "That didn't sound involuntary."

Cadwalledar looked pained and embarrassed, prompting Sharon to lash out again on Eddy's left arm.

"Owwww, when are you going to stop doing that?"

"When you stop being a prick!" snapped Sharon.

Madbul continued to glare with loathing at Eddy, which prompted his exit from the storeroom.

"I think we'd better be getting back to the party," said Eddy with a sigh. "Thanks for the help, gentlemen; please lock this bugger up and throw away the key."

"I don't think you need fear that you'll be seeing Madbul again," said Masters.

"And thank you for helping flush this guy out," said Johnson.

"Give our regards to Ms. Tzin," said Kinsey.

"Cunting motherfucker," chimed in Cadwalledar.

This prompted a fresh outbreak of giggles from Eddy. Eddy could see that Sharon strained to maintain her composure. They left the storeroom, reentering the ballroom.

At the threshold, Malcolm beckoned them over and spoke close to their heads to be heard above the pounding techno-beat.

"You'll never guess who's just walked in; well, been wheeled in?" said Malcolm.

CHAPTER 60

SURPRISE

"No, surprise me," said Eddy.

"You might want to sit down first," said Malcolm.

"C'mon, who?"

"Bill Blake. It's a long time since I've seen him, but I'd know him anywhere."

Eddy shrank at the mention of Bill's name. He wished he could take refuge behind Cynthia. Sharon noticed the change in Eddy, whose color had faded from tan to pale gray. His knees actually shook and looked like buckling. Sharon grabbed him by the elbow and tried to stiffen his resolve.

"Come on, Eddy, he can't hurt you now, especially not here. Anyway, you've got your Chinese fairy godmother to keep you safe," said Sharon.

Eddy, Malcolm, and Sharon made their way through the crowd to the ballroom entrance where Tiger Tokugawa and his party had just arrived, complete with Bill Blake in a wheelchair. He was fitted with a neck brace to support his spine and minimize movement. One of Tokugawa's men was pushing the wheelchair. At Tokugawa's side was a thin, pale Japanese woman who rested her hand on Bill's shoulder.

Zhang was informed that Tokugawa had arrived with an unexpected guest. He and his entourage approached Tokugawa's group. On the periphery stood Cynthia, with Ah Chu at her shoulder.

He had changed out of the waiter's uniform into a black tunic and trousers. Eddy, Malcolm, and Sharon moved to join them. Tokugawa's party all bowed in unison.

Tokugawa spoke, pitching his voice above the music.

"Konichi-wa, Magnesio-san, congratulations on your twenty-fifth year in business. I hope you will not mind if I bring my men in with Miki and myself. In addition, Magnesio-san, I bring this Englishman, Mr. Blake, who my partner Miki found in Astana. She adopted him like a stray kitten. I think you may be the one that lost him, Magnesio-san, and so we return him to you."

Eddy had been studying, Bill who still looked as menacing as Madbul even when sitting in a wheelchair. He had lost weight over the past few months but was still a powerful physical presence, and his eyes still conveyed the madness within. Eddy tried to conceal himself behind Malcolm, but Bill, who had been scanning the faces assembled around him, spotted him. He sat up straighter in his chair and, staring directly at Eddy, spoke in a loud, clear voice.

"I will call upon the Lord, who is worthy to be praised: so shall I be saved from mine enemies."[17]

Bill continued to focus on Eddy, whose innards quailed under Bill's manic glare.

"He said to Sharon in a small, shaky voice, "I've got to stop pissing off all these bad guys."

He felt Sharon grip his left arm more firmly, while a familiar voice said in his right ear, "Buck up, Edward. This bogeyman cannot harm you."

---

[17] Psalm 18:2–4.

CHAPTER 61

PRODUCER

Zhang stepped forward and dismissed the arrogant Japanese introduction.

"Welcome to the party. I am also hosting a small soiree in Function Room B; feel free to join us, but also feel free to take your time."

He walked away, and the others drifted after him leaving the Japanese and Bill. Eddy felt it best to be wherever Cynthia and Ah Chu were. He followed Zhang's entourage into Function Room B. He could feel Bill's stare boring into his back as he walked with Sharon, almost leaning on her for support as his legs quivered.

The small room afforded a degree of privacy and relief from the music. Guests engaged in conversation amid the clinking of glasses and the toasting of Magnesio.

Sol Silberstein collared Magnesio to educate him about the film industry. He had been alarmed to hear that Zhang was thinking of getting into the movies.

"I tell you the film industry is not something you want to invest in. Talk about financial shenanigans, those grifters and snake-oil salesmen. They dip into your pockets like street urchins. They will tell you bare-faced lies. I have been there, my friend. Let me relate an account of my own doleful experience. I am in Cyprus; I am talking to Spiro Aristonis; his father was a metal trader. The father disappeared, almost certainly kidnapped, was never seen again. Spiro should have inherited the money, but he could not lay his hands on it because they never found the body of his father. Anyway, the son wanted to get into the movies. I now know why—starlets. He had this idea that he could operate the casting couch.

"I knew his father well; he was a decent man. He convinced the Italian government to pay me to take over a union-infested aluminum refinery in Sardinia. I'm obliged to do what I can to help. I am thinking the son is a loser; the son is going to be in over his vacant head. I know this, but I am a sentimental man, so I forward him a few million, lend it to him at below prime rates. He invests in three movies. They're all big hits at the box office—huge box office sales. But Spiro comes back to me and says they lost money; the producers have no payout for him. Why? What is going on here? I see the lines at the movie theaters. I see the revenue figures, many times more than I had lent. I am aghast. Somebody explain, please. Why?"

Sol stood with his arms held wide apart.

"Well we know who the culprits are—the movie production company accountants. The producers see a winner coming; they allocate you all the costs from the films they already financed that bombed. You're left with a loss-making blockbuster. I recommend you stay clear of the movies, dear friend. That reminds me, Thomas."

Another thought completely unconnected with the sad tale of film financing had struck him. Thomas was standing there next to him rigid, not listening to anything at all, just fixated on other end of the room.

"Thomas, why are you standing there like a fucking aspidistra plant? Did you speak to Reuben's people?"

Sol followed his gaze to a corner of the room where a large-screen projector was connected to a laptop. Sol recognized that Thomas was mesmerized.

Boddy Woo bent over the laptop, her posterior wrapped in a tight skirt. She was swaying gently while her long, nimble fingers massaged the mouse pad. Sol knew that nickel trading was the last thing on Thomas's mind. No wonder his assistant was constantly poleaxed by the sight of Boddy Woo.

Sol was about to make some withering remark to Thomas when

a video image flickered onto the screen. Peeking into a webcam were two people. One was a man with black curly hair and thick horn-rimmed glasses. Next to him was an elderly, plump, stern-faced woman with gray hair tied back in a bun.

The woman shouted, "Solomon! Solomon!" and proceeded to release a barrage of Sephardic Yiddish. The man in the video put a hand on her shoulder and said, "Mama, Mama," before issuing some calming words in the same language.

Zhang recognized Sol's brother, Ephraim, and he interrupted the old lady's verbal onslaught.

"Ephraim, Ephraim, my friend, it is so nice to see you and Mrs. Silberstein. How are you?"

Ephraim said, "Magnesio, my esteemed friend, thank you for the invitation; if only we could be there with you in person. My apologies for my dear mother's outburst; the well of her sorrow is deep. The burden of our exile here in Zug is a burden no mother should have to bear. She feels there is injustice in our enforced émigré status here while my wonderful brother travels freely the globe.

"I tell her, 'Mama,' I tell her, 'you do not have to stay; you are free to leave.' But her duty to family knows no limits. We toil, and we serve, not that you don't, Zhang, my friend. Nobody has been more dedicated in his industriousness than you, but we toil in service of the market and this is what we get—those ingrates at the IRS and the US Department of Justice. I tell my mother not to be so harsh on Sol but—"

Sol interrupted. "Okay, brother, okay. I don't think anybody is interested in the story of our family tragedy."

He whispered through the corner of his mouth to Thomas.

"No wonder they call him Motormouth. He never fucking shuts up."

Sol carried on the conversation with the video conversation. It was quickly descending into mayhem as all three simultaneously exchanged words and gestures that nobody understood, challenging the bandwidth of the communications link.

CHAPTER 62

LANGUAGE

The party began to leave them to their disagreements. and this gave Thomas a chance to go over and talk to Boddy Woo.

"Those Mandarin lessons, can we practice some?"

Thomas had been working hard ever since Boddy had promised to help him improve his language skills.

"I suppose so."

Boddy smiled, revealing a set of perfect white teeth.

"Practice makes perfect."

Despite the budding romance, they were both pragmatic types, and so the focus of today's lesson was the metals markets.

Boddy began. "How do you say, 'five hundred metric tons at the average LME three-month settlement price'?"

Thomas slowly spoke a series of words. He knew the pitfalls a speaker of nontonal languages can have with the Chinese languages. A foreigner struggling to find the right tones can easily mispronounce a word that translates to something completely different from what was intended.

When Thomas had finished, Boddy laughed.

"Not quite right, Thomas. But that was a very nicely and politely enunciated request you just made."

"What did I say?" asked Thomas, nervously.

You said, "Please retarmac my supervisor's driveway."

Thomas blushed.

"Oh, dear, that's not a phrase one would use very often, is it?"

"On the contrary," said Boddy, "I had cause to make that very request not two weeks ago when Mr. Zhang returned from his visit to Beijing and saw that a runaway lawnmower had carved up the driveway at his Ascot estate. Let's try another; say this: 'Ten million dollars. You call that a line of credit?'"

Thomas tried again, this time with a little more confidence.

"Not bad," said Boddy, "but it did sound a little like you were asking somebody to phone for a spinach-flavored fishing rod. Okay, try this: 'It looks like the zinc shortage is going to be around for some time.'"

Thomas was more confident than ever this time as a fluid succession of syllables rolled from his tongue. Boddy raised her eyebrows, a smile on her face.

"What was that?"

Thomas repeated the sentence.

Boddy said, "That was nothing like it. You said, 'Your lips are luscious red cherries—succulent, and tempting—and I long to devour them.'"

"I know I did," said Thomas with a smile, "and it's true. Shall we go somewhere quiet and peaceful where we can validate my hypothesis?"

Boddy did not reply. She just took Thomas's hand; they walked away together, through the crowd and in the direction of the lobby. An elevator stood, awaiting their entry and ascension to her room above.

CHAPTER 63

NERVE

Sigurd had been invited into Function Room B with his white tiger. He was sitting at the end of the bar, conversing with Eddy and Sharon. Eddy was glad to be somewhere, anywhere, other than in Bill Blake's presence.

Sharon asked, "I hope I'm not being insensitive, but is there no one else that could work with you?"

Sigurd smiled and shook his head. "Everyone asks that question. No, Leroy and I are in a relationship beyond the stage show. We came out as gay years ago, though I think it was obvious to most people. Some others use large cats in their conjuring shows, but we raised our cats from cubs, so they know us. I know you want to ask about the mauling. All I can say is it was an accident. Even the most loving pets can lash out or bite. When it's a tiger, well, we saw what happened."

As the evening wore on, guests began to leave, and eventually there were only a few people left in the room. Sol and Magnesio were deep in conversation. They were sitting in a pair of armchairs smoking Havana cigars and lamenting the sad state of the metals industry and the endless interference of the regulators. Cynthia and Nancy Liu sat adjacent to Sol and Magnesio, engrossed in conversation. Ah Chu stood to one side, attending to the two women and keeping the room in constant surveillance.

After talking with Sigurd, Eddy, Sharon, and, latterly, Eric Dwyer were sitting at the bar, growing ever more drunk. A barman served cocktails, wine, and beer. Eric had just shown up. He was attending a metals conference in Detroit. He heard the Knockney crew were in Vegas and flew down to see the great Sol Silberstein.

A gentle word in Cynthia's ear had secured his entrance through hotel security and into the inner sanctum. Nigel Owens put his decks on automatic and came to congratulate Sharon on her election win. Sharon introduced him to Eddy, Eric, and Malcolm, and he stayed to have a drink with the Knockney expatriates. He regaled them with the latest misfortunes to befall the council.

Sigurd was still sitting in the corner, gazing forlornly at his tiger, occasionally stroking its head and muttering something in its ear. The Knockney folks were talking about Bill. Eric and Eddy were intrigued to hear what Sharon told them about Clore being Bill's brother. However, the major topic was that Bill Blake was in town, in this very hotel, accompanied by a bunch of Japanese gangsters. Eddy relayed the whole story about the metal sting in Kazakhstan and Bill's eventual rescue, exactly as Cynthia had reported it to him.

Eric said, "It was me that led him into that Kazakhstan deal; I must say I didn't know how it would turn out. I just assumed that he would end up in a shitload of trouble and that would be the last we would see of him. He has a fiendish way of bouncing back. I sometimes wonder if he is human. Do you think he knows that I knew it was a scam?"

Sharon said, "He'll assume you did. In his book, everybody is guilty. In his psychopathic view of the universe, we are all guilty of original sin, and we are all in need of redemption. Fortunately, he's presently confined to a wheelchair, so he can't personally do much to you."

"I didn't like the look of those Yakuza dudes, though," said Eddy.

There was a flood of sound as the double doors at the entrance burst open. Bill Blake's wheelchair rolled into the room, pushed by an unseen hand that clicked the doors closed behind him.

The wheelchair occupant looked around the room, moving his head slowly due to the neck brace. Everybody in the room looked toward him.

"I've come here to deliver a sermon," intoned Bill from his chair. Bill pulled out a sleek pistol from under his jacket and pointed it first at Sol.

"Now, normally firearms are not my preferred form of punishment, unless it's driving a nail through bone and flesh. But given my temporary disability, I'm somewhat restricted in my movements, and so I'm left with no choice."

"And you would be?" asked Sol with contempt as he stood to look at Bill.

"You know who I am. Hong Kong? Crap metal deal?"

"Ah, Bill, my friend," Sol said with a laugh, "join us. What are you drinking?"

"I don't drink," said Bill. "When you are encamped against your enemies, keep away from everything impure."[18]

"I was so sorry to hear of your accident."

Sol remained unperturbed and appeared to have no fear of Bill at all.

"Kazakhstan is a difficult place to do business. There are many pitfalls. Or in your case, pratfalls."

Bill ignored him and said, "How fortuitous that I should find all my enemies assembled in one place. I owe my Japanese friends a lot. They are decent people who have been a great help to me through my recent tribulations. In fact, in their kindness, they have arranged for us to be left in peace while we reconcile our various ledgers. Don't try to leave; that door stays locked until we're done."

Zhang came forward. "Bill, Bill, if I understand correctly, you consider one of us or some of us to be responsible for your misfortune. Is that correct?"

Bill ignored this too and turned his wheelchair to face the Knockney group standing by the bar.

"You, Relish, you little fucking punk. How could you possibly think you could escape? I own you. Look at you, Dwyer. You're just

---

[18] Deuteronomy 23:9.

like your loser of an uncle, a two-bit nobody who thinks he's arrived just because he's done a bit of business here and there."

Then he turned to Sharon, "Hello, Sharon. How are you, my dear? You know, they always said you were a smart one, but it seems you're just as much of a dumb fuck as all those other Knockney bints, hanging around with tosspots like this."

Bill continued as the Knockney people shriveled nervously and averted their eyes. Eddy thought that Bill could not possibly take out all of them with one gun. If they rushed him together, somebody would be hit, but they could overwhelm him. However, who would be willing to take that risk?

As it turned out, there was one such brave party in the room. Sigurd and his tiger had observed events from the end of the bar. The tiger had a moral compass and recognized a villain. It leapt into action heading straight for Bill in his wheelchair.

Bill did not see the tiger coming until the last moment. He managed to move his gun in the tiger's direction, but it was too late. The tiger had Bill's elbow in his mouth and a couple of bites later, Bill's forearm had fallen onto the blanket on his lap. He tried to fend off the tiger with his other arm, but the tiger took the hand off that arm. There was blood everywhere. The tiger then tore into Bill's throat, silencing his cries of alarm. It dragged Bill by the head out of the wheelchair and onto the floor. The tiger shook Bill's helpless body back and forth and tore bits of flesh from various parts of his fragmenting frame.

As the tiger settled in to feed, Eric said, "Somebody should go and get help."

Sol asked, "Didn't Mr. Blake say the door was locked?"

"I think he did," replied Eddy.

"Which means that we can't get out of the room to summon assistance," said Zhang.

"Indeed. Anybody got a cell phone?" asked Eddy.

"I've got one," said Sol. "Let's see if there's a signal …"

He looked down at the phone. "Can't see without my glasses.

Here," he said, handing the phone to Eddy, "can you read it? Oh, I'm Sol Silberstein, by the way."

"Pleased to meet you Sol. I'm Eddy Relish."

The tiger had a piece of Bill's thigh wedged between his front paws and was chewing on it.

"You're the wunderkind they were all talking about back there? Congratulations on your relaunch; mind your engines don't fail."

"I'll try; thanks so much," said Eddy as he punched in some numbers after studiously scrutinizing the display.

"Well, is there a signal or not?" asked Sol.

"Nah, the reception's nonexistent under all this concrete," he said, passing the phone back.

"Shaz, do you have your cell? Maybe it's on a different network."

"Ooh, gross." said Sharon.

The tiger delicately removed what looked like a kidney from the Reverend's torso with its tongue.

"What did you say? My cell? No. I mean, yes, in my bag. But the battery's flat."

Zhang summed up the situation.

"Well, ladies and gentlemen, it seems there is nothing to be done. We shall just have to wait until the authorities notice our absence and let us out. We tried our best, but there was nothing in the end we could do to save this unfortunate fellow."

Sigurd was standing immobile and pale, some distance from the group. He had not restrained the tiger when it leapt at Bill because he had seen the pistol. Now he was in a panic.

"My God, My God," he said.

He walked slowly to the exit and opened the door. It had been unlocked all along, and Sigurd yelled for assistance.

CHAPTER 64

CHALK

Eddy watched the police and crime scene investigators arrive. They anaesthetized the now placid and satiated tiger. The guests made statements; CSI photographed the position of the corpse and chalked on the wooden floor. CSI specialists scooped portions of Bill into a body bag to be shipped off to the morgue.

The shaken throng emerged from Function Room B. Tokugawa's party confronted them.

Nancy Liu and Cynthia stepped out ahead of the group to converse with the Japanese. Eddy saw Ah Chu stood a little behind the two women, poised and alert. He wondered if there was any real danger from Bill, given the professional espionage talent in Function Room B.

He remembered Ah Chu, Cynthia, and Nancy all being in the room before Bill arrived. However, he could not recall any details of where they were before and after the tiger attack. Another tale for the next time he and Cynthia had a tête-à-tête over a glass of whiskey.

Nancy Liu spoke to the Yakuza in Japanese. Eddy saw surprise on the Yakuza faces on the story of Bill Blake's demise. Tokugawa reached out and took hold of Miki Ogamura's hand, interlinking fingers. The conversation between Nancy and the Yakuza continued in a stilted formal manner, until Tokugawa spoke tersely, bowed, and turned to go. Miki kept turning and glowering at the assembled group.

Cynthia drifted over to Eddy, Sharon, Eric, and Malcolm.

"Goodness! That was a little tense. China-Japan relations are never very smooth at the best of times. Nancy explained the circumstance behind Mr. Blake's demise. You may imagine we expected them to be a little upset that their guest had met such a ghastly end. We were expecting that young hellion, Miki Ogamura, to overreact. She is Tokugawa's personal bodyguard, as well as his lover. She can be a very nasty piece of work with a blade in her hands.

"I suspect that she could give even Ah Chu a run for his money. Thankfully, I believe Tokugawa was secretly pleased that the situation resolved itself and accepted that it was Bill's karma to die through the tiger attack. He told Miki that it was a hero's death in the face of his enemies; she should be glad for him. I am not sure that this argument swayed her. You may have noticed him take her hand, more to restrain her than to give her solace."

"I'd like to know how the hell a low-rent Knockney gangster like Bill Blake gets mixed up with the Yakuza?" asked Malcolm.

Cynthia glanced up at the tall, gangly Englishman.

"I am sure all will be revealed in time," said Cynthia.

CHAPTER 65

FAMILY

Eddy and Sharon bumped into Clore in the hotel lobby as they returned to their room.

"Inspector," said Eddy.

"Hello, Relish," said the inspector. "I heard that Bill was back. Somebody told me he was seen coming into the hotel in a wheelchair."

"Well," said Eddy, "on that score, I have some good news and some bad news. The good, yes, your brother did arrive in one piece this evening. The bad news is that he's already left, in considerably more pieces."

Sharon's fist drove into Eddy's already bruised left arm, causing him to wince.

"When are you going to stop doing that?"

"Like I said, when you stop being a prick," said Sharon.

Eddy nursed his bruised arm while Sharon took Clore to one side, sat down with him in the foyer, and, holding his hand, related what had happened to Bill.

"Inspector, I'm really sorry you lost your brother again."

"I can't believe it," said Clore. "I only wanted to see him and say hello, brother. He was the only family I had left."

"Maybe it's all for the best. Bill would never have accepted you as his brother. He would have made your life a misery. You've spent your police career navigating around Bill's crimes."

"I know. I've never had the guts to confront him."

"I think it's time you stopped daydreaming about TV detectives and pursuing easy targets such as Eddy. Think of it as a new start; you never know, you might get a promotion before you retire."

Eddy sulked and brooded on his lost decade, while he fed coins into a dime slot machine. Out of the corner of his eye, he saw Cynthia and Nancy Liu walking arm in arm and chatting in Mandarin.

They spotted Eddy and joined him. This was the first time he has seen Nancy up close. She was a little taller than Cynthia, almost his height, and looked to be about the same age as Cynthia. She was clad in expensive silks and jewelry like Cynthia. Though not delicately beautiful as Cynthia, she was nonetheless a striking and formidable-looking woman.

Cynthia spoke to Eddy while Nancy scrutinized him with eyes like two chips of polished obsidian. He noticed that while the two women were friends, Cynthia was deferential to Nancy, suggesting that she ranked higher in the hierarchy of China's intelligence service.

Cynthia said, "I expect you're wondering, Edward, why we didn't try and catch Madbul when he came to the Lucky Lotus."

"Actually, as it happens, I wasn't, but since you ask …"

"We knew a superior operative like Madbul would likely spot a trap. He called the day before, and that was not enough time to make watertight preparations. I guessed he would be looking, at a minimum, for a weapon and money, so we had the blank cartridges prepared. Remember, Edward, we wanted Madbul alive to hand to the Americans. Now they are in debt to me and by extension to China."

Eddy thought for a moment. "That makes sense, but he might have checked the ammo and gone off and got himself the real thing."

"Ah Chu kept close to Madbul all the time, even when he was driving from Los Angeles to Las Vegas."

"How did he—"

"Trade secret, Edward. We might have taught Madbul many of our secrets but not all them, as he found out this evening."

Cynthia said in a low voice, "Nancy has just informed me that she ordered the execution of Bill in Astana. Nancy felt that you are far too valuable. We did not want you squandered by the murderous whims of an English psychopath. As we know, that operation in Astana failed, but thanks to our feline friend, all's well that ends well."

Eddy glanced with shock into the stern, unblinking, unsmiling face of Nancy Liu.

Feeling that some response was required, he stuttered, "Oh, err, well, gosh, thanks, um Nancy, I mean Ms. Liu."

A smile played across Nancy Liu's stern face, as she spoke in English.

"Yes, I do see how you could become quite enchanted by Mr. Relish."

Cynthia smiled and, to Eddy's surprise, flushed a little.

Before he could respond, Cynthia recovered and said, "Enjoy the rest of the evening, Edward."

Both women leaned forward, kissed him on his cheeks in unison. He was left in a haze of perfume and confusion. The twin kisses attracted a freezing glare from Sharon. Clore gave a startled yelp as Sharon tightened her grip on his hand.

CHAPTER 66

THREADS

Eddy and Sharon retired to bed just after 2:00 a.m. after a nightcap with Malcolm. Eddy and Malcolm hated dancing, but they were dragged out onto the dance floor by Sharon, Liz, and several actresses from the Venereal Awards, who were very persuasive in gaining entry.

Christ, what a night, thought Eddy Relish. A new chapter of his life was beginning. Cynthia vanquished the bogeymen and monsters haunting the last ten years. Her espionage activities caused him some qualms. There were news stories about the FBI catching agents in the pay of the Chinese. He broached the subject with Cynthia, who said it was no more than a lover's tiff. Eddy knew better than to press the point further. He gingerly massaged his left arm, where Sharon's punches had left it tattooed with little bruises.

Sharon seemed to have forgiven him for Cynthia. The two of them had gone to the bathroom together. Eddy remarked on this to Malcolm, who laughed when Eddy suggested it might be a good thing.

"Mate, the last thing you need is two women comparing notes about you."

Eddy had been too tired to argue.

Sharon gave Eddy a good night kiss, before collapsing into the huge king-sized bed and falling asleep. She had told Eddy that she had to get back to Knockney. The council was in disarray following the cannibal incident. She was the only opposition member in the council chambers, but she had to enlarge the breach in the politburo wall. She hoped that the next round of local government elections would see the incumbents tossed out.

Eddy yawned and reached out to turn off the bedside lamp. His muted cell phone buzzed on the bedside table.

"Yeah, hello?"

"Edward, good evening, I'm sorry to disturb you when it's so late. I understand that you will be going to Romania soon. Please come and see me at the Lotus before you leave."

Here we go again, thought Eddy Relish.

CHAPTER 67

FIN

It was 3:00 a.m. Sol had been strolling 'round the hotel lobby with Zhang as they spoke to various trading desks around the globe. They both finished their calls simultaneously. Zhang's face was a picture of calm. Sol's was still fading back to its normal olive color from furious beetroot red They were targeting an oil trader whom Sol personally blamed for OPEC quota cuts and screwing up his short oil position.

Zhang appeared to be disappointed that the party had ended the way it had. Sol commiserated with him.

"That business with the gangster was really a shame, my friend. Spoiling the party like that, I said to myself from the moment I first set eyes on him, I said this loser is bad news. I mean, letting himself be devoured during such a joyous occasion. Does the man have no sense of decorum?"

"These things happen," said Zhang. "I have no regrets. Now I know exactly what I would like to do. Let us finish the day by taking a late snack at the New Shanghai. My cousin says it is highly recommended, specializing in some delicacies from our home village. Would you care to join me?"

"Of course," said Sol, "but I am paying."

They headed for the exit and walked to the curb as a limousine materialized. They drove away from the Strip to the New Shanghai restaurant on Spring Mountain Road. They were attended by an elderly Chinese couple, with whom Zhang had a brief conversation. After they had taken their order, Zhang told Sol that the couple had recently returned from an extended vacation to England. They had visited their son and daughter-in-law who ran a Chinese takeaway in Knockney.

They ordered shark's fin soup, which was not a menu item and was illegal in the state of Nevada. The conversation turned to the film industry.

"What I said about film financing is true, you know," said Sol. "You aren't really going to invest, are you?"

"I might," said Zhang. "But I will bear in mind your helpful comments and keep an eagle eye on the executive producer."

"Well, I suppose you can handle it. Let's be honest, a person who can get me to buy them shark's fin soup at four in the morning could make mincemeat of those Hollywood pussycats. More to the point, anyone who can dispatch his creditor by having him eaten by a white tiger in front of his guests at his anniversary celeb ..."

Sol paused, and a thought suddenly occurred to him. Sol looked at Zhang. "You planned it, didn't you?"

Zhang's face was a picture of calm.

Sol continued. "That was a public announcement that nobody fucks around with Magnesio, wasn't it?"

Sol was grinning widely now.

Zhang's face was a picture of calm.

"Oh, my life, you are something else, Maestro; Tinseltown will not know what hit it."

"We'll see," replied Zhang, "but actually, you know, the movies are only one thing. I have another diversification plan."

"Tell me."

"Exotic medicines; with China's growing wealth, the demand for traditional remedies will increase. As you know, the supply of exotic animals is limited. The ban on rhino-horn sales means the world's rhinos are all disappearing. Nobody has an incentive to preserve them. Anyway, I will not touch rhinos; they are too hot. I will be focusing on antelopes."

"You will be focusing on antelopes. Now I have to admit, that is not something that had ever occurred to me. What are you going to do, corner the antelope market? Are we going to have to rename you Antelopio?"

Zhang continued. "I am serious. Do you have any idea how big that market is? People pay fortunes for their aphrodisiac qualities. Do you know the worth of an antelope penis?"

"Do I know the worth of an antelope penis? Let me think," said Sol.

He stared into Zhang's eyes.

"To me, nothing; to the antelope, I would think it would be worth the whole world."

Printed in the United States
By Bookmasters